The Road to You

The Road to You

A Wildflower Novel

ALECIA WHITAKER

poppy

Little, Brown and Company
New York   Boston

Poppy

Hachette Book Group
1290 Avenue of the Americas, New York, NY 10104
Visit us at lb-teens.com

Poppy is an imprint of Little, Brown and Company.
The Poppy name and logo are trademarks of Hachette Book Group, Inc.

The publisher is not responsible for websites (or their content) that are not owned by the publisher.

First Edition: July 2015

Wildflower was conceived by Kathryn Williams and developed by Aerial Publishing LLC.

Library of Congress Cataloging-in-Publication Data

Whitaker, Alecia.
The road to you : a Wildflower novel / by Alecia Whitaker. — First edition.
pages cm
Summary: "Rising country music star Bird Barrett is on a national tour where she meets a cute roadie, and the two start to date, but when Bird moves to LA, she is swept up in the Hollywood lifestyle and the mounting pressures of her professional music career begin to affect her personal life"— Provided by publisher.
ISBN 978-0-316-25140-2 (hc) — ISBN 978-0-316-25141-9 (ebook)
[1. Musicians—Fiction. 2. Country music—Fiction. 3. Dating (Social customs)—Fiction. 4. Fame—Fiction.] I. Title.
PZ7.W57684Ro 2015 [Fic]—dc23 2014032150

10 9 8 7 6 5 4 3 2 1

RRD-C

Printed in the United States of America

This one's for Jerrod—glad the road led me to you

1

"Bird!" a group of fans shout as my dad holds open the back door of a radio station in Baltimore, Maryland. Maybe two dozen people wait with Sharpies and posters, CDs, magazines, T-shirts, their own forearms, anything that I might be willing to autograph. Not too long ago, I would have been surprised at the crowd, might even have turned my head to see what the fuss was about, but in the past two months, since my album, *Wildflower*, has been out, I've come to expect this craziness as part of my new life. "Bird!" they cry, bodies pressed close as they angle for position behind a barricade and a bored police officer. "Bird, over here!"

"Go get 'em," my dad says with a grin as we step out into the sunny parking lot. This is my favorite part—interacting with my fans. *My fans!*

The whirlwind publicity tour Anita Handler put together has had a sink-or-swim feel as she's whisked me from TV interviews to public events, from benefits to radio stations like this one. It's been exhausting but exhilarating—especially since the album is performing beyond anyone's expectations. When Dan Silver, the president of my label, Open Highway Records, called to tell me that *Wildflower* had sold over thirty thousand copies on iTunes in the first week, I was so shocked that I dropped my phone and cracked the screen. He made sure to break the news about my second single, "Sing Anyway," in person: It topped both the Hot Country and Hot 100 charts. Seeing my name on top of *Billboard* for "Notice Me" was amazing, but seeing it a second time was the most incredible feeling I've ever had. Like it wasn't a fluke. Like I was meant to do this.

"Hi!" I call to the crowd, reaching out for a CD and a marker.

"I want you to know, it's like you wrote 'Yellow Lines' just for me," a young girl gushes as other people squish in close to her. "My dad's in the military, and I've already been in, like, seven schools."

"Yeah, moving around can be hard," I reply.

"I am obsessed with 'Sing Anyway,'" a girl next to her says.

"Oh, thanks so much," I say. I move on, working my way down the line. I know that Anita will try to drag me off soon, saying that we are on a tight schedule and that I should "always leave them wanting more," but it's hard to pull away. I'm so motivated hearing that people connect with my music.

Speaking of my publicist, I kick it into high gear when I catch a glimpse of her approaching out of the corner of my eye. I grab for CDs and posters, smile in the direction of camera phones, and sign *Bird Barrett* as fast as I can, my signature a *B* with a loop to another *B* followed by a squiggly line as I scribble quickly, trying to get to everyone. I want to reach them all, and I hate that inevitable moment when Anita click-clacks over to me in her heels to lead me off.

"Thank you all for coming," she says now, her harsh New York accent always a little jarring. She puts her arm around my waist, expertly positioning herself between my fans and me, beaming at them as we pass. "Be sure to follow Bird on Twitter while she opens for Jolene Taylor's Sweet Home Tour this summer," she calls. "Tickets are on sale now at BirdBarrett.com."

I'm being wrangled toward a black Lincoln town car waiting for me at the corner, but a girl in a wheelchair desperately reaching over the barricade stops me in my tracks.

"Hi there," I say.

"Bird, I love you! I'm your biggest fan, I swear!" she says in a raspy voice.

Anita tugs on my arm, but I don't budge. I very rarely give her any pushback—after all she's the pro, and to put it frankly, Anita's pretty intimidating—but there's something about the girl who's calling out to me now. Her friends look to be about my age, so I'm guessing she is, too, but her eyes are too big for her sallow face and her cheeks are sunken. She fiddles self-consciously with her oxygen tubes as she speaks.

"I'm your biggest fan, Bird. Biggest. By, like, a million percent," she declares. "I know every word to every song, and 'Sing Anyway' is my absolute all-time favorite. I bought the download *and* the CD, which—could you please sign?"

"Sure," I say as she hands it to me.

"B-E-X," she dictates as I scribble a note on the case. "When I started chemo, I made my dad find me this wig," she says proudly. "I call it my Bird Barrett look."

"Oh, wow," I say, noticing her long, golden-red tresses. "That's a wig? Dang. My hair looks better on you than me."

She beams. "My dad's driving me and all my friends up to Philadelphia when you come through on Jolene Taylor's tour. It's pretty much the greatest present I've ever gotten."

I frown. "Hmmm. Better than backstage passes?"

Bex blinks. One of her friends grips her forearm, and their smiles vanish in shock. "Backstage? Are you serious?"

I grin. "By about a million percent."

Anita links her arm through mine again, and I know

it's time. I can read her mind: *Plane to catch*. But for once, I stop still and stare a hole through her, giving her the opportunity to read mine: *Do something*.

"Yes, yes, of course," Anita finally says in a huff. She shakes her head as she pulls a business card from her purse, then she turns toward the girls with an obviously forced smile that nearly makes me laugh out loud. "How about this?" she asks Bex. "You e-mail me at this address, and I'll send you all-access backstage passes for Philly. You can even tour Bird's bus. She helps out her biggest fan, and you become the talk of your high school for something other than your cancer."

I cringe at her bluntness, but Bex doesn't even blink.

"That's amazing," she says, clutching Anita's business card to her chest. She falls back in her chair as if she's just fought twenty rounds of boxing and won. "Thank you. Thank you so much."

"See you later this summer," I say as we end our exchange. I wave at the crowd as we walk toward the car, hating the disappointment I see on the faces of the people whose stuff I didn't get to sign. My dad holds open the door, and I duck inside, Anita right behind me.

I buckle up and look out the tinted window at the fans, my focus falling on Bex and her friends. I can't believe *my publicist* actually said *for something other than your cancer*. I shake my head.

"What's wrong, Bird?" Anita asks as if she can read my mind.

"Nothing really," I say. I turn toward her and try to choose my words carefully. "It's just that—Anita, you know I love you. But you're so...direct. Like, I know you meant well with that girl, but—"

"But I made her dream come true?" Anita interrupts. She wears a look of satisfaction as the car starts moving. Then she holds up her phone. "Sounds familiar, doesn't it?"

On her screen is a text from Dan:

Billboard in. "Sing Anyway" holds #1 for 4th week!

And although I may question Anita's methods, she doesn't leave room for anybody to question her results.

"I don't think I'll ever get over the unlimited cookie selection," I say as I grab a snickerdoodle from the flight attendant's tray. The label has rented a private plane for us a couple of times to get me between appearances, and I still can't get used to it. "To think some people would kill for a bag of peanuts on a flight."

"Oh, Bird, not again with the guilt," Anita says, sliding her window shade closed and squeezing a lime into her gin and tonic. I've finally discovered the kryptonite of my tough-as-nails publicist: flying. "I've told you over and over that we are developing your image. Your *aura*. Regular people fly coach, and you are no longer a regular person. You'd be mobbed if you flew commercial."

"Did you text your mother?" my dad asks, settling into the seat across from me.

"Yep. They should be here any minute."

"There's your silver lining, Bird," Anita comments. "Think of the gas we're conserving by letting your mother and brothers hitch a ride today."

I roll my eyes, and she smirks.

"Back on the Internet again, huh?" my dad comments, indicating the iPad Anita got me. He grabs his book of Sudoku puzzles from his bag. "I swear, if you're not writing or performing, you spend every other waking moment online. Do they have a sleep app?" he teases.

"Oh, that's genius," Anita pipes up. "I'd pay big bucks for an app like that." I look up at her and laugh even though she's not joking. Anita's entire life consists of work and running *my* life, and I'll tell you one thing: I'm glad she's in my corner.

I pull up Twitter and scroll through the mentions, retweeting and favoriting some as I go. "I know you guys think I'm crazy, but this is the best part."

Anita leans across the tiny aisle and reads over my

shoulder. "'Hashtag whythehype for at BirdBSings? She should lead summer camp sing-alongs, not open for legend Jolene Taylor. Hashtag overrated.'" Anita smirks. "That's the best part?"

My chest burns from the insult. Those comments hurt—they really do—but they're the minority. For every negative comment, there are fifty positive ones. "Well, not that exact tweet," I say, "but interacting with my fans." Then I reply to the mean tweet aloud as I type. "I love summer camp!"

Anita rolls her eyes. "Waste of time," she mutters, taking a sip.

"Maybe I want my *aura* to be friendly," I say.

Anita harrumphs just as the rest of my family walks onto the plane.

"Let's get this party started!" my oldest brother, Dylan, yells by way of greeting. He, my mom, and my other brother, Jacob, are boarding the private jet for the first time, and their faces say it all: *This* is the way to fly.

I stretch and have to admit that while I sometimes feel guilty flying private, it has been nice to be on a plane that can actually accommodate long legs like mine. And the comfort of the small cabin takes me back to the days when my family and I traveled the country in an RV playing bluegrass music at honky-tonks and festivals. Plus, it's pretty sweet getting both a window and an aisle, the leather seats and the little TVs are awesome, and I can't complain about skipping all the lines at the airport.

But as much as I have come to enjoy these flights, tonight it all feels different. That last tweet reminded me of our destination: the CenturyLink Center in Omaha, where I will be the new opening act for country music goddess Jolene Taylor and her Sweet Home Tour. Ever since Dan called me with the news that I'd be joining the last leg of her tour, my emotions have gone back and forth from excited to anxious, pumped to be onstage again and terrified that I won't be good enough. Jolene is a Nashville fixture and a member of the Grand Ole Opry. To open for her is a life-changing opportunity, and I'm worried I won't live up to the high expectations. What if I screw it all up? What if the fans don't like me live? I mean, they're mostly going to be Jolene's fans: middle-aged women with car pools and careers. What if they hate my stuff?

I pull up the *Billboard* website. It's both mind-blowing and comforting to see my name at the top, to see "Sing Anyway" right there above Justin Timberlake, to realize, as my best friend, Stella, pointed out, that that means J.T. knows who I am. That guy brought sexy back, and he *knows who I am*.

And although this Thursday is a good one with my single still on top of the charts, I can't help but feel my stomach flip when I see a *Billboard* story about new country artist

Kayelee Ford. I click on the article and read about her album; her label, Great American Music, and its president, Randall Strong, who originally tried to sign me; and how her first single, "Be Like Me," is already climbing the Hot 100, inching its way closer to mine. I know I shouldn't, but I do a Web search of my competition and gasp audibly when it takes me to a tabloid's side-by-side comparison of the two of us. There is a picture of me singing in the studio in my Open Highway sweatshirt right beside a picture of her singing to a crowd of spring breakers in a bikini, with the headline FORD FLIES AFTER BIRD, BUT WILL SHE CATCH HER?

I gulp hard and scan the article as the plane taxis to the runway. Then I close the browser window and immediately go to my fan forum. As we prepare for takeoff, I upload a selfie from my radio interview today and promise my fans a major autographed-swag giveaway if I get one hundred thousand "likes" by the time I land in Omaha. It doesn't take long for the post to gain momentum, and when the comments start to pile up, I take a deep breath and feel better. I look out the window as we race down the runway, gaining speed until the landscape is a blur. Once we're in the air, once the plane has taken a couple of dips as we gain altitude, once we're steady and above the clouds, I allow myself to refresh the page. I smile when I see that I'm already halfway there.

Catch me if you can.

2

"RIGHT THIS WAY, Miss Barrett," Jordan, the stage manager, says as she directs me through the back halls of the CenturyLink Center Omaha. Our footsteps echo on the polished concrete floors as I follow her past huge speakers and instrument cases, past roadies in black jeans and black T-shirts, and into the bright, cold stadium. My heart is racing. My pulse is pounding. My grip is tight on my fiddle and bow. I step over taped-down wires and think how different everything feels in the arena, how massive it all is, how many greats have come before me, how important it is that I live up to this gig.

The band waits for me onstage, and I follow Jordan up a set of narrow steps, eager to join them. It feels slightly reckless that we're meeting for the first time this morning and performing together for the first time tonight, but when Dan Silver wants something, he makes it happen.

When Jolene's tour started at the end of May, the opening act was another band on her label. According to Anita, though, Jolene was pressured into replacing those guys because her people felt she needed "a young artist to attract a younger fan base." Dan worked his magic, booked me for the remainder of her tour, and lined up these backing musicians. In an ideal world, I'd have a few days to rehearse and get to know the band, but with the timing of my publicity tour, we don't have that luxury. It's go time.

Jordan walks to the middle of the stage, motioning my band leader over as she announces, "Hey, everybody, this is our new opener, your lead singer, Bird Barrett."

I follow her to the center microphone stand, where I meet Monty, the lead guitarist, an older rocker who reminds me of a not-so-anorexic-looking Steven Tyler. "We've been rehearsing around the clock, Miss Barrett," he says, offering his hand for a shake. "I think you'll like what you hear."

"It's Bird," I say. I smile and shake his hand enthusiastically. "And I'm sure I will."

"Let's get to it, then," Jordan says, checking her sporty black wristwatch. "You have the stage until five, then Jolene will come in for sound check. And she doesn't like it when her openers run over."

I nod and take my place behind the mic. I'm a bundle of nerves even though I've performed live music for over half my life. The first song on the set list is "Yellow Lines," and as I look out over the empty arena, following the aisles into the upper decks above, I can't help but feel a tad overwhelmed.

"How many people will be here?" I ask, pulling my lucky rock pendant out from under my shirt and clutching it tightly.

Jordan adjusts her headset. "It's a sell-out crowd, so I'd say eighteen thousand three hundred." She winks. "Approximately."

"Oh," I reply, not wanting to make a bad first impression. I gulp down the panic in my voice and plaster on a smile. "That's a relief. Nineteen thousand would've been a little daunting for my first arena performance, but a measly eighteen thousand three hundred? Child's play."

Both Jordan and Monty chuckle, and we all settle into our places. Thank God I have Maybelle, my fiddle, the one thing that is tangibly familiar in this surreal moment. As Monty counts us in, I close my eyes and take a deep breath. Then, right on cue, I attack the fiddling pass, completely thrown off when a fiddler in the band starts in at the same time. My eyes fly open, and I spin around, the other guy grinning broadly as if I'm supposed to like the fact that his style is totally different from mine and that two fiddles before the first verse packs way more introductory punch than the song calls for. But I just grin at him and turn back to my mic, determined to finish the entire song before I start ruffling feathers. Surely Monty hears it, too.

When the first verse comes around, I relax my arms and let the other fiddler take over the easy stuff, knowing I really do need to focus on my vocals. I smile out at the empty arena as I start to sing, trying to project energy all the way to that fan who will be in the upper decks:

"The wheels are rolling down the highway.
The county lines are all a blur."

This is what I love about rehearsals. Even though the stage is bigger and the stakes are higher than during my days in the Barrett Family Band, rehearsals are the same. They're the grace period, the creative space, the free zone to play around with the show and figure out what will work when the seats are full. This song is fast paced and fun, so I snatch the mic off the stand and walk toward the front of the stage, bolstered by the music blaring from the speakers and filtering into my earpiece. I remember the way I felt the first time I publicly performed "Notice Me" last year at Stella's school and try to recapture that high. I was a wild woman that night.

As I sing now, I get pumped up imagining her friends

filling the seats right here in Omaha. I run from one side of the stage to the other, giving it all I've got during the chorus:

"Another school, another town,
Another round of good-byes.
Adventures wait and life unfolds along these
    yellow lines."

And then, before the bridge, I holster the mic and bring Maybelle to my chin. If the other fiddler joins me, I don't even notice because I play that pass like it's my territory, my moment, my time.

After the first song, the nerves are gone. I am alive with anticipation. Tonight, this whole place will be filled with people who love Jolene Taylor's classic country sound, but I'm going to do everything I can to leave them wanting to hear more of *my* sound: new country with a bluegrass twist. When Monty counts us in on "Notice Me," I raise the mic and do it all over again, gearing up to give a performance worthy of a headliner I've idolized for years. I only get forty minutes tonight, and I'm determined to make them count.

"Bird," Monty says, abruptly cutting the song. "Your enthusiasm is catching, but you've got to have a voice tonight."

"Oh," I say, blinking.

"You don't have to prove anything to us," he says with a grin. "Save something for the ticket holders, okay?"

I nod, feeling both scolded and flattered at the same time.

For the next couple of hours, I sing with discipline, strong but smart, stopping when Monty directs us to rework instrumental breaks and add in moments for vocal riffs. We decide to strip "Before Music" down to bare bones, going completely acoustic, and we also switch up the set list so that we open with fan favorite "Notice Me."

By the time I end the last song, I feel like I've been through boot camp. My hair's falling out of my ponytail and my shirt clings to me, but I'm invigorated.

"That was incredible!" I say to the band. "Thank you!"

Monty approaches me, smiling and looking every bit as spent as me. He reads from scrawled notes on the back of his set list. "Not bad, guys. We need to talk about getting Bird a break between the second and third songs, and listen, we need to..."

But he trails off midsentence when Jordan hustles toward him with a worried look on her face. Over her shoulder, I see Jolene Taylor, winner of a slew of awards, including at least four Grammys, and the person who sang one of the very first songs I ever learned on the guitar.

I smile broadly, self-consciously tightening my ponytail. I've been dying to meet Jolene Taylor. I wonder if she heard any of my set.

"Let's go, guys," Jordan commands the crew brusquely. A group of roadies make their way onstage, rearranging equipment for Jolene's band.

As for the music legend, she frowns and makes a show of pulling her cell phone out of her pocket, glancing at the screen, and tucking it away again.

"Okay, gang," Monty says. "We'll meet up in the dressing room in fifteen to go over some notes."

Hurriedly, my band puts their instruments away. I grab Maybelle and my set list and follow Monty off stage right. As I get closer to Jolene, I can't believe that she's actually prettier in person. That just doesn't seem possible. Her dark brown hair is in a stylish shag and her trim body looks great in a yoga getup, but it's her eyes that take my breath away, light blue and bright as if LED lights power them.

"Hi, Miss Taylor—or Jolene—or—" I stammer, holding the mic out to her. *Get it together, Bird.* I shake my head. "Gah, sorry, I'm just nervous actually meeting you in person. I love your music. I've been a fan of yours since I was a little girl. Seriously. I am so excited to be on the Sweet Home Tour. Thank you for—"

"Glad to have you," she says, cutting me off and giving me the vibe that she doesn't quite mean it. She offers a closed, tight-lipped smile and takes the stage, accepting a rhinestone-covered mic from Jordan and leaving me standing by the stairs holding my arm out like an idiot.

Confused, and a little shocked, I look at our stage manager wide-eyed.

"I told you she doesn't like her openers to go over," Jordan whispers as she relieves me of the plain black mic in my hand.

I pull out my own cell phone. "By three minutes?" I ask, incredulous.

"That's Jolene," Monty grumbles as he walks past.

Disappointed, I follow him down the stairs to the backstage area. As her band strikes up a hit song that I used to blare in the RV, I realize this is the first time in my life that I haven't wanted to sing along.

3

"SURPRISE!"

I look over the shoulder of my makeup artist, Sam, who, like me, jumped when the door flew open. He pulled his mascara wand away faster than a hand on a hot stove, smearing some on my cheek.

"Oh my gosh, what are you doing here?" I scream when I see my best friend, who's supposed to be back in Tennessee, standing in the door of my dressing room, arms open wide.

"I came to see your first professional football game," Stella teases, gesturing to the black line under my eye.

"Ha-ha," Sam deadpans.

I jump up, and we meet in the middle of the room. Stella's giant hug is just the thing I need to distract me from the ticking clock and the thousands—*thousands*—of people taking their seats in the arena at this very moment. Then her mom walks in behind her.

"Shannon!" I shout, and I rush her for a big hug as well.

"Oh, Bird, it's good to see you," she says, her dangly earrings tinkling in my ear as we embrace.

"I can't believe nobody told me y'all were coming," I say as Sam politely yet firmly leads me back to my makeup chair.

Stella leans toward my mirror, straightening her thick bangs. "We wanted it to be a surprise," she says with a grin.

When I signed with Open Highway at the end of last summer, Dan paired me up with an established songwriter, Shannon Crossley. She helped pen a lot of the songs on *Wildflower* and really took me under her wing. That's how I met Stella, and honestly, I don't know what I'd do without either of them.

"You look amazing, Bird," Stella says as Sam finishes the touch-up. "Like yourself, but even better somehow. It's like you're glowing."

I turn toward the mirror and take myself in. I see a tall, skinny girl with long, wavy, coppery hair wearing a jean jacket, white tank top, magenta shorts, and an incredible pair of custom-made Justin boots.

"What'd your dad say about those Daisy Dukes?" Shannon asks with a sly smile.

"He doesn't like them, but apparently he doesn't get a vote," my dad answers as he walks into the room with my mom and brothers.

"Was she surprised?" Dylan asks as he throws an arm around Stella's shoulders.

"Totally," she says, quite smug, crossing her arms.

"You two and your schemes," I say, pointing at them accusatorily. Last Christmas I thought I lost my lucky rock—one I'd found the day I was offered a record deal and carried with me all the time—but in reality, Dylan had swiped it when I wasn't looking. He gave it to Stella, who encased it in silver wire and attached it to a long silver chain, making it into a necklace so I'd always have it with me. It's the best gift I've ever gotten. No matter how my stylist dresses me, I never take it off.

As my brothers help themselves to the contents of my minifridge, and everybody else settles in around me, I realize that my nerves have morphed into excited energy. I feel revved up, ready, like a car gunning its engine at the starting line. I have people here—*my people*—and I'm ready to do this thing!

"Bird, it's almost time," Jordan says, knocking on the door.

"Okay, thanks."

She vanishes, on to her next stage-managing duty.

"Well, gang, it's been a wild year, that's for sure," my

dad says as he circles us up. I squeeze between Dylan and Jacob, and we join hands just like the old days when we were touring together as the Barrett Family Band, playing honky-tonks and dive bars almost every day of the year. "I've gone from Bird's father, to her band leader, to her manager, and to who-knows-what next! But let me tell you something, that girl is happiest with this group of people around her."

My eyes blur all of a sudden, and I look up, blinking rapidly, determined, as my dad goes on, not to cry, even if they are happy tears. Then both of my moron brothers squeeze my hands, and it happens anyway. I lean over and dab a wet cheek on each of their sleeves, and they pretend to hate it.

"And I'll tell you one more thing," my dad continues. "She has a level head, even with all this craziness. You all are our family"—I look over at Stella, who flashes me a megawatt smile—"and all this success is due in part to your support. So we thank you." He looks at the clock on the wall and turns back to our group. "We've got to wrap it up and get this girl onstage, so let's bow our heads."

I take advantage of this minute of peace—of pause— to thank the Big Guy Upstairs for this career, this unexpected success, and, most important, these amazing people I call family. And as always, I remember my little brother, Caleb, who died too young, but who ultimately led us all to music. We end the prayer as we did in the days of the Barrett Family Band, and join in with my dad, "Take good care of our boy. Amen."

"All right!" Dylan says, clapping his hands loudly before lifting me up and spinning me around.

I hug the rest of the group one by one, and the crowd thins until it's only my Open Highway team, who has shown up at the door. Anita barks orders at somebody on her phone while Dan talks to Monty about the final number. My stylist, Amanda, tears off a new sheet on her lint-brush roller; my hair stylist, Tammy, tests the curling iron; and Sam is at the ready with a makeup sponge.

"Wait, Stella!" I call, grabbing my phone and passing it to her. "Here, will you text Adam? It feels weird that he's not here for all this." Adam was my muse for "Notice Me," the only guy I've ever really liked and the one person I would do anything to see right now. We shared an amazing kiss in January, and I know he was as into me as I was into him, but I got so busy with my career that I somehow lost the opportunity to be with him. That was six months ago, though, and tonight's a big night, and, well, I miss him.

"What should I say?" Stella asks, eyes wide.

I frown. The last time we talked on the phone, Adam told me I'd hate myself for putting a guy ahead of my music. We've played phone tag and texted back and forth a little since then, but without him really in my life, my music hasn't been the same.

I close my eyes as Sam sets to work fixing the smudges. Then I slowly dictate a text, trying to figure out what to say as I go. "Put 'Hey, Adam, I'm about to play the Century-Link in Omaha, which made me think of that dive bar here, Lucky's, where the fountain Coke wasn't half bad. Remember? Anyway, wish you were here to share one with me after this show. I'm pretty nervous, and there are going to be, like, a million people out there, and I was thinking of you and thought I'd say hey and hope everything's going well in Austin. Or I think Jacob said you might be back in Nashville this week. Wherever.' "

I pause, my eyes still closed and my fingers gripping my lucky pendant tightly. "I can't think of anything else, Stel, so just put something like that. Or is that too much? Should I just put 'Hey, how's the road?' or 'How's the demo?' and leave out anything that's too 'I miss you' sounding?"

"Um..."

I open my eyes as Sam moves on to my lips. "What?"

Stella holds the phone in her hands like it's hot. "I thought you meant that's what you wanted to send. I just typed as fast as I could and sent it. I mean, I—"

"You sent all that?" Sam asks, arching one perfectly plucked eyebrow and looking aghast.

"Mmm, mmm, mmm," Tammy tsks, shaking her head as she smooths the hair on mine.

My face pales. "Is it awful?"

"I'll tell you what it is," Stella says, throwing my phone into my lap and edging into my mirror to check her own lips. "It's done. And who cares? He's lucky you're even texting him at all."

I try to look down at my phone, but Sam keeps my chin up with a remarkably strong pinkie finger. I sigh and close my eyes, hating how awkward things are with Adam. Everything was always so easy with him before, comfortable, and now I second-guess texts and secretly stalk him on Twitter. It's pathetic.

Sam pulls away, and I open my eyes again. He studies my face while Stella grabs one of my hands. "Listen, you are going to kill it tonight, Bird. Murder it. Annihilate it. I don't know what Adam would say right now to make you feel better, but take it from your best friend on this planet: You are going to be phenomenal. You are beautiful and your songs speak to everyone. When you're onstage, people can't help but feel happy, and I can't wait to get out there and cheer you on."

I grin. "Thanks, Coach."

"And you're opening for a le-gend!" she adds, stomping a turquoise vintage cowboy boot. "I mean, Bird, come on! Jolene Taylor is one of the greatest stars of all time, and *you* are her opener! Can you even fathom that?"

I shake my head. No. I actually can't.

"What's she like, anyway?" Stella prods. "I mean, I was kind of hoping to get a pic with her. You'd better not get any ideas about replacing me."

"Ha." I laugh dryly, thinking back to the brief encounter I had with Jolene today. "No worries there. I don't think she's as excited as we are about my being on her tour."

Stella's entire demeanor changes. "Screw her. She's old and washed-up. And she wears *rhinestones*. Please don't let them put you in rhinestones, okay?"

"Never," Amanda says, disgusted at the mere mention of bedazzlement. "I have a reputation to uphold."

"Looks like you're surrounded by good people, Bird," Stella says, clapping me on the shoulders. "Now I've got to get out there so I don't miss a single second. I heard the show opener brings the house down." She winks and blows me a kiss before heading out.

Then my dad comes over with Dan and Anita, who wish me luck, and there's nothing left to do but sing.

4

I TAKE A deep breath and rush the stage, climbing the steps two at a time, putting one boot in front of the other and hoping these butterflies will carry me through the show. Even though this is Jolene's tour, a few pockets of people in the crowd go wild and I spot some homemade signs meant for me.

I grab the mic and stare into the bright lights, willing myself not to freeze. The last time I had stage fright like this was the first time I sang lead for the Barrett Family Band at the Station Inn, but Dylan helped me through and Adam was in the front row. It was the night my whole world changed. I glance over at my dad in the wings now. He gives me two thumbs-up. I gulp and look back out into the arena. I wish I knew where Stella was sitting, or my brothers or my mom.

"I love you, Bird Barrett!" a young girl screams at the top of her lungs.

It's just the jolt I need.

"How you doing, O-ma-haaaaa?!" I shout into the mic, lifting it off the stand and walking to the front of the stage with one hand at my ear. The crowd swells. "Hello, up there at the top!" I call to the nosebleed section. "Can you see me?" I wave. "Do y'all... *Notice Me?*"

I hear a few squeals as I turn around to cue Monty. He's smiling, and it feels like we're off to a good start. As the music flows through my earpiece, I connect to the rhythm and give my fans everything I've got.

My set is a fantastic blur. I have always loved performing live, but singing in an arena this size is a whole new level of wonder. Rather than being paralyzed by my nerves, I am energized by the venue and crowd. I sing, clap, and dance. I laugh out loud when the wave takes off all around me and soak up my fans' excitement like a sponge. I tell them about writing "Tennessee Girl" last winter when my family put down roots again for the first time in seven years. I briefly mention Caleb when I bring things down a notch and share the inspiration for the ballad I cowrote with Dylan called "Before Music." And for the last song, when the stadium is finally good and full, I hold the mic out during the chorus of "Sing Anyway." They sing along to every word, and it takes my breath away.

By the time I take my final bow, I am exhilarated...and exhausted. My heartbeat is strong and thumps in my chest like a huge tom-tom. The baby hairs at my temples are drenched in sweat, and if my water bottle is any indication, I'm sure my lipstick has completely worn off. I wave to the fans as I exit, beaming at my mom, who waits for me off-stage. I close my eyes, for just a second, to mentally record this moment as the greatest of my entire life.

Then I nearly fall.

"Oh!" I cry, grasping for the handrail by the steps.

"You okay?" a roadie asks, holding out a hand as he lunges from behind a big light.

I grip the handrail and glance over at him. His open palm is smudged in scribbles from a ballpoint pen, his black T-shirt fits snug to his lean, muscular body, and his chiseled face looks adorably worried. Whoa. I feel my cheeks flame. "Yeah, I'm good," I say, hustling down the rest of the stairs. "Thanks."

"Bird, sweetie, you were incredible!" my mom calls, her arms open wide. As we hug, I spin her around to get another look at the cute roadie. He looks about Dylan's age, a little taller than me, with smooth olive skin. The kind of guy Stella would call Category 4.

"Nice job," Monty says, grasping my shoulder as he walks past.

I let myself get swept up in the crowd of people filing

offstage. "That was crazy. Wild. Ah-mazing!" The guys in the band give me fist bumps and head nods, and the backup singers offer big smiles and high fives. I feel like I'm floating.

"Where's Dad?" I ask.

Mom sighs as she links her arm through mine. "Had to take another phone call so he texted me to come back and meet you. I think this manager stuff is a lot more work than he expected." She clutches me tighter and gives me a death stare. "But don't you dare repeat that."

I laugh. "He's doing great. And there's nobody else I'd trust to take care of me."

"Well, he's been doing it all his life, so I'd say he's the most qualified."

"True," I say, nodding. "Very true."

We're almost to my dressing room when my mom stops short and points in the least discreet way imaginable. "Oh, Bird, there's Jolene Taylor!"

"Mom!" I whisper urgently, pulling her hand down.

"Well, I've been hoping to get her autograph, and now she's right there in her dressing room with only a couple of people around. I could just run in real quick—"

"I wouldn't," a woman's voice warns from behind us. We turn around, and my mom gasps, totally starstruck. We are face-to-face with Bonnie McLain, a country singer who was super famous in the late nineties and is one of my mom's all-time favorites. She looks over our shoulders in Jolene's direction and chuckles. "Jo's not what you'd call friendly on even the best of days, so talking to her right before she takes the stage would kind of be like poking a hornets' nest with a stick. Bad idea."

"Bonnie, my name is Aileen, and I am a huge fan. Huge." Bonnie graciously offers a hand to shake; my mom takes it in both of hers and keeps laying on the praise. "I have every one of your albums. I even saw you in concert when you came through Houston in '77. In fact, I always sing your song 'Stop and Take a Minute' at karaoke."

I am mortified that my mom is going on like this, but Bonnie's bright blue eyes are gleaming and the crow's-feet beside them are crinkled up in amusement. Even with her graying blond hair and dated feathered bangs (another thing she and my mom can bond over), I am struck by how pretty she is. Her smile is infectious, and she emanates this genuine warmth, like she would give great hugs.

"What are you doing here?" my mom asks. "A surprise performance? Maybe a duet with your old buddy Jolene?"

Bonnie shakes her head emphatically. "Oh no, no, no. When I left the industry, I left it for good. I'm just here to see Jolene perform and spend time with my husband's grandkids. They live right here in town."

"Bonnie, while we've got you, would you mind signing my CD?" my mom asks, fishing in her bag.

"You've got one of my CDs with you?" Bonnie asks, incredulous.

"Well, no," Mom admits, blushing. "It's Bird's, but these are like a dime a dozen around my house."

"Gee, thanks, Mom," I deadpan.

Bonnie laughs out loud and takes the marker my mom offers. "This is a first," she says, chuckling as she scrawls across the *Wildflower* cover. "I haven't signed an autograph in half a lifetime, and I've *never* signed another artist's merchandise."

"Oh, 'half a lifetime'—please," Mom says. "You haven't aged a bit."

"Well, that's kind of you to say, but I'm chubby and old and happier than I've ever been. I just celebrated my forty-tenth birthday last weekend."

"Happy birthday," my mom and I say at the same time.

Jordan comes through the hall, knocking on dressing rooms and giving a call for Jolene's set. Musicians grab bottles of water, a few stretch or finish cell phone calls, and roadies hustle to complete the changeover from my show to Jolene's.

"Isn't it amazing how much work goes into getting a single show up?" I marvel, watching a man frantically try to find the end to a big roll of tape. "Without these guys, concerts would be a disaster."

Bonnie nods her head and looks at me with appreciation.

"You know, Bird, I like your music, but it's good to know that you've got a heart that's likable, too."

I smile, warmed by such a nice compliment.

"Do you think I could take your picture together?" Mom asks, pulling out her cell phone.

I cringe, but Bonnie says, "Love to."

The former country music icon puts her arm around me as my mom fumbles with her pass code. "Thanks for doing this," I say quietly as we wait for Mom to pull up the camera app. "You know she's going to want one with you next, right?"

"This ain't my first rodeo, kid," Bonnie says, smiling. "But, listen," she adds, getting serious. "This life—it's wild. Trust me, I know. Everybody loves you, but nobody knows you."

"Say cheese!" my mom yells, waving her hand over her head.

"Cheese," we say simultaneously.

My mom takes the picture, then pulls her reading glasses down from where they were perched on top of her auburn hair. "Let me just check it."

Bonnie relaxes her hold and turns toward me, continuing her sage counsel. "I don't mean to get too deep on you or anything," she says. She pokes my sternum with her finger. "It's just very important that through it all, you remember who you really are."

I nod, not knowing how to respond.

"My turn!" Mom says, shooing me away and handing me her phone. "We've got to hurry. I just saw Jolene's entourage whisk her away."

I take a few pics, and then we say our good-byes. As Bonnie walks down the hall, I can't help but wonder why she gave everything up. She used to have all that fame, had lots of big hits, and is clearly a charismatic woman. How can someone like Jolene Taylor still be at the top of her game while a person like Bonnie McLain is on the sidelines?

My mom babbles on and on about the celebrity run-in as we hustle to my dressing room. I heard a little of Jolene's set during sound check, and I'm actually excited to get out of wardrobe and watch her show from the wings. I pull up one of Bonnie's old songs on my iPhone, and while I change, my mom crashes on the couch, singing along happily and uploading the pics to her Facebook page.

"Why'd Bonnie quit singing, Mom?" I ask as I lay all my show jewelry on the velvet roll Amanda left out for me. "She was pretty great, right? And she obviously had a following."

"Oh, I don't know, Bird," Mom says, sighing heavily and looking off to the side. "I think she just got mixed up in some bad decisions."

I consider probing deeper but don't want to be a buzz-kill. Instead, I text Stella and invite her to watch Jolene's set with me backstage. "Come on," I say to my mom as I pull her up from the couch. Jolene's voice is blaring down the hall.

As she sings "Two Men Too Many," my mom and I sneak into the wings. Jolene is a firecracker onstage, and her fans are going ballistic. She's twenty years older than me but still smoking hot in a rhinestone tank top and skinny leather pants. I daydream, thinking about head-lining my own tour one day and taking home Grammys like Jolene.

My mom closes her eyes and starts to sing along. I take the opportunity to glance behind us for another peek at the cute roadie who helped me earlier. He is manning a big light, and I find myself admiring the cut of his strong arms. He glances over, and I look away quickly, mortified that I was caught staring and then even more so when I realize that my mom is swaying with her arms in the air as if she just found Jesus.

"Mom!" I say, grabbing her arms.

"Bird!" Stella squeals, hugging me from behind. "You were so good!"

I hug her back, and then she pulls up a crazy pic on her phone: me in midair, jumping at some point in my set.

"I jumped?" I ask loudly in her ear to be heard above the music.

"You were wild!" she screams back. "You were amazing!"

She hugs me again, swinging me from side to side, and I laugh out loud.

I pull my phone out to show her the pics with Bonnie McLain but am thoroughly surprised to see a text from Adam:

Break a leg, Lady Bird.

A grin slides onto my lips. And the night just keeps getting better.

5

"THANK YOU, CONNOR," I say to the head of craft services the next day. The food on this tour is no joke. I mean, this man is serving *Top Chef*–style fare. "I can't get over how delicious these green beans are."

"Thank you, Miss Barrett," Connor says, but his attention is quickly diverted to one of the road crew using his hands to pick out a pork chop. "The tongs! Use the tongs!"

I laugh—as does the cute roadie who saw me trip after my show last night. The minute he got in line behind me, I tensed up. I couldn't think of anything to say, so I just smiled and grabbed a plate. Now, he nods toward the green beans and says, "It's the bacon, by the way. If you want veggies to taste good, just add bacon."

"Ah," I say. *Play it cool. Stay cool.* "I always thought butter did the trick."

"Well, you're definitely onto something there," he answers in all seriousness. "I'd say you could cover your bases by piling on both."

"Now you're speaking my language," I say, grinning as I grab a roll. "You know, my great-grandpa used to sit at the table with a tub of butter right next to him, and for every single bite, he would knife a dollop out and smear it on."

"Wow," the boy says, his expression a mixture of impressed and grossed out.

"He lived until he was ninety-four, so if anything, I'd say a case can be made *for* butter."

He laughs as we make our way over to the drink station, and I linger while he grabs a bottle of water from the cooler. I look out over the crew, huddled around tables for the preshow dinner, and wonder where he's going to sit... wonder if it'd be weird to sit with him.

We are both walking slowly as we inch away from the buffet, trying to look casual and therefore appearing anything but. He lays his plate on an empty table, looking hesitant as to whether he should sit down. I get the feeling that he wants to sit with me, too—that he wants to keep talking as much as I do—but feels just as awkward. So I set my plate down next to his and say, "So, where are you from?"

He pulls out his chair, looking adorably relieved, and

I join him, feeling the same way. "Los Angeles, born and raised."

"Oh, really?" I say. "My brother Jacob's going to school at UCLA in the fall. He took a campus tour, but all he could talk about when he got back was In-N-Out Burger."

I roll my eyes, but he chuckles. "I get that," he says. "It's addictive. But tell him the Mexican food out there is top-notch—the most authentic he'll find anywhere."

"Well," I say, cocking my head as he takes a drink, "except maybe in Mexico."

He nearly chokes. "Touché," he says, his dark eyes twinkling as he laughs. "Touché."

I laugh along, and we start to eat, listening to the conversations like white noise around us. I get goose bumps when he cuts his pork chop and his arm brushes against mine.

His cell phone buzzes, and he tilts a little away from me to pull it out of his jeans pocket. I glance over and catch a glimpse of what is, at the bare minimum, a six-pack under that T-shirt. "Sorry," he says as he texts a reply. "My mom's always checking up on me."

I nod and think, *I'm just happy it's not a girlfriend.* "So you're a momma's boy, huh?" I ask with a grin.

"Actually, it was just the two of us for a long time, so yeah," he admits with a slight blush, "I'm a major momma's boy."

His candor surprises me. "Oh," I say.

"But when I was a freshman my mom met Matt, my stepdad, who's a good dude. He legally adopted me when they got married, even though I was already, like, seventeen. He makes her really happy." He wipes his mouth with a napkin and grins at me sheepishly. "And now, Bird Barrett, you know my life story."

"But I don't have a name to go with it," I point out.

He pauses and then frowns. "Well, that's disappointing," he says in a hushed voice. "Jolene Taylor went out of her way to learn all our names when the tour started. She had us submit snapshots and short bios so she could really give the Sweet Home Tour a family vibe."

I pale. "She did?"

"I mean"—he gestures to the crew—"do you know anybody's name?"

I look around. "Jordan. Monty. I think the fiddler is Jeff...or Eric?"

He shakes his head. "It's already been more than twenty-four hours, and that's all you got? Wow."

He stares at me intently as I process what he's just said. I feel awful. Here I've been judging Jolene for snubbing me and judging the crew for kissing up to her when in reality, I've been the jerk. I really liked this guy, and now he probably thinks I'm a snob.

"I—I don't—" I stammer.

"Yeah, right," he finally says, busting out laughing. "Come on, you believed that?" He's laughing so hard that he has to set his fork down, and I feel blood rush to my face and down my neck. He got me. He got me good. "There are, like, a hundred of us, and it's only your second night with the tour. Come on, Bird, really?"

He takes the cap off his bottle of water and collects himself before taking a drink. I don't know whether to be mad or embarrassed, but I smile at him, sure of one thing: "Revenge is sweet, boy. Now I owe you one."

"Boy?" he asks, clearly flirting. "Now it's just 'boy'?"

"Well, I don't know your name!" I say, exasperated.

"I'll give you three guesses," he says.

I shake my head. "You want me to guess your name. There are, like, a million names, and I'm supposed to just guess."

"Hey, I'm giving you three tries," he says, dark eyes gleaming.

I take another bite and chew thoughtfully, accepting his challenge but playing with him. "Hmmm...you kind of look like a Fred."

He nearly chokes on a bite of pork chop. "Fred?"

"Okay, okay, not Fred. But you're from LA, so your mom probably liked the Lakers," I muse. I know I'll never really guess his name, so I toy with him. "Is your name Shaquille?"

He looks at me straight-faced and shakes his head. "I am not even going to dignify that with a response. And besides," he adds, clearly enjoying himself, too, "I'm a Clippers fan."

"Okay, okay, okay." He's a cutie with a sense of humor. I can't wait to text Stella. I pretend to think hard, going along with his game.

"Bird," he says, startling me by putting his hand on my forearm. I look down at it, charged. He has a worker's hands, the calluses on his palm just barely scratching my skin, sexy. "This is your last guess. Look at me." I do. His eyes are so dark that I can barely see the difference between his irises and his pupils. "I am sending you a telepathic message, repeating my name over and over." He furrows his brow; I do the same.

"Ah, yes," I say, nodding. "It's coming to me now."

"You can hear me?"

"Loud and clear. You're on the Sweet Home Tour, so you must love country music," I say, closing my eyes as if receiving his message. "I'm going to go with Garth. Final answer."

I open my eyes, and he hangs his head, sighing dramatically. But he doesn't remove his hand right away. And I don't want him to.

"Garth? Seriously?"

"Well, come on," I say. "There's no way I'm going to guess. I've only known you, like, five minutes!"

"You're right," he says, removing his hand and straightening an imaginary bow tie. "Hello, Miss Barrett. My name is Kai. Kai Chandler. It's nice to meet you."

He holds a hand out, and I shake it. "Nice to meet you, too."

Really nice.

"So I hate to burst your bubble with that last guess," he says, lowering his voice, "but I don't really *love* country music."

I pause. "Um, bubble burst."

He smiles. "Sorry, that came out wrong. I mean, I love *your* stuff—"

"Yeah, yeah," I say, taking a drink of pink lemonade and looking away.

"No, really," he says. He touches my arm again. I look back at him. "You don't understand. What I meant is that while country music is okay, this is just a job for me. If I'm in my car jamming out or something, I prefer to listen to indie bands, like Bedlum or Zane and Cass, you know?"

I shake my head. "Who?"

He nods, almost as if expecting that. "They're small bands out of New York and LA. Do you know Hard Break for Bugsy at least?"

I shake my head again, feeling like things are going downhill. "I listen to everything, though," I say. "I try to keep my mind open to all kinds of music, so I'll definitely check them out."

"Cool, cool. Electropop is kind of the thing now, making its way into a lot of indie stuff." He shrugs. "I'm not loving the fad since mainstreamers grab on to anything that's easy to imitate, but I do like it mixed with honest lyrics. Weighs down the pop part. I like music with depth, you know? Soul."

I nod, not understanding one hundred percent what he means but able to agree that every song I write needs to have a little piece of my soul woven in.

"The melancholy of 'Emma's Watercolors,' for example." He looks over my shoulder, almost far away. I feel both moved by his passion for music and lost at the same time because I don't know these groups. He looks at me and says, quite frankly, "I cried the first time I heard it."

My face must register my surprise. No guy I know would admit to that.

He grins. "Like a baby."

I look down at my plate, completely wowed by this boy. He's into music, beautiful, fit but not macho, he's... perfect.

I notice the tables around us starting to thin out and check my phone. I need to go back to my dressing room to get ready for the show tonight, but I don't want to leave, at least not on such a deep note.

"You know," I say, looking up and leaning in conspiratorially, "the first time I heard Jolene Taylor sing 'Pink Pumps and Purses,' I cried, too."

He is so surprised that he guffaws, drawing the attention of a few guys nearby.

"Because you liked it so much?" he asks, playing along.

I shake my head mischievously.

"Because you hated it?" he whispers.

I nod.

He leans in close, our faces inches apart. The lines of his nose and cheekbones are so straight and perfect, his jawline hard, like it's etched in stone. He is the definition of handsome.

"You know, I've worked a lot of shows, and I could tell you things you'd never believe. But Jolene?" He glances over his shoulder. "Oh man, she's the biggest diva I've ever seen. She brings her own Pilates studio with her on tour and demands that everything in her dressing room be pink, even the yogurt and vitaminwater stocked in her minifridge." He glances around again before going on. "And get this: There was this lighting tech that got fired a few weeks ago because Jolene thought the lights made her look older than she is."

"Are you serious?" I whisper, totally stunned.

He nods dramatically. "But you can't tell a soul, or I could get fired, too."

"My lips are sealed," I say, zipping them up.

"Well, you'll probably need those tonight for your show," he answers, barely touching the corner of my mouth when he "unzips" my lips. It takes everything I've got to keep my composure. "Just keep it confidential."

He gathers his trash, and I do the same, snapping out of it. I follow him to the bins, admiring his lean, hard build. I am shaken up. Worked up. Cannot wait to get out on that stage and let loose, give these feelings an outlet.

We walk down the corridor side by side, quiet. A few paces before my dressing room, he touches my arm again. This boy and those hands...

"I really love 'Before Music' by the way," he says. "It's so honest. It's my favorite part of the show."

I feel warm all over. "Thank you, Kai."

"Break a leg," he says, heading toward the stage. I watch him go, dazed, feeling like maybe I just dreamed the last half hour. But I can still feel his warmth on my forearm, and I know that we had a connection. I smile, floating into my dressing room on a cloud.

6

"BIRD, YOU WERE even better tonight!" Stella says the minute I step offstage. "I didn't think that was possible, but you were amazing."

"You do wonders for my self-esteem, Stel." I give her a giant hug, and as the band files past, I spin her so that she's looking in Kai's direction and say softly, "Look at the boy behind me and get ready for details later."

"Which one?" she asks. "It's dark."

"Okay, okay, never mind, then," I say, pulling away. The last thing I need is to be caught drooling over a boy . . . *by* the boy.

She squeezes my hand, eyes wide. "You vixen. What have you been up to?"

I don't leave out a single detail once we're safely in my dressing room.

"So how hot is he, exactly?" she asks.

"Really hot."

"Is he taller than you?"

"A little. Shorter if I'm in heels."

"Fine. So you become a sandals girl. Although the cowboy boots might be a problem." Her eyes light up. "Oh! Was there ever, like, that sudden, quiet almost-kiss moment?"

I laugh out loud. "Stella, it was just one conversation! It was only half an hour or something."

"Great romances have started in less time."

There is a knock at the door, and I glance at the time on my phone. Jolene's set starts soon. We leave for LA tomorrow, so I'm sure my glam team is ready to pack up and punch out.

"Hey, guys, sorry—" I say as I open the door. But I am completely shocked to see that the person standing outside is none other than Kai himself, looking adorably nervous with something in his hand.

"Bird. Hey."

"Kai!" I say. In my peripheral, I see Stella bolt to attention. "Hey."

"Sorry, I know this is totally out of the blue," he says with a sideways grin. "And I don't have a lot of time before

I have to get back out there for Jolene's set, but I copied a few tracks for you after dinner. That song 'Emma's Watercolors' is on there, and some of the other bands I was talking about before."

"Oh, wow!" I say, taking the flash drive from his hand. "That's so nice."

"It was no big deal."

"Thank you. Really."

"Sure."

Pause.

Pause.

I can't think of anything else to say. He rocks back on his black boots and glances over his shoulder as a couple of guys from the crew pass, but they're walking in the opposite direction of the stage, so we still have some time.

Pause.

Should I invite him in? Or is that weird? Kai's so good-looking that I feel self-conscious around him, like I don't know what to do or like I might say something stupid.

Then Stella clears her throat dramatically, snapping me to my senses. "This is my best friend, Stella," I say, looking at her with immense gratitude as I step back into my dressing room and gesture for him to follow. "Stella, this is Kai. He works lights for the show."

"Nice to meet you," she says, standing up and offering her hand.

"You too," Kai says as they shake. I slip the flash drive into my purse and turn back to him as he takes it all in. I try to see it from his eyes: the clothing rack full of more wardrobe options than I'll ever possibly need, the big mirror with a few pictures of me with my family and Stella tucked into the frame, the rows of shoes and accessories, all the makeup, the hot irons and hairbrushes. I realize I must look very high maintenance.

"If I didn't know better," Kai says, "I'd say you were kind of a big deal."

"It's crazy," I say, waving it away.

Pause.

"So Bird tells me you're from LA?" Stella pipes up. Kai grins and glances over at me. I could kill Stella. She might as well have said, *So Bird hasn't stopped talking about you since you met.* I feel a furious blush creep up my neck. "That's the next stop, right?" Stella continues, oblivious.

Kai nods. "Yeah, I'm really looking forward to getting back. I've been with the Sweet Home Tour since it started, so it'll be good to be home for a few days."

"I know exactly what you mean," I say, finally finding some common ground. "I loved growing up on the road, but sometimes it's nice to stay put for a little while."

"Definitely," he says. "Are you guys going to check out the city while you're there? I could suggest a few good spots, you know, like record stores, coffee shops..." He shrugs and flashes me a bold grin. "The places the *cool* people go."

I melt a little.

"Not me," Stella says with a frown. "I'm tagging along on the bus, but my mom has a gig back home this weekend. I'm headed back to Nashville with her once we get to La-La Land, but you should totally give Bird a list. She and her mom are going to explore while y'all set up the stage."

"Oh, really?" he says, pulling out his phone. "What's your number, Bird? I'll text you some must-sees."

I feel a little breathless as I give Kai my number. While he punches it into his phone, I glance over at Stella, who is clearly satisfied with herself.

"Okay, got it," Kai says. He pulls a pen from his front jeans pocket and scribbles a reminder on his palm. "I'll put a good list together. You'll definitely want to check out Spring for Coffee. And Makana for dinner. Oh, and go to Jet Rag if you like vintage."

"I adore vintage," Stella says. Then she looks at her phone and says, "You know what? Dylan just texted me that they're making dinner reservations, so I'm going to step out and call him back." She holds her phone up. "I can't seem to get a good signal down here."

I try to suppress a smile as she makes a hasty exit and then it's just Kai and me, alone, in my dressing room. It feels like when Stella left she took all the oxygen along with her.

Kai actually seems to have the opposite reaction. He looks a lot more relaxed once Stella is gone, and he walks over to my guitar. "May I?"

"Oh, sure," I say.

He picks it up and lets out a slow whistle. "This is gorgeous."

"Do you play?" I ask.

He shakes his head. "Not really. I know a couple of chords, but that's it."

"That's all Johnny Cash knew," I say. "And look at his career."

Kai grins at me. "Well, I am dressed in black every day." He walks over and sits next to me, holding my guitar out. "Play something?"

I am taken off guard. "Um, well, okay," I say, taking the guitar from him. "What?"

He shrugs. "Anything. What are you working on right now?"

I bite my lip. The song that I've been stuck on lately is one about Adam ditching Nashville—and therefore a future with me—for Austin, but it's not ready and it's not something I want to share with Kai.

Although I *am* inspired.

"What chords do you know?" I ask.

"Um, a few," he answers sheepishly. "C, F, G. I don't know. I'm definitely more of a music lover than a music player ... or musician, I guess."

"Okay, so let's see," I say, strumming. "Hmmm ..." Something comes to me, and I decide to go with it. "All right, so this is off the cuff, okay? Don't judge me."

Kai puts his hands up. "No judging."

I only have one line in my head, and it's going to be so obvious that this song is about him, but I'm going to go for it. Stella would tell me to, I know it. And if I learned anything from my short-lived attempt at a relationship with Adam, it's that if I want a guy to know how I feel about him—even from the start, even if I embarrass myself, even if he doesn't feel the same way—I just have to go for it.

"Fill up my plate with Southern cookin'," I sing to the tune of Johnny Cash and June Carter's famous duet "Jackson." *"Pile it on in great big heaps,"* I continue. *"There's a boy in black, standing at my back,"* I sing. Kai chuckles, but now I've strummed myself into a corner. Heaps. What rhymes with *heaps*? *"Got me thinking he might be for keeps."*

Oh my gosh, what the—?

My cheeks flame, so I look down at my fingers as if I need to see the strings when, really, I just don't want to make eye contact. Surely there's another word I could've rhymed with *heaps*. I shake my head and just keep going:

"Oh, teach me 'bout music.
You tell me what moves you.
Yeah, show me your music.
I'll learn a thing or two."

I cut it with one big strum and laugh nervously. "Ta-da!"

Kai claps. "Wow, you just made that up? Like, right now?"

I nod self-consciously, fiddling with the tuning keys. "Just joking around, though."

"Wow," he continues. "That's talent. Seriously."

I shrug. "Eh, I was inspired."

"Well," he says with fake swagger, "I tend to do that to the ladies."

I look up at him and laugh out loud. It suddenly feels like I've known him forever, when only minutes ago, I didn't have a thing to say. As our laughter dwindles to smiles, he holds my gaze a little longer than would be considered just friendly, and my heart flutters.

"Oh, man! What time is it?" Kai says, suddenly serious as he stands up and pulls his cell phone from the front pocket of his black jeans. "I have to go."

"Yes, of course!" I say, also standing. Time does weird things with Kai, like thirty minutes at dinner and we are already good friends; five minutes in my dressing room and I get the feeling we could be more.

"Listen to the songs on the flash drive, okay? I want to

know what you think," he says, hustling out. "There will be a quiz!" he calls, backpedaling down the hall.

"I'll be ready!"

Smiling, I walk down the hall in the other direction, where Stella is leaning against the wall. She looks up, and I can see the approval on her face. "Bird, my friend, you weren't lying. Team Jacob, baby."

I laugh. "He does look a little like Taylor Lautner. But cuter I think."

"Cute?" She fans herself dramatically as we push open the back doors and step out into the summer night. "Try hot. Face of Taylor Lautner and body of Taylor Kitsch. Suh-mokin' hot. I can't even."

I laugh at her theatrics but couldn't agree with her more.

My phone beeps, and my stomach flips. Kai texting me this soon is definitely a good sign. But when I look at the screen, I am surprised to see that the message is actually from Adam:

So, Lady Bird, how's life back on the road?

"Kai?" Stella asks, wiggling her eyebrows.

"Um, Adam," I say.

Her jaw goes slack, and she looks over my shoulder as I reply:

So far so good.

I push SEND and then let out a heavy sigh.

"You okay?"

I shrug, taken back to the moment when Adam suggested we slow things down, the day he broke my heart. "It's a little weird to be texting again."

"Maybe your mega message last night reopened the door," she says.

I hip-check her. "Yeah, thanks for that."

Adam writes back.

Just like the old days?

Not exactly, I think.

We left things between us so weird over the winter, and honestly, I miss Adam. But now, as I glance over my shoulder back toward the arena, where I know Kai is manning a big light at stage right, I can't help but think that I'm looking forward to the *new* days.

I text Adam a smiley face and a thumbs-up, loop my arm through Stella's, and open my heart for wherever the highway will take me next.

7

"We're like a moving city," Jacob says as the sun climbs into the sky.

"This is nothing, son," the bus driver says. She's almost sixty, smokes an electronic cigarette, and goes by Sissy. She's rough and country, full of crazy road stories; I'm so glad she was assigned to my bus. "You should've seen the way Madonna toured. Woo-ee! Now that was something."

Grinning, Jacob glances back at me over his shoulder, and I giggle. While the Barrett family is accustomed to life on the road, this is a scale of production none of us has ever seen: four buses, nine big rigs, and lots of vans and cars. We've covered some distance from Omaha to Los Angeles, but having my family and the Crossleys on board has made the time fly. We had a jam session yesterday, we've watched a few movies, and I've demolished everybody at the alphabet license plate game.

"Phew!" my dad says as he walks out of the back bedroom and heads for the coffeepot. We've barely seen him, which is pretty bad considering we're all crammed in one bus. "This is great, huh? The whole family on the road again."

"Can you imagine if we'd traveled the country in this thing, though?" Dylan asks. He is lounging on the leather massage chair, eyes closed.

"Her name is Dolly," I remind him.

"I beg your *Parton*?" Stella chimes in, right on cue. We lose it, falling over each other on the couch, while everybody looks at us like we're crazy...or mildly annoying. Let's just say that the joke was hilarious the first time, but we seem to be the only ones who still find it funny after a few days on the road.

"The bus is nice. Don't get me wrong," my dad says. "But we did all right on Winnie. Hey, you guys want to—" His cell phone rings, cutting him off. He looks down at the screen and sighs heavily. "Sorry, let me just..." He trails off as he heads back into the bedroom. "This is Judd Barrett."

"I can't believe you guys are flying out today," I lament to the others. We'll be in LA in a couple of hours, which means I'll get to perform again tomorrow. It also means that my entourage is flying home.

"Sucks," Stella says.

"Can't you push your flight back?" I ask, batting my eyes at her mom. "Shannon, don't you want to see me play the Staples Center?"

Shannon smiles. "I'd love nothing more, Bird, but I've got a spot at the Bluebird tomorrow night."

"Oh, that's right," I say, bummed for me but happy for her. Playing in the round at the Bluebird is a big deal, especially on a Friday night.

"Bird, don't start missing us before we're even gone," Stella says, throwing her arm across my shoulders. "You didn't even know we were coming! And at least I got to see what life on the road is like for big stars like you. I feel like a freaking Rolling Stone."

Dylan snorts and opens his eyes. "Yeah, you're a regular Mick Jagger, Stella." She rolls her eyes, and I laugh. As they start talking about their summers—she has an internship; he has a job—I stare out the window, thinking about how much I'll miss my family and how weird it'll be to tour without them. Only my parents are sticking around.

Suddenly my phone pings with a new text message, and I can't get to it fast enough. I didn't get Kai's number, so the ball has totally been in his court. Besides the fact that I like him and it's been torture waiting for him to text me, it really would be nice to see LA from a local's point of view.

I smile enormously when a text from a 323 number comes up:

Kai Chandler's unofficial official LA tour, for VIPs only.

His message is a long list of his favorite underground spots: record stores, coffee shops, art galleries, and dive music venues. No wonder he didn't text me right away; he really put some thought into it. I pass my phone to Stella under the table, and she reads the text. I take a big breath and fill my lungs with this energy, this feeling that I'm on the verge of something special, as the road leads me somewhere entirely new.

"How was it, Bird?" Dad asks when he meets Mom and me later for dinner. When our massive caravan pulled in this morning, the roadies sprang to life, unloading the trucks and beginning setup in a way that said, *We've done this before.* My dad, on the other hand, started running around like a chicken with its head cut off, and it was clear to me that if Mom and I hung around, we'd only be in the way. So we called a car service and went sightseeing.

After a full day that included LA musts like the Hollywood Walk of Fame and Sunset Boulevard, we are now at

Makana, a restaurant Kai suggested. It's Hawaiian, which is cool, something I've never had before. The place is stylish. The tables look like they're made of reclaimed wood, and the dim lightbulbs are encased in old glass buoys. It's rustic and romantic. I don't know what made Kai suggest this place, but it's a home run. And as much as I love my folks, I can't help but wish I were here with him instead.

"We had a great day," I say, taking another bite of the special: a spicy fish stew with something called poi. It's divine. "We didn't make it to the Hollywood sign, but we saw a lot of LA, Beverly Hills, and some of Santa Monica."

"You wouldn't believe how friendly the people are out here, Judd," Mom says. "We stopped at a trendy little coffee place Bird's friend recommended, and I actually left my wallet right on the counter—"

"Aileen," my dad says, shaking his head.

"Well, now listen," she continues. "This boy with those circle earrings that stretch out your earlobes came running up to me in the parking lot and gave it back. Then, he wouldn't let me buy him a coffee or anything for thanks!" My dad looks impressed, but I'm annoyed. I want to ask why his earrings have anything to do with it, but I bite my tongue. "You should've seen his tattoos, Judd. All the way up and down both arms. Looked like a color-by-number type of thing. But he was nice. That just blew me away— how nice he was."

"Wow, so you can't tell a person's character by the way he looks?" I finally say. "That's odd."

"Bird," my dad cautions.

My mom purses her lips. "You know that's not what I meant."

"Right," I say. They exchange a look like I'm somehow the brat in this situation, but determined not to fight, I change the subject. "I wish you could've come with us today, Dad."

He shrugs. "Me too. But my boss is pretty demanding."

"Ha-ha," I say dryly, and he laughs. I tell him about the rest of our day, Mom and I both effusive about our gorgeous drive up Highway 1 toward Malibu. It was enchanting, with the Pacific Ocean sparkling blue under the bright sunshine. I rolled down my window and took it all in, the surfers and paddleboarders, the amazing beaches, and the stunning houses perched on the hills and nestled in the valleys.

"Wow, I'm jealous," he admits. As dinner progresses, his phone beeps so much that it gets obnoxious. He was never that guy before, and it's pretty hypocritical since the Barretts have a "No Screens at the Table" policy, but again I bite my tongue knowing all the messages probably have to do with the tour and me.

"LA sure is something else," my mom remarks. "Everybody dresses so casual and tries to act laid-back, but the cars all zoom down the freeway." She's right. The traffic is intense. "Nobody can slow down these days."

I glance over at my dad and sigh. Here we are at an absolutely wonderful restaurant, and he can't see beyond the texts and e-mails blowing up his phone. Judd Barrett is supposed to be a banjo player and father, but looking at him now, I see only my manager.

When my mom says California feels worlds away from Tennessee, I have to agree. But that's also what I like about it. There's an almost palpable vitality here. I thought LA would be so fake, all stretched, plastic faces and flashy snobs, but I had a blast today and loved every minute. As we went from tourist stops to local favorites, even getting stopped a couple of times for an autograph or picture, I couldn't help but think about how many big dreams have come true along these busy boulevards.

8

"ANYBODY HOME?" ANITA calls from the front of Dolly. She wasn't at all interested in a road trip from Omaha, but there's no way she or Dan would miss my first show in Los Angeles tonight.

"In the bathroom!" I holler back.

I hear her making herself a cup of coffee as I spit out my toothpaste. Winnie got us where we needed to go and I love that RV, but life on Dolly is a whole new level of mobile living. This bathroom may be small, but it's nicer even than the one we had in our old house in Jackson.

"How was your flight?" I ask, meeting Anita out in the lounge area.

She shrugs. "Terrible, as usual. How do you like California?" she asks.

"Oh man, I love it," I gush, packing my bag for another day out. "My mom and I went down to the Chinese Theatre yesterday. I can't believe I'll actually be there for a movie premiere on Monday!"

Anita worked hard to get my song "Beautiful to You" on the sound track of the latest blockbuster starring Hollywood It Boy Jason Samuels. She even set us up on an awkward coffee date, which was infuriating at the time, but now that the movie is being released and I get to walk the red carpet, all is forgiven. Besides, Jason ended up being cool. A little pretentious about his "craft," but a good guy.

"Are your parents here?" she asks suddenly, looking over my shoulder.

"They went into the arena to check out the stage," I answer, unplugging my phone from its charger. "I'm supposed to meet my mom in a few minutes. She's flying back to Nashville on the red-eye tonight, so this is our last chance to see the Hollywood sign. I know you're probably worried that I'll be worn out before the show, but don't be. We won't be gone long."

Anita smiles. "Oh, I'm not worried. That's your manager's job."

"Well, my manager has a billion things to think about besides whether I go sightseeing, so I think I'll just use my best judgment."

"Wonderful," she says, taking another sip of coffee. "Soak up all this California sunshine."

"Right?" I say, remembering to grab my sunglasses. "My dad says he likes having all four seasons, but I say a girl could get used to having a tan all year-round."

"You know, Bird," Anita says, placing her cup in the little sink, "Open Highway is in the process of setting up a second office out here. A lot of country singers try to keep a foot in both Nashville and LA. You could always relocate, even if for only part of the year. It could really go a long way toward opening up crossover opportunities for you."

I finally stop moving and consider her. "Relocate?"

"Just part-time. Something to think about," she says, heading toward the front door of the bus. By the time her stilettos hit the pavement, she's already on her phone and I've forgotten to ask why she stopped by in the first place. But living in LA? How would that work? Would my folks even let me? Definitely not on my own, but would they be willing to make the move?

I shake the thought from my head and get going. Home is this bus for the rest of the summer, and that's about as far as I can think right now. I pull on my Beats and listen to the playlist I made from Kai's flash drive as I walk across the parking lot, California dreamin'.

"Wow, you guys," I say to Dan and Anita later as I join them in the nosebleed section of the Staples Center. "If you want, I can talk to my manager about getting you better seats."

They both laugh. "Bird," Dan says, pulling the seat down beside him, "have a seat. See what the fans see."

When I settle into the last row of the uppermost deck of the arena and look out over the sea of empty seats, I feel so small. It's kind of trippy since when I'm out on that stage, I feel like a giant, full of power, fearless. Suddenly, a light-bulb goes off in my head. "I ought to tape some signed CDs under these chairs and then announce it during the show. If I were a fan, I'd be stoked."

Dan turns to Anita, who looks impressed. "I'll get some up here by the time we're through with this chat," she says, and begins typing on her phone, presumably sending someone to meet us with CDs.

"You could just text my dad," I offer. "He's on the bus, I think."

"Actually," Dan says, propping his elbows on the armrests and steepling his fingers at his chin, "we really wanted to take a moment alone with you, Bird. Just to have a quick talk."

"Oh," I say. I pause. "My dad shouldn't be here, then?"

"Probably not," Dan says, crossing one leg over his knee. "This isn't really a meeting. It's more like a conversation."

"*Oh*-kay."

"First of all, I couldn't be happier with the success of *Wildflower*," he says with a genuine smile. "The tour is off to a great start as well. The crowd ate it up in Omaha, and I have no doubt that the LA audience will love you this weekend."

"Adore you," Anita says.

"This tour with Jolene," he continues, "is going to launch you into a whole new stratosphere."

"Everyone in America will know who you are by the end of the summer," Anita says, pointing a manicured finger my way. "Mark my words."

I believe *her*, but I sometimes still can't believe *it*.

"Which brings me to something I've been meaning to talk to you about," Dan says, readjusting himself in the seat once again. Something about this whole "conversation" has me filled with anxiety. Dan runs one hand over his bald spot and goes on. "It's a delicate topic, I admit, but Anita and I have been talking a lot about your future, your next steps, where we see you in a year, five, ten, and so on."

Wow. I barely think beyond tomorrow.

"And you're only going to get bigger, Bird," Anita says.

"With that in mind . . ." Dan says, clearly uncomfortable. My throat tightens. Something's not right. "We strongly feel that it would be in your best interest—and this is just business, not personal—to hire a real manager.... sooner rather than later."

"Huh?" I say, stunned. They want to replace my dad?

"I love that your parents are so supportive, Bird. I do," Dan says.

"They're amazing people," Anita adds.

"But you're in the big leagues now, and your dad has..." Dan pauses. "Let's just say he's dropped the ball on a few things."

"Well, he's learning," I say, caught off guard. "We're new to all this. I think he's doing pretty well, really, for somebody who's never been a manager before."

"Listen, Bird, there's no doubt he has your best interests at heart," Anita says, leaning forward to look me in the eye. "But the facts are these: He's had trouble staying on top of things, he's coming to us with a lot of stuff that we don't have time to sort out for him, and you're only going to get bigger, so he's only going to get busier. There's just not time for a learning curve. I'm not being mean, just honest. Your dad's great, but this is business."

"You need a professional, Bird," Dan says. "I'm telling you this as your friend, not as your boss. I actually have an excellent manager in mind, if you think this is something you want to at least consider, but he lives in California."

"If he's in California, then how's he going to do a better

job than my own father, who'll be right on the bus with me?" I ask defensively. Probably not the best way to talk to the president of my music label, but this all feels wrong: hiding out at the top of the arena, talking about my dad behind his back.

"Well, that's actually something else we wanted to talk to you about," Dan continues. "We think you need to have a presence out here. A strong presence in LA will really help you cross over from the country scene into mainstream."

"So, you want me to...ditch my dad...and move to California?" I ask slowly, my head spinning.

"That's not *exactly* what we're saying," Dan says.

I think about my dad this morning, how it looked like he'd gotten hardly any sleep and how everything he does these days is for me. I think about what he's sacrificed since that night last year at the Station Inn when I was first discovered. I think about music, what it means to him and to my family, how it saved us...how the Barrett Family Band stopped touring because of me, and how if I replace my dad as manager, I'm shutting him out of it all completely.

"No way," I say, standing up. I could never hurt my dad like that. "Is that it? I need to get backstage."

"Certainly," Dan says, uncrossing his legs and standing up. "It was just something to consider. We didn't mean for you to make any sudden changes. I'm sure Judd will figure things out and be a pro in no time."

I nod as we walk to the escalators, but a twinge of doubt niggles at the back of my mind. *Will he?* Just this morning he was frustrated that it took him seven calls to get the right guy on the phone for a merchandising situation in San Diego. How many phone calls would a seasoned manager have had to make?

"And California isn't something we're suggesting happen right away, either," Anita says. "But Dan and I are heading back to Nashville after the premiere Monday night, and we wanted to have a conversation before then about where you are and where we see you going."

"I'm looking forward to the premiere and seeing Jason again, actually," I say, changing the subject as we file onto the down escalator.

"It will be an incredible night," Anita says. "Your first major red carpet, Jason and his Hollywood friends, and the clothes—oh, Bird—wait until you see the gowns I'm having sent over."

I smile, the tension from just moments ago already lightening as I think about it.

When we hit the first level again, we walk toward the doors to the backstage tunnel and one of Anita's "people" meets me with the surprise upper-deck CDs to sign. After I scrawl my signature across the cases, Anita smiles knowingly and hip-checks the doors wide open. "Get ready, Bird Barrett. You're about to see how much fun LA can really be."

9

"Bird! Over here! Bird, Bird, you're gorgeous! Bird, here! Right here!"

"This is insane," I say as I accept my dad's hand and step out of the limousine. The cameras and paparazzi are a blur, everybody crowding around one another to get a good shot. I link my arm through my father's and we look right, smile, look straight, smile, look left, and smile. Anita coached us on red-carpet tips like that, as well as a few poses I could use in front of the step-and-repeat—the wall of sponsor logos in front of which everyone gets their picture taken—but when it comes to the microphones jutting forward and TV cameras rolling, I haven't got a clue. "There are so many people calling my name I don't even know where to look," I say through clenched teeth.

My dad isn't much help. He looks like a deer in head-lights, and as we start to take a few steps down the red carpet, it is abundantly clear that he's as lost about proto-col as I am. Luckily, Anita hangs in my shadow, looking absolutely stunning in a sleek black Marc Jacobs dress, her dark hair slicked back in an elegant bun. When we make eye contact, she knows instantly what I need and maneu-vers down the carpet ahead of us to direct me toward the reporters she'd like me to talk to.

"Bird, who are you wearing?" an *Entertainment Tonight* reporter asks, holding her mic out to me. I smile and walk toward her, thinking to myself what a stupid question that is. I want to respond, *I'm wearing someone? Dad, check my back. Do I have a stowaway?* But I know Anita would kill me, so I look down at my gold-and-black dress and say demurely, "Calvin Klein."

"It's beautiful," she says. "But I have to mention, I'm surprised to see you without your trademark footwear." *Huh. I have a trademark?* "Where are those cowboy boots we never see you without?"

I look down at my high, high heels and think how much more comfortable my apparent trademark would be, but I smile and answer in the way I think my publicist would want me to: "Well, Jason Samuels was voted Sexiest Man Alive, not Most Likely to Host a Hoedown." The reporter chortles, surprised by my answer, and I laugh with her, feeling like I nailed it; but then I make the mistake of glancing over at Anita to gauge how I'm doing and she's wearing the expression of someone who's been pinched. I gulp and try to read her. *Too frank?* I thank the reporter and step away as people around her clamor for an interview.

"Bird! Bird, one question!"

"Phew," I whisper to my dad, my smile unwavering. "This is crazy, right?"

But before I can talk to another reporter, Anita cuts me off. "What was that?" she snaps.

"I thought it was funny."

"It wasn't. You're a country music singer, so try not to insult the entire cowboy boot industry, okay?"

I feel my cheeks flame. "But you said the Louboutins were sexier."

"They are, but I didn't put it in a press release."

I sigh heavily.

Anita softens, placing both of her hands on my arms. "Bird, calm down. Don't overthink the questions or try so hard to impress. You look gorgeous and everyone loves you. Just be yourself." She turns and leads me back toward the press line.

I plaster on a smile and try to follow her advice, but it's hard to "be yourself" when that doesn't seem to be what anyone wants at all.

"That movie was so good!" The screening is over, and our limo is now joining the line of cars dropping people at the after party. "My voice—*my song!*—while Devyn Delaney pines over Jason-freaking-Samuels? I can't. I can't! Stella is going to die."

"Well, the critics aren't so enthusiastic," Anita says, holding up her phone. "Rotten tomatoes across the board."

"Seriously?" I say. I'm about to defend the wartime biopic but am distracted when I look out the window. "Wow," I murmur as we stop in front of Lure, a big LA club where the after party is. "Look at the line."

"We'll be on the list," Anita says airily.

It's all so exciting, even more so now that Anita and Dan are my chaperones instead of my dad. After the movie, he got a call about the merchandise situation and had to go ahead to San Diego to fix it. We'll meet him there tomorrow with the tour. I loved taking him as my date tonight, but no girl wants to go clubbing with her father.

We step out of the car and are gracious with more smiles to the paparazzi, but move quickly inside. The place is packed, but it's like the parting of the Red Sea as the hostess leads us through the crowd to the VIP section.

"Poor Jason," I say, scanning the scathing comments

about the movie on my Twitter feed. "All that hard work and then everyone just turns their backs on him."

"That's show biz," Anita says simply, her eyes scanning the room. "But your song is safe. The *Hollywood Reporter* said 'Beautiful to You' was the best part of the movie."

I let her words sink in. If that's show biz, it could be me with my next album. It could be me with my next single. I think about everything my family has sacrificed and even the relationship I could've had with Adam. If fans can be so fickle, can turn on us so quickly, then everything I've worked for could disappear in a flash. A shiver runs down my spine. I have to keep making good music. I cannot let up.

"Bird!" Jason yells when we cross the VIP rope.

"General!" I call back teasingly, referencing his character.

He stands up from the booth, leaving behind four clearly disappointed model types, and walks over for a hug. His thick brown hair is pulled back into a low ponytail and his face is covered in stubble, scratching my cheek the tiniest bit when we embrace. My pulse quickens. *People* magazine doesn't have anything to explain to me—Sexiest Man Alive? Abso-freaking-lutely.

Anita and Dan congratulate him on his performance and quickly move on to other movers and shakers in the room, directors and publicists their age, but I stay with Jason, determined to give him the kind of reception I would want after I played a big show. I think about my songs, how hard I work on them and how personal they are, how nerve-racking it is every time one is finally released and how terrified I was when my album first dropped. The littlest criticisms stung, so I can't imagine how he must be feeling if he's been online at all.

"I loved the movie," I say over the music, nodding effusively and flashing my most encouraging smile. "Seriously. I cried."

He smiles, putting his hands together and bowing a little like people do in yoga. "Thank you, Bird."

"You're welcome."

"Come," he says, suddenly linking his fingers through my own. He leads me through the party like I'm an old friend, and I try to stay cool, as if I hold hands with A-list actors all the time. At the food table, he lets go and passes me an appetizer plate. He speaks loudly into my ear. "You look ravishing, by the way," he says with a half grin.

I blush. "Thank you."

I can feel people watching us as we load our plates with fruit, cheese, and crackers. I am the center of attention, sharing his spotlight. A photographer approaches us and we pose, Jason wrapping his arm around my waist as if it were the most natural thing in the world.

"Congratulations on *Wildflower*," he says before dipping a piece of kiwi in the chocolate fountain. "It's a terrific album."

"Wow," I say. "Thanks a lot."

"We have much to celebrate. Jason Samuels with a new movie and Bird Barrett with a chart-topping album," he says. I grin when he refers to us both in third person. A waiter passes with a tray of champagne, and he reaches for two glasses. "Cheers," he says, holding one out to me.

"Oh," I say, surprised. Instinctively, I glance around the room, looking for my chaperones, but they are busy schmoozing the movie's producers. I've never had a drink before, even though—and maybe because—I've played honky-tonks and dive bars for years, but I don't want to be a buzzkill. And I doubt Jason Samuels often hears the word no.

We clink glasses and I bring the bubbly to my lips, so excited to be at this after party that it feels like my heart is thumping in time to the beat the DJ is spinning. The champagne is sweet, but it burns a little going down. And I doubt it's the alcohol already, but I feel light-headed. Jason Samuels is smiling at me devilishly, almost the way he does at the girls in his movies, and people I recognize from *Us Weekly* are all over the place. This is unreal.

"How long are you in town?" he asks over the music.

"We leave tomorrow," I answer. "San Diego."

"Ah." He nods. " 'America's Finest City.' You'll love it."

I shrug. "I won't get to see much of it. We're only there for one show and then moving on."

"Breakneck," he says.

"What?"

He leans in closer to be heard over the music and again, my heart skips. I'm not the one with the celebrity crush—it's Stella who calls herself Mrs. Jason Samuels—but he really is good-looking. And so close that his shirt collar brushes the bottom of my chin. It's like, *intimate.* "Breakneck," he repeats. "The tour. The pace. Breakneck, right?"

"Oh, yes," I say. I nod, hoping the dim lighting will disguise the intense blush I can feel on my face. "Yes, totally. Crazy."

He smiles, then clinks my glass again, downing the rest of his champagne. "It's really good to see you again, Bird Barrett. LA could use a little more of you."

I giggle, tossing my hair back and settling into this conversation. I can't believe Jason Samuels is flirting with me, but I might as well return the volley, just for the fun of it.

"Well, actually, my label is opening a—"

"Oh no," he interrupts, his smile gone as he looks past my head. "Um, I need to go talk to my manager about... something. I'll catch you later, Bird."

He squeezes my arm and cuts through the crowd, leaving me alone in the middle of the room. I look over my shoulder to see what could've shaken him up and spot an intimidating posse of gorgeous, bejeweled girls entering the VIP section. Devyn Delaney, Jason's costar and supposed ex, leads the pack, the definition of queen bee. She is stunning, her dark skin flawless and her smile radiant. She locks her almond eyes on mine and from the look on her face, it's as if she's hit the bull's-eye. Now whether that's a good thing—

"Bird Barrett," she declares, her entire group of friends encircling me with matching smiles and model poses. "I'm Devyn. I've been dying to meet you, ever since you did that PR thing with Jason."

"Oh, right," I say, figuring she must mean our coffee "date" in Nashville. "Hi."

"Wasn't that the worst, how it got blown up?" she asks, her intensely made-up eyes narrowed.

"Oh my gosh, yes!" I say, nodding vigorously. I know I'm overdoing it; I just can't make myself stop. "The worst! I was mortified. I mean, not that Jason's not nice, but the tabloids calling me his 'Song Bird'? It was so fake."

"Yeah," she says, cracking a smile. "Especially since he and I were totally hooking up then."

My jaw drops. "Oh," I manage. "Right. Especially."

"The press," she says, shaking her head dramatically. *"God."*

I nod, not really knowing what else to say. Anita told me that Devyn and Jason broke up weeks ago but have to pretend otherwise for their publicity tour. I can't imagine how badly that would suck, and yet, I don't think it's the best topic of conversation.

"Um, I loved the movie," I say instead. "I cried. You two were perfect together."

"Tell him that," she responds bitterly. Then, as if catching herself, she quickly recovers and laughs out loud as if it were a big joke. "Just kidding. I'm so glad we're over." Devyn grabs my wrist and pulls me a little closer. She smells like one of the heavy-perfume pages from *Vogue*. "It's hard though, you know? Working together and doing all this press when he's obviously still not over me." She shakes her head. "It's sad."

"Really? Oh, wow."

"Hollywood is such a small world, though."

"Right," I agree, just trying to keep up.

I know nothing about her life, about her relationship, or about dating in the Hollywood world, but it's pretty evident that Devyn Delaney is a big part of the in crowd out here. A waiter passes by with a tray of champagne and her friends all grab glasses. They start talking about Miley Cyrus's most recent train wreck, and although I have nothing to add to the Hollywood gossip circle, I laugh along with them. Devyn totally tunes out the conversation and texts on her phone, which is pretty impressive since she's also holding a glass of bubbly and her clutch.

None of the other girls introduce themselves to me, so I bob my head to the music and scan the crowd. It's kind of bizarre; all the faces here are familiar, but I don't *know* anybody. I catch Anita's eye across the room and can tell that she's pleased to see me "networking," so I take a breath and try again with Devyn. She has a song on the sound track, too, so I start there. "I loved your song, by the way. You have a really beautiful voice."

"OMG, thank you, BB," she says, placing one hand over her heart. "You are so sweet to say that. I love yours, too."

"Thanks," I say. I take another small sip of champagne, feel the burn, and try to disguise it. It's decided: I'm already over this stuff, but I don't know what to do with my glass and everybody else has a drink in hand.

"I downloaded your whole album and really like 'Sing Anyway,'" she goes on. "That is *so* the story of my life."

"Aw."

"You know, like everybody's watching. Always. And we have to sing anyway," she says, pulling a long strand of black hair out of her heavily glossed lips and smoothing it back. "Oh, ussie while we're standing here!"

"Ussie?"

"A selfie with both of *us*," she explains. "Duck lips!"

She holds her iPhone out and stands on tiptoes. I lean down and smile but realize too late that she's making a pouty kiss face. I try to change expressions, but she snaps the pic too quickly. "Gorg!" she squeals. "I can't wait to tweet this out!" which she does right away, before I can suggest a do-over. "Anyway, we should hang out sometime. How long are you going to be in LA?"

"I leave tomorrow."

She puts on an exaggerated pout. "Of course. Right when we become friends. So here, give me your number. We'll get lunch or go shopping or something the next time you're in town."

"Oh, that'd be great," I say. I give her my number and surprise myself with the nervousness I feel. It's so amazing to be making friends with these people. I mean, I've paid real money to see Jason and Devyn in the theater before. Now we're hanging out. *What the what?*

"I just texted you," she says. "The three-one-oh number is me."

I give my still-full glass of champagne to a cocktail waiter walking past and get my phone out of my clutch. "Got it," I say, firing back a smiley face.

"Perf," she says, saving it in her phone. Then she looks up and says, "Oh, there's Selena." She gives me an air kiss on both cheeks, says, "Ciao," and walks across the room, her posse of cocktail dresses in her wake.

If California seemed like a different country before, it feels like an entirely different *planet* now. But it was good to see Jason again and surprisingly pleasant to meet Devyn.

I kind of suspected that she'd be high maintenance, but I wasn't expecting her to be so friendly. It would be nice to know another girl my age who's dealing with the spotlight, so I save her number and retweet the pic of us, even if it's not my best, and even though I cringe at her hashtag: #hollywoodhotties.

I think about my conversation with Dan and Anita in the nosebleeds yesterday, when Dan called this "the big leagues." As I look around at the glamorous young stars and swanky VIP room—of which I am now somehow a part—the one thing I do know is that I'm certainly not in Nashville anymore.

10

"Just us girls now, right?" Sissy asks when I stomp down the bus stairs. She's smoking a real cigarette outside before our two-hour drive down the coast. Since it's a big deal that somebody like Jolene is letting her opener sell anything at her shows, I get why my dad had to go ahead and smooth over whatever is messed up with merchandising, but it's a little weird to be on my own. My mom and brothers are back in Tennessee, as are Dan and Anita as of this morning.

"Yep, just the two of us," I say. I pull on my sunglasses and stretch. People are milling around the parking lot, ready to roll.

"I've been wanting to tell you about my European tour with Kiss anyway," she says.

"Oh, wow." I walk over to the side of the bus and get my guitar and fiddle from underneath. Now that the place is cleared out and I'll have some time on my hands, I want to work on that song about my pseudo-breakup with Adam. "I'd love to hear about that, but actually—"

My cell phone pings with a text alert. I pull it from my back pocket, surprised but thrilled to see a message from Kai:

Did you get to everything on the list?

I smile, writing back:

No, but I did my best.

"But actually, what?" Sissy asks.

"Huh?"

"But actually...what? You got a boy you going to try to sneak on here?" she asks with a half grin. "Don't worry. I'm not a suit and I'm not your mom. You do what you want and I'll just keep her between the lines," she says, patting Dolly on the side as she walks toward the door.

"That's not what I was going to..." I call after her, but my words trail off.

Distracted, I put my instruments back under the bus, my pulse quickening as I text Kai:

I saw your hometown. Want to see the way I grew up?
Bird Barrett's unofficial official tour of RV living. For VIPs
only.

I stare at the message, my jittery thumbs hovering over
the screen as I wait for his reply:

Sure. When?

I lean against the side of the bus and type my invitation
before I have the chance to chicken out:

Now?

He writes back instantly:

On my way.

I do a little jump before I realize that I don't know
which bus he's on right now and therefore he may be able to
see me. Playing it cool, I slip my phone back into my pocket
and stroll toward the door of the bus, then race up the stairs
and head to my bathroom. I don't have time to put on full
makeup, but I do swipe on a little mascara, take down my
ponytail, and fluff my hair. Then I smear on pink lip gloss
and kiss a piece of toilet paper so it doesn't look too fresh.

Finally, I grab a peppermint from the tub up front before I hear a knock.

"Permission to come aboard?" Kai asks when I swing open the door. He is a vision, his skin smooth and tan with the sunlight pouring in around his frame.

"Permission granted," I say, stepping back up the stairs ahead of him. I take a deep breath and try to keep control of myself.

He climbs up into the RV and looks around, clearly impressed. "Nice digs."

"Yeah," I say nodding. "Our Winnebago wasn't as nice as this, but my family and I lived in a rolling home since I was nine, so I'm used to cramped quarters."

He grins. "This doesn't feel cramped."

"Well, there were five of us on Winnie, and she was way smaller than Dolly."

"Did you say Dolly?" he asks.

"Yeah," I say, blushing a little. "That's what Stella and I named her."

"Ah," he says, nodding.

I think about our punch line, but in front of Kai it feels corny. I change gears. "You want something to drink?"

"Sure," he says. "I'll take a water."

I squeeze around him, just barely brushing his forearm with my own, and shiver. This is the first time I've seen him in something other than the required all-black roadie wear, and while I didn't think it possible, he looks even better in street clothes. His style is casual but put together. He's wearing a snug white cotton shirt that looks soft and comfy, like it's been washed a million times, with slim-fit jeans and plaid Converse sneakers. His black hair is longish on top and looks like it might have some product in it, and he wears a woven band around his wrist. A silver chain is tucked under his shirt, and I wonder if the necklace is lucky like mine.

"Do you play poker?" he asks, walking over to the table. He picks up the case of chips we'd been using on our way to LA.

"I know the basics," I say, setting our drinks down. "My brothers love cards." The bus starts to roll forward and we sit, Kai opening the case and pulling out the deck.

"I prefer Texas Hold'em," he says, shuffling. "You've got to know the rules of the game, but poker is about so much more. It's about reading people. Come on, let's play. You'll be ready to empty the Vegas vaults by the time the tour rolls through there."

A girl doesn't grow up in an RV with two older brothers and not learn a thing or two about reading people, but I don't tell Kai that. I think it's cute that he wants to teach me how to play. He deals and I pick up my cards. I would normally fold the two of diamonds and nine of clubs right away, but we're not playing for money so I ante up to see the flop.

"I loved 'Emma's Watercolors,' by the way," I say when he turns over the first three cards. A couple of low diamonds but nothing worth staying in for.

"You did?"

"It's gorgeous," I say. "So sad, though. The first time I listened to it I was in bed and then I couldn't fall asleep."

"I told you," he says knowingly. "It tortures me."

"Yeah, and the crazy thing is that it's not just the words. The music itself is—I don't know. If there weren't a single lyric, it would still be depressing."

"No, you're totally right," he says. He is so enthusiastic that he doesn't even realize he's holding his cards faceup. I was going to fold, but his hand is as bad as mine so I stay in. "What else did you like?"

"Oh," I say, looking up. "One of the songs reminded me of 'Some Nights' by fun., but with a slower tempo."

"Really?" He frowns. He looks down and throws in a chip, clearly bluffing.

"Yeah, a little." I match his bet, and he burns a card before flopping over another. It's a king of diamonds.

"Probably 'Restless,'" he says, clearly not liking the comparison. "I guess I can see that." He frowns at his hand as if he's not sure what to do and then baffles me by throwing in a stack of red chips.

"Seriously?" I ask.

"What?"

"Um," I stall, looking away. He doesn't know that I know he's bluffing, so I cover. "You seriously don't see the similarity between Zane and Cass and fun.?" I look at my cards and pretend like I don't know what to do. Once I feel the appropriate number of seconds has ticked by, I match his bet. He looks up at me, arching his eyebrow as if that were the last thing I wanted to do. I have to look out the window to keep from laughing out loud.

"I guess, now that you mention it," he says nonchalantly as he burns another card and turns over the river, "but fun. is so...mainstream." The queen of diamonds smirks up at me, but I study my cards as if still stumped. I know he has nothing, but I can feel him trying to read me...and failing miserably.

"I never really thought of them as 'mainstream,'" I say, knocking the table with my knuckles to check. "Have any of the indie bands you like made it?"

"Well, it depends on what you mean by 'making it,' I guess," he says, frowning again. He looks up at me almost apologetically as he pushes his chips forward. All his chips.

And now I'm in a pickle. I know I've got him beat, but I don't want to stop playing. I like having something to do with my hands, having something to focus on besides his absurdly cute face. If I luck into a weak flush on the very first hand, will he even want to play again? I mean, he's trying to teach me and I don't want him to feel bad.

"Whoa, too rich for me," I say, throwing my cards down. "I fold."

His shoulders relax and his lips stretch wide into a beautiful smile. "I was bluffing," he admits, showing me his cards. He rakes the chips toward himself, and I shake my head as if I can't believe it.

"Oh, man!" I say, picking up the cards for my deal.

"You have to really study me to figure out my 'tell,'" he explains. "The 'tell' is something people do unconsciously when they're bluffing."

"Ah," I say.

"Wait, let me see what you had."

Kai grabs my cards before I mix them into the deck, and I gasp. "Hey, don't—"

His jaw drops. He takes a beat and then looks up at me with a half grin. "Are you hustling me, Bird Barrett?" he asks slowly.

I blink. "Huh?"

"You've got a flush," he says. "You folded a flush."

His dark eyes search mine and I cringe. "I just thought when you went all in that if I smoked you on the first hand you'd feel bad."

He shakes his head. "Of course you play poker," he says, chuckling now. "Cool girls always play poker." I shrug and smile, and he tosses the cards back my way. "I accept the challenge, Doc Holliday. Deal 'em and don't hold back."

Smiling, he sorts the chips and evens out our stacks again while I shuffle. I pay the big blind and we get serious about cards, but over the next hour, we also talk more about music, about our families, and about the places we've been. He is obviously passionate about the underground music scene, but it's a little puzzling. It seems to me that what he likes more than the music they make is that no one knows these bands. I am much more interested when he talks about his mom working two jobs until she met his stepdad and how disappointed they were when he decided not to go to college. We also bond over our travels.

"I've never been to Europe," I say. "Or abroad at all, actually."

"Have you been to Hawaii?" he asks. I shake my head. "My mom grew up on the Big Island. It's awesome."

"Well, if they had RVs that float, the Barrett Family Band would've booked a gig, no doubt."

He grins. "You're ridiculous."

I smile and look down at my cards, hoping that's a compliment. Kai's legs brush mine from time to time, and his body is so close in the kitchenette that I feel like I can't get a good breath. Even though the conversation has flowed, I still can't get rid of the constant jitters around this boy. *I never got this worked up around Adam.*

"Your go," Kai says, nodding at my cards.

I cringe as I raise him. He has to surrender his last

chip and he does so slowly, dramatically, which makes me laugh out loud. We turn over our cards and examine them, look at the five in the middle of the table and the two we each have, and he hangs his head. I've beaten him, fair and square.

"Bird Barrett!" he says, reaching his hands over and grabbing my head. He pretend shakes me, his muscles rippling. I laugh and fake trying to escape, swatting at him.

"Sorry!" I say, dragging the chips my way when he lets go.

"Oh yeah, 'sorry,'" he mocks, dramatically pantomiming sweeping piles of money across the table and into his lap. He tosses imaginary stacks into the air and I giggle uncontrollably. He affects a high-pitched voice. "'So sorry, Kai. Please show me how to play poker.'"

"Hey, I never asked you to teach me," I say.

He grins, so hot. "I know, I know. I'm just kidding."

We sit there looking at each other, until I can't return his gaze and turn my focus to putting the poker chips back into the silver case. He hands me the deck of cards and then I click the case closed and stand up to put it away.

"You want a snack?" I ask, walking up front and opening the cabinets. "Cashews, granola bars, chips and guac?"

"Nah, I'm good," he says. Then he stands and stretches, his shirt rising up with him so that I catch a peek of smooth brown skin at his waist. He walks toward me and crashes on the couch, lounging at a diagonal with his legs stretched out.

I sit, too, folding my own legs up underneath me, hyper-aware that he's so close. "So what else does Kai Chandler do in his free time, besides teach clueless girls how to play poker?"

"Funny," he says wryly. "Actually, I'm really into photography. When I'm not touring, I spend a lot of time shooting or editing."

"Have you done anything, like, professionally?" I ask.

"A year after my mom and Matt got together, he asked me to take some pictures that he could use on the menus at his restaurant."

"Oh, that's cool."

"Yeah, really cool because I was only fifteen and had this old, crappy camera. Matt could've, and probably should've, hired a professional." It feels like he's sharing something really personal with me, and he's not at all hesitant. It's something he did the first day we spoke, too. "And then that Christmas, he and my mom bought me a really nice camera, and I was hooked. I saved up and eventually got a great computer and taught myself to edit my pictures and convinced everybody in my family to pose for me. I think they're all pretty sick of being my guinea pigs."

"I bet they love it."

"Well, five years later and Matt still uses those first

pictures on the menus," he says, shaking his head. "I've taken more for advertisements and the walls, but he won't change the menu. I'm like, embarrassed, you know? My work is so much better now!" He smiles. "But my parents—they're sentimental like that."

"I think that's amazing," I say. "My parents are super supportive, too. I feel really lucky."

"I'm sure they feel the same way."

I thank him with a shy smile and we sit together in silence for a minute, enjoying the closeness. I could so easily lean against him, rest my head on his shoulder, rock with the bus with him as my pillow. When he talks about his life in Los Angeles, I can't help but imagine myself as a part of it. Not that I'd let a boy influence a major life decision like moving to California, but still . . .

"What did you think of the menu, anyway?" Kai asks, breaking the silence.

"What do you mean?"

"At Makana," he says, smiling mischievously. "What did you think of my pictures?"

I stare at him, dumbfounded. "That was your parents' restaurant?"

He nods.

"Oh my gosh, Kai, I could kill you!" I say, swatting his rock-hard arm. "What if I'd said it totally sucked or something? What if I'd said the owner was a jerk?"

"I knew you'd like it," he says, his chocolate eyes glittering. "And I know he's not."

"I cannot believe you sent me in there without telling me that," I say again. "I would've looked closer at the pictures and tipped the waitress more or something."

"My mom said you're a great tipper, so don't sweat it."

"That was your mother?!" I exclaim, my eyes bulging.

He nods his head, clearly enjoying himself, while I, mortified, think about my dad asking whether the fish head was still attached on the fresh catch. "I could kill you. I could just kill you."

"Aw, Bird," he says, putting his arm around my shoulders, sort of like you would with a best pal and sort of like you would with a best gal. I melt into the sofa, the feeling of his arm at the back of my neck sending a warm surge across my entire back. "But then who would you pummel at poker?"

I cross my arms and fake pout, but snuggle in anyway. It feels amazing to be so close to a boy, to a boy I really like. For a second, I am taken back to that day in January when Adam and I first kissed. I think about how even though I've known him for years, I never met his parents—how he'd change the subject whenever they came up—how he was always on the road alone.

But I snap to, shaking my head and pushing him out of my mind. I'm here now with Kai. He pulls up a song on his phone, and as the music fills the bus, I find myself wishing that Sissy could let off the gas a little. We're at the San Diego city limits already, but I could drive all the way to South America like this.

Once we arrive, Kai heads off to set up. I know I should probably get my journal to write, but I grab my cell phone instead and call Stella, rehashing the last two hours with Kai.

"So where is he right now?" she asks.

"Walking across the lot to one of the vans." The sun paints the parking lot a brilliant yellow hue, yet he is the brightest spot on the landscape, like a spark of fire, heat, energy. Oh man, my heart's already writing poetry about this boy.

As soon as we turned into the lot of the Valley View Casino Center, I had to swallow back a groan. It's not that I'm dreading my performance—not that at all—it's that I want more time alone with Kai. Why couldn't my dad mess up the merchandising between two farther stops, like here and Phoenix? And Kai certainly didn't linger. Once Sissy put her in park, he thanked us for the ride and bounded down the stairs, all business. I can appreciate that he takes his work seriously—I do, too—but it all felt so abrupt.

"And he didn't kiss you?" Stella asks.

"No!" I almost wail, walking back to the bedroom.

"*So*, does this mean maybe you're finally over Adam?"

I chew my lip and think about it. "I don't know. I do know it sucked when he decided to leave town," I say. "But just because we're texting again—occasionally—doesn't mean I'm going to pass up this chance with Kai." I grin just saying his name. "Stella, he's so...deep. I mean, on a whole other level. He's sort of got this brooding, mysterious vibe about him, like the minute he walks into the room I'm intimidated."

"Well, probably because he looks like a Versace model," she cracks.

"But it's more than just his looks," I say. I sit on the bed and pull my lucky rock pendant out from under my V-neck, running it back and forth along its chain. "He's so passionate about music. Oh! And when I told him that guys never really noticed me before, which was the inspiration for my first single, he said, 'Then you must've been hanging out at a school for the blind.'"

"Wah-wah," Stella responds dryly.

"Whatever," I say, laughing. "It was cute. Oh! And that restaurant he suggested? Makana?"

"Yeah?"

"That is his family's restaurant!" I cry. "I met his mother and stepfather and didn't even know who they were!"

"Stop it," she says. I can imagine the look on her face and it makes me smile. "Bird, that was totally a test. He wanted to get their honest opinion of you. Like, *you've met his mother already*. Let that sink in." She pauses for dramatic effect. It works. He wanted me to meet his family, see his roots, *know* him. "Kai likes you, Bird. Majorly."

I smile from ear to ear, throwing myself back on the bed. "Well, I like him, too. Mega majorly."

"I liked Adam and all," she goes on, "don't get me wrong. But you know what makes Kai a way better match for you?"

"What?"

"He's *there*," she says. "Like, you can see him every day if you want."

I sigh. "I know. It's amazing."

"Moving on to *my* love life," she says now. "Is my future husband, Jason Samuels, single or still with that blah Devyn Delaney? *TMZ* says they're back together."

I laugh out loud. "Oh, Lord. At first, I thought you'd really met someone."

She laughs, too. "Nah. The only guys I hang out with these days are your brothers and my friend Ty, and we both know I'm not that hard up," she says.

"I don't know," I tease. "You and Dylan looked pretty close on your Instagram the other day."

"Oh, gah," she groans. "He came to my mom's show,

Bird. That's it." Then she gets fake serious. "And I would never cheat on Jason."

I laugh again. "Okay, well, he and Devyn are definitely not together, no matter what it looks like. Anita told me it's a publicity thing."

"I knew he still loved me," she says dramatically.

"And, not to be disloyal or anything, Stel, but Devyn was actually really nice at the premiere last night."

"Bird!" my dad calls, pounding on Dolly's door.

"Hold on," I say, giggling as Stella pretend gags over the Devyn comment.

I walk up front and unlock the door for my father, who looks furious.

"You care to explain this?" he asks, storming up the stairs. He thrusts his phone in my face, and I'm confronted with the pic that Devyn took of us last night... except there is a giant red arrow pointing to a huge red circle around the glass of champagne I was holding. My stomach drops.

"Dad, I only took one sip," I say, putting my phone down to my side. I am in so much trouble.

"You're sixteen!" he booms. "One is one too many!"

"I didn't even like it," I say. "It's just that everybody at the party was drinking and I didn't want to—"

"Oh, so if everybody jumped off a bridge, you would, too?" he asks, the vein in his forehead bulging.

I force myself not to roll my eyes, and to play the penitent daughter, but it's hard. "No," I say quietly.

"You look pretty intoxicated to me," he fumes.

"Dad, seriously, it's just the picture. I was smiling and then changed to a serious expression at the last minute. My eyes are a little closed, but I'm not drunk. I swear." I grab my dad's arm and look him straight in the eye. "Dad. Please. I didn't get wasted last night. You have to believe me. I would've never retweeted that pic if I were doing something wrong. It's just, somebody handed me a glass of champagne and I didn't know what to do with it."

He pauses a second, looking back and forth at my eyes, before I finally see him decide to trust me. "Fine. I believe you. But will the fans? Will your fans' parents?"

"I—" I don't have words. I never considered how holding a glass of champagne at an after party could affect my image.

"You know, Bird, this is bad," he says, raking his hand through his longish blond hair. "Anita called me this morning because that Kayelee Ford girl is running with it, and Anita is furious. She gave me the chance to talk to you first, but she's not happy, Bird, and neither is Dan. Although to tell you the truth, I'm not exactly happy with them. Where were they when all of this was happening?" he says more to himself than to me. "And your mother—" He stops himself, shaking his head. "I should've been there. I thought I could trust you to make smart decisions, Bird."

"You *can*, Dad," I say as hot tears sting my eyes. I'm upset that I disappointed him, but I'm also starting to get a little ticked off. "I *did* make the smart decision *not* to drink, and yeah, it looks bad and I'm sorry, Dad. I really am. But you can tell Dan and Anita and Mom and stupid Kayelee Ford and whoever else cares so much about my life that you know the truth. I didn't get drunk last night. I didn't."

My dad presses the bottoms of his palms into his eyes and takes a deep breath. Then, calmer, he looks at me and says, "Bird, you have to remember that you're a role model now. You've got a responsibility to—" Just then, his phone rings. He looks at the caller ID and his expression is that of sheer fury. "I have to take this," he says as he walks down the stairs, "but this conversation isn't over."

"This is Judd Barrett," I hear him say crisply into the phone as he stalks off.

I bring my own phone back up to my ear, my mood starkly different from when this call began. "I guess you heard all that, huh?" I ask Stella.

"I'm looking at the picture now," she says somberly. "I didn't even notice the drink when you tweeted it last night, but now it's on *TMZ*, and—ooh," she says, dropping her voice.

I'm afraid to ask. "What?"

"Kayelee Ford retweeted it to all her fans with hashtag oops and hashtag goodgirlgonebad."

My mouth hangs open. "What?" I ask again, this time heatedly. I head straight for my iPad, pull up the damaging pic, and groan. "I bet Anita is livid. She's always talking about my image, and it really doesn't look good for my dad," I say, thinking about our conversation in the upper deck of the Staples Center. I bite my pinkie nail. "Dan thinks I need to get a new manager—a real one."

"Whoa."

"Yeah, I know. At first, I was, like, 'No way. I'm not going to hurt my dad like that.'"

"Totally."

"But now, especially after he just went berserk over this fake scandal, I can't help but think that maybe it's not the worst idea in the world."

"Really?"

"Really," I say. "I mean, do you think a professional manager would attack his star like that? Over one tiny sip of champagne?" I fall into the leather massage chair and close my eyes. "I mean, obviously people seeing me out drinking is not great, but I think my dad just went off on me more than a regular manager would. And that's not his job."

"Well, I mean, it sort of is . . ."

I pick at a loose thread on my jeans. "It's not the job he gets paid for," I amend.

"Right," she says, "but how do you fire your dad?"

I exhale loudly. "Exactly."

11

WHEN DAN AND Anita said Jolene's Sweet Home Tour was going to be intense, they weren't joking. Over the past two weeks, Dolly has wound her way across the country, stopping in Phoenix and Kansas City—which reminded me of Adam, since that's the last place we both played before I was signed—and then on down to Little Rock. After that, we trucked all the way to Atlanta for a couple of shows before playing a doubleheader in Washington, DC. I was hoping to get to do some sightseeing in our nation's capital, but Anita squashed those plans when she flew up and jam-packed my schedule with interviews and appearances. It feels like I've talked to everybody who's ever worked in country music...well, except for my tour partner. Jolene still seems hell-bent on pretending I don't exist.

Now we're in Philadelphia, a quick stop but one I've been looking forward to ever since meeting Bex in Baltimore the day before I joined the tour. I peek out through the curtains and see her sitting in her wheelchair surrounded by a posse of her girlfriends, all wearing bright pink *Bex Friends Forever* T-shirts. It's really sweet.

"Break a leg, boss," Kai says behind me.

I glance over my shoulder, smile, and then put my game face on. He matches my expression, and we segue into my favorite part of each night: our preshow routine at the stage steps right before I go on. He squeezes my shoulders, like a personal trainer for a boxer, while I shuffle my feet in place. When my band files past and the lights change, he whispers, "You got this. You got this!" right in my ear and I bolt onto the stage like shot from a cannon, charged from contact with that boy.

"How y'all doing tonight?" I call into the microphone. The crowd explodes, and it's crazy how different the energy is on the tour now. The arena is pretty full, and while a lot of the fans are still from my mom's (or Jolene's) generation, it looks like everybody with a ticket is on their feet. They know me. They are here to see me, too. "Oh, Philly," I call, waving them off playfully. "I bet you treat all the girls this way."

They go nuts all over again. I laugh into the microphone, throwing my head back, totally in my element. This is where

I belong. All that traveling my whole life only to discover that the stage is where I am most at home.

"Let's start things off with one you ought to know!" I call.

I turn toward Monty and we're off, the band picking up the first number with palpable enthusiasm. As I start to sing, everything feels special tonight. There are cell phones in the air and signs in the crowd that say things like I HEART U BIRD and BB 4 EVA.

I love my fans.

My set is amazing. The band gels perfectly, and we float through each song with ease; it's as if I'm just hanging out with thousands of my best friends. My time is almost up, so I step back and take off my guitar. Openers don't get encores on Jolene's tour, but Monty and I have worked it out so that at this point in my show, we take a deliberate break, almost as if we're through. I step back and wave, leaving the fans a little frenzied. I grin my face off as they lose it, screaming maniacally, begging for one more song. They want "Sing Anyway." I know they're expecting it and it's my favorite part of the show, too. I always love hearing the massive chorus sing along.

I walk to center stage and take the mic off its stand. "What's that, Philadelphia? One more?" Their reply is deafening. I smile down at Bex and her friends, cupping my hands into a heart sign at my chest, pumping them in her direction. They return the gesture and that feels like as good a time as any to wrap this party up. I raise my mic and my band starts playing softly as the lights dim.

The dark arena flickers to life the way fireflies lit up my backyard right after sunset at our old house in Jackson. And we sing.

On the way to Buffalo I should sleep, but I can't put down my iPad. My Twitter feed is blowing up with mentions by my fans of the behind-the-scenes videos that Bex and her friends just posted. They came backstage after my set, chilling with me in my dressing room before Jolene's show and watching it from the wings with me. Then they hung out on Dolly for a while. They were a lot of fun, telling me how much they liked the concert and showing me pictures of guys they like or are dating at their school. We're the same age, but our lives couldn't be more different.

They asked me what inspired my songs, and I admitted that it's almost always a boy. This led them to questions about my love life at present, and I was so caught up that I wanted to spill, but honestly, I don't know what Kai and I are. I've seen him every day since San Diego, and he's hitched a ride on Dolly a couple of times, but with my dad on board it's not like we've had a lot of alone time. I look for him at meals and love bumping into him in the back hallways of the venues we play. We text nonstop and talk on the phone for hours when we're on the road, like we've known each other forever. Sometimes we laugh until we can't breathe, and a couple of times, I've woken up to a dead cell phone on my pillow after we've both fallen asleep talking late into the night.

But what *are* we?

I lay my iPad on my lap and lean back on the couch cushions, staring at the dark window and thinking about chemistry and connections and having *the* conversation. The DTR. But how do I "define the relationship" when he hasn't even kissed me yet? It's been nothing but a series of quick touches: brushing a hair from my face backstage, squeezing my arm at dinner, leaning against me playfully when we pass in the arena corridors. What does it even mean?

As the bus rolls down the highway, I pull my lucky rock pendant from under my shirt and study it: just a black chunk of asphalt with tiny silver flecks, but Stella turned it into so much more. It reminds me of when I was beginning this life—of being on the cusp of something amazing. I feel like that again now with Kai, but I don't know if he feels it, too.

I have no answers, so I call the one person who always does.

"Before you worry, nothing's wrong," Stella says by way of greeting. She sniffles. "I'm watching *The Notebook*."

I chuckle. "Say no more."

I hear the movie go mute and she asks, "What's up, woman?"

I sigh. "I'm thinking about Kai, *of course*, and what we are to each other, *if anything*, and it's frustrating, you know? He still hasn't kissed me or made any kind of obvious move. Is it possible I'm misreading it?"

"It doesn't sound like it," she says, "from what you've told me."

"Yeah, he acts like he likes me, but how do I know for sure?" I ask. "And he's supposed to make the first move, right?"

"Not necessarily."

"Well, in this case, he is," I say. I can't imagine myself making the first move. If he didn't reciprocate, I would maybe crumble into a pile of dust on the spot. I close my eyes and rock with the sway of the bus. "Dating is like an impossible riddle."

"You ought to write about it," Stella suggests. "You always seem to say things better with your music. And lots of girls feel the way you do in that in-between stage. Oh! Write a song and call it, 'Do You Freaking Want My Body or Not?' I would blast a jam like that."

"You're crazy," I say, laughing. "But to be completely

honest, that's not much worse than the stuff I've come up with lately. I've had writer's block so bad this summer, which really sucks since Dan wants to hear something new by the end of next week. I don't know what's wrong with me. I was always inspired on the road growing up."

"And there's even a boy!" Stella says. "A really hot boy. You should have ten songs by now!"

I roll my eyes. "You're not helping."

"Sorry."

I sigh heavily. "No, you're right. I'm happy and busy and falling for a great guy, but everything I write is so forced."

"Well, then, maybe the guy is the problem."

I frown. "What do you mean?"

"Maybe you're spending so much time texting or talking to Kai that you're not allowing yourself the creative space you need to work."

"Kai is *not* the problem."

"Okay, sorry," she says. "I just know my mom never writes hits when she's happy."

I chew on my lip and consider that.

But then I think it's bull crap. I've got writer's block because the label wants a pop sound and my roots are in bluegrass. I don't know how to make my stuff fit their marketing strategy. And I'm on a breakneck tour schedule. And some days you just don't have it. But it's definitely not because of Kai.

I force a yawn, not mad at Stella but suddenly ready to get off the phone. "I'll try this 'who makes the first move' idea."

"Do it," she says. "Do both. Write the song *and* make the move." Then, "Oh no."

"What?"

"Um, are you still online?"

"Why?" I ask, reaching for my iPad. But before she can answer, I gasp. "'At BirdBSings is so fake,'" I read out loud. "'Pimping out cancer patients for press. At least at KayeleeFord keeps it real. Hashtag belikeme.' What the—"

"It's terrible," Stella says. "And Kayelee is retweeting all kinds of stuff like that. What's your show have to do with her? Ugh, I hate that girl."

I know it's not helpful, but I read through Kayelee's feed and feel sick. I know I burned a bridge with her label the minute I turned them down for a deal last year, and I know that the media is fanning the flames of a supposed rivalry, but to accuse me of exploiting a girl with a terminal illness, basically saying that the whole thing was staged for good press? I am fuming, my face hot and my pulse rapid. "I would never," I say softly. "I'm not like that."

"Obviously," Stella says. "And your true fans will know."

I scroll down the page, hoping that's true and wishing it made me feel better.

12

"KNOCK, KNOCK," KAI calls from the front of the bus.

I slap the strings of my guitar quiet and look up from where I'm writing on the couch, giddy just at the sound of his voice. When the tour pulled into Buffalo, we got the day off, and I played tourist with Kai and some of the crew before our show at the First Niagara Center the next day. Then it was back on the bus to play Cleveland before heading over to Chicago, where I had the most amazing time sightseeing with Kai. He took loads of pictures as we explored Millennium Park and the Riverwalk, and while he still hasn't kissed me, he held my hand as we walked along Michigan Avenue. And tonight at the end of our preshow routine, he gave me a good-luck peck on the cheek before I bolted onto the stage. It's been more than enough to make me feel better about the potential of *us*. Chicago is now one of my all-time favorite cities.

"Come in!" I call as he ascends the stairs.

He hesitates at the top. "Oh, you're working?"

"No, it's nothing," I say, setting my guitar and journal on the end of the couch. My dad is off somewhere making calls before we head out for a special show for the troops at Fort Campbell. It's crazy to me that I've only got Indianapolis and Tulsa after that before the final stop of the tour, three shows in Nashville...which means that Dan will be waiting for me, ready for new material. But I shake my head. That can wait. "What's up?"

He holds out his laptop and sits next to me, the scent of the Moroccan oil he uses making me swoon a little. "Last night I edited some of the pics from Saturday, and I wanted to show you a few of my favorites. We don't leave for another half hour, so—"

"Yes!" I say. "Totally. I'd love to see them."

"Okay, so these first ones are from 'the bean,' " he says. I move in closer as he clicks through the images and am blown away. He captured the cityscape brilliantly, distorted by the curves of the enormous bean-shaped sculpture. He also took some amazing candid shots of couples laughing and children squatting at the base, mesmerized by their contorted reflections in the stainless steel.

I settle in against his side, and he puts his arm around

me. He scans through the pictures quickly, only stopping on a few that he thinks are worthy. If I could get my hands on his computer, I'd take my time with each image so I could slip into his brain. His photography isn't like any I've ever seen. Duck feet sticking out of the Chicago River; my hands strumming my guitar before lunch; my toes in the grass at the park; Maybelle nestled into my neck, only showing my chin and forearm. There are very few of my face, some only showing my profile, my eyes, my mouth, but not my whole face—this famous face that I see online as much as in the mirror these days. These other parts of myself, or maybe the way he's brought attention to them, feel much more intimate.

"I feel like you really see me," I say quietly.

He turns his head and kisses my forehead, his lips lingering there. I gulp, hard. We are so close, my nose at his neck, and I don't know if I should tilt my face up and bring my lips to his—if I should make the move.

He turns back to his computer, and I lay my head on his shoulder. Of course now my heart starts writing a song. I know I should grab my journal or my guitar, but that would require pulling away. Then I think about what Stella said, about Kai being more of a distraction than an inspiration, and I exhale loudly.

"What's wrong?" he asks.

"What?" I look up at him. "Oh, nothing. I was just thinking about my next album."

"How's it going?"

"I don't know," I answer honestly. "It's like—I've gone from bluegrass to country and now they're pushing for pop, which isn't really me. I mean, I play the fiddle!"

He shakes his head.

"*And* they're not calling it pop; they're calling it 'crossover,' " I say with air quotes.

Kai cringes. I knew he would hate that.

"Exactly," I say. I pick up my songwriting journal and frown. "I think I'm finally onto something, but I'm just not in love with this song yet. It was never this much work before!"

"Can I hear it?"

"Oh," I say, glancing up at him in surprise. The song is about Kai—so clearly about Kai. I feel my neck redden just thinking about playing it for him. "I don't know. I've only got the chorus, and it's really rough."

"Bird," Kai says. "You can trust me. I just showed you my photographs. I get how hard it is to share your art, and I promise, I'd never judge, especially in this early stage."

I don't have the guts to kiss him, to make that kind of move, but maybe Stella is right: Maybe I need to put myself out there, maybe I need to make *my* kind of move.

Reluctantly, nervously, worriedly, I scan the page, the lyrics scribbled and scratched out like a mad scientist at work, and hand it over.

"Okay," I say. I reach for my guitar. "So I'm fooling around with the idea of relationships and when they go from friends to something more." My voice is shaky.

He looks over at me with a knowing half grin and my entire face heats up, so I look down at the strings and start to strum. "I think I'm onto something maybe. So...anyway...it's called 'Friends Don't.' Here goes:

"Never knew that you could say so much,
With just a single move, with just a touch.
Friends don't brush a hand against my skin.
Friends don't send my heart into a tailspin.
I just want something more to let me know
Where this could lead us and how far we could go."

I let the last note fade away and then we sit still for a few seconds that feel like an eternity. I'm waiting for Kai's response, for him to say something—anything—but he's staring a hole in my notebook, contemplative.

"I'm dying here," I finally say.

"Sorry." He looks up and smiles. "Sorry. I was just in my head." He pauses, wearing the expression of someone carefully choosing his words. "It's just...I feel like I really know your stuff now, Bird. I mean, I've been on tour with you for weeks. And I also feel like I really know you."

He puts his hand on my knee and squeezes. I feel a shiver from my head to the tips of my toes.

"But I don't—" He stops and looks up at me, hesitant.

Oh no. He doesn't feel the same way. I've totally read him wrong. I've read it all wrong. Oh sweet Jesus, kill me now. This is my worst nightmare.

"I just don't feel like this is really *you*."

I blink. "What?"

"This song. The lyrics. I just—" He stops and scratches his head. "I think you should stretch yourself. Seriously. Don't get boxed in." He picks up one of my hands, turns toward me, and locks his eyes onto mine. "Listen, this song is definitely commercial, and maybe this is what your label wants, but your sophomore album will solidify your reputation in the music world. Other artists are skeptical of your staying power, and your fans are waiting to see what else is in there." He points to my heart. "And I feel like some of your songs, like 'Before Music,' are so raw and powerful that they set you apart from the other girls in the business. I feel like you need more stuff that's...profound...you know?"

I swallow. "So what do you suggest?"

A small grin plays at the corner of his mouth, and he softly says, "I say listen to your heart. I say be true to yourself."

He drops my hand and brings his to my shoulder, brushing away the hair there and rubbing the side of my neck with his thumb. My throat is suddenly dry and it feels about a billion degrees hotter on the bus. And then, as if my life were in slow motion, Kai leans toward me. I grip my guitar and hold my breath, watching him close the space between us, then shutting my eyes when his lips meet mine. It is a soft kiss, a sweet kiss, almost like an introductory kiss. My shoulders relax and my body goes limp. I sigh and my fingers brush down the guitar strings as if of their own accord. I feel his lips stretch into a smile. He pulls away.

"I've been wanting to do that since the day I met you," he says softly.

I feel like my heart could burst in my chest. "Me too."

His hand is firmer on my neck as he moves toward me again, and I tilt my head, my heart pounding big African drums, but then the door to Dolly swings open and we both fly back to opposite sides of the small couch. My dad walks up the steps on his cell phone, sees us, and does a double take, then walks toward the back of the bus, clearly agitated, glancing over his shoulder as he goes.

Kai checks the time on his phone. "Guess I should get going."

"Yeah," I say quietly.

He stands up, and I do, too, following him down the stairs and out the door.

He turns back to me, and I hold his steady gaze. It looks like he might kiss me again, but then he glances up at Dolly and steps back, clearly worried about my dad. I wave as he trots toward his bus.

And I think again about the manager Dan knows in LA.

The sun has just dipped below the horizon, and twilight envelops the parade field where the stage was erected in Fort Campbell. It's sticky hot, but my palms are cold. Somebody, somewhere, convinced Jolene Taylor to sing the national anthem with me, timing it perfectly as the sun set. It did not go well.

"A big thank-you to all the military families here in Fort Campbell, Kentucky!" Jolene calls into her rhinestone-covered microphone, blowing kisses as we exit. "I love you so much. Be right back, y'all!"

The audience cheers, and I wave halfheartedly as the stage lights go red, white, and blue all around me. The lighting guys shoot off fireworks, but I don't stick around to marvel. I can't get backstage fast enough. Unless somebody changed the lyrics of "The Star-Spangled Banner," then I had a total lapse in brain power and flubbed the last line.

We rehearsed this afternoon, but I was a bundle of

nerves. Jolene insisted on singing the melody and instructed me that my harmonies be soft. She also demanded that neither of us go higher than E-flat on the big "free" that the Mariah Careys of the planet send into orbit but that the mere mortals of the world struggle to hit. She stopped me during the rehearsal several times, asking things like, "Is that how you're going to sing it tonight?" and "Is there a reason you're holding that note out?" She kept flashing me that tight-lipped fake smile, and every time I tried to inter-act with her onstage, she walked away. By the time I got back to my dressing room to get ready, I was wound up like a top.

It was impossible to enjoy my set tonight. Not only did I let Jolene get into my head, but it was hard to get pumped up onstage when there weren't as many butts in the seats as usual. This concert was meant to be small, only for mil-itary and their families, and I was stoked to support the troops, but then half the ticket holders didn't trickle in until it was almost time for Jolene to come on. I missed the cell phones and signs in the air, the occasional "I love you, Bird!" screamed by an enthused fan. I tried to engage the sparse crowd, but it was an older bunch, and they didn't know my music. It felt like they were bored, like they were just humoring me until the real star came on.

When it was finally time to perform together, Jolene started off by genuinely thanking all the servicemen and women for their sacrifices. Then she began the anthem without cueing the band or me. I caught up on the second word, and although neither of us was excited to sing together, I have to admit that we sounded amazing, her low, loud belt complemented beautifully by my softer tone. I actually got cold chills at one point. Jolene flashed me what appeared to be the first sincere smile in our month-long relationship, which made me feel like we'd finally had a breakthrough, but it was in that euphoria that I lost focus. When we reached that climactic moment in the song, "And the home of the—" I sang the word *free* again before quickly correcting to *brave*.

Jolene flinched but lifted her shiny mic higher, belted louder, and held that final note—and held it and held it—until I started wondering if she was punishing me. Then, *finally*, she cut the song.

"Bird," my dad says now, holding his arms open. Truthfully, I could use a hug, but Jolene is right behind me and even if I goofed—and maybe because of it—I want to look like a professional. So I take the bottle of water from his outstretched hand instead, pretty sure that it was his and not meant for me, and I chug it. "That was really beautiful, sweetheart," he says.

I nod. "Uh-huh. Thanks, Dad."

He pats my back uncertainly and nods at a smug-looking Jolene as she passes. I mimic her signature tight-lipped smile and follow her entourage backstage, purposefully not looking over at Kai. It's all I can do not to cry as it is, so I don't need my dad to hug me and I don't need the boy I like to pity me.

"Bird, that was incredible," Monty says, catching up.

I purse my lips and nod. "Thanks. You guys sounded great tonight." The band circles around me when I get to the back lot behind the stage, giving me props on the anthem. My stylists chime in, too.

"Seriously, thanks, y'all," I say. I'm appreciative of their graciousness, but it's only making me feel worse that everybody's pretending like I didn't mess up the last line. "But honestly, I'm really tired and I've got a headache. I think I'm going to head back to the bus, okay?"

The guys nod, Sam and Amanda exchange glances, and my dad suddenly takes a phone call. Everybody knows why I really want to be alone. They know I'm just barely holding it together, which makes me feel even worse as I weave through the group, like they all think I'm being a baby or something. I know it was good; it just wasn't perfect. And it was my first time performing with a multiplatinum Grammy winner in front of men and women who defend our country. It meant a lot to me, and I feel like I blew it.

I get pretty far away from the stage area before I crouch down in the grass, as if inspecting the clover. I pluck one of the little white flowers and watch it blur as my eyes fill with tears. My phone pings with a text message, but I don't look at it. Instead, I stare and stare at the little flower in my hand and berate myself, wondering how I could screw up the first chance Jolene has given me.

"Bird," Kai says, his shadow falling next to me.

I turn around, shocked, as he drops to his knees in the grass. "What are you—"

"That was incredible," he says, holding my cheeks and wiping under my eyelashes with his thumbs. "I saw the look on your face when you left the stage, though. You know you sounded amazing, right?"

"Kai, I messed up the words to the *national anthem*," I cry, feeling a tear escape and run down my cheek sideways, following the curve of his palm.

"*A* word," he corrects. "And it was the last one when everybody was already screaming. I guarantee nobody noticed."

"Yeah, right." I groan. "People love YouTube anthem bloopers."

"Bird, I swear to you. Nobody noticed," he says. He's staring at me so intently, his dark brown eyes full of concern. "Jolene was belting like an opera singer, and the people were going crazy. You sounded incredible. I had chills, and it's, like, ninety degrees outside." He lifts my chin. "You know I don't lie about music."

I grin despite myself. "I know."

"I have to go," he says, one hand on my knee. "Are you okay?"

"Yeah," I say with a forced smile.

He picks a tiny strand of wet hair from my cheek and smooths it back into place with the rest of my hair. And then his fingers work their way into my mane and lock themselves urgently behind my neck. He pulls me toward him with need, his eyes on mine until we are so close that our noses nearly touch. When our lips meet, he is firm and deliberate, as sure as if he's kissed me a million times before. I close my eyes and wrap my arms around his broad shoulders, feel my body relax, absent of any tension or sadness as he holds my face, as he kisses me deeply, steadily, his thumb tracing a circle on my cheek.

I forget the stupid anthem—forget anything other than this perfect boy kissing me. He lifts me up and pulls me close, squeezing me tight. "Bird," he whispers between kisses.

Finally the crowd roars, signaling that Jolene has taken the stage again, and Kai reluctantly pulls away. He drags me all the way back to the concert area and leaves me by the stairs, where my dad looks at us both sternly. I don't care. I clutch the little white flower to my chest. Kai is aiming his light toward Jolene, but he looks down at me and winks. My heart leaps, *soars*, as if vaulting from my chest, and as it falls, I only hope that this boy catches it and keeps it safe.

13

"Boooooooo!" Kai is pretending to be an angry fan at Tulsa's BOK Center. I keep singing, but he doesn't stop heckling me. "I can't see a thing!" he yells. "Is that even the real Bird Barrett?"

Abruptly, I stop singing and shout, "Lights!" and Kai flips them on. I smile at the flipcam recording on a tripod in front of me and say, "It takes a lot to run a tour. Today I want to introduce you to one of our lighting techs, Kai Chandler."

Kai walks over and waves at the camera. Then he reaches out and presses STOP. The second the red light is off, he kisses me—again—for the twentieth time in the past ten minutes as I'm *trying* to record this behind-the-scenes video for my website. It's only supposed to be a couple of minutes long, but filming has been met with a few challenges today...mainly to do with focus and, no, I do not mean the lens.

"Kai, come on," I say, pulling myself away and swatting him playfully. "I didn't have any of these distractions with the sound guy I interviewed last week."

Kai cocks an eyebrow. "You better not have."

A few other crew members appear, and I check the time. Sound check is soon, so Kai and I walk back to my dressing room for the rest of the interview. When he plops down on the couch, I aim the tripod and camera toward him and remind him to be professional. We have to keep it platonic when the camera's rolling because (1) Kai doesn't want to be in *Us Weekly*, and (2) although I haven't shared this with him, Anita has strongly hinted that if I have a romance brewing, it shouldn't be made public.

I press RECORD and sit down. "Okay, Kai, these questions are rapid-fire. Ready?"

"Shoot."

Even though we talk and text every day, the interview is eye-opening for me, too. I ask him about his job: What is the best part about being on tour and the worst. What does he do in his time off? What's the craziest thing that's ever gone wrong during a big show? We have fun with it, stopping and restarting a few times when one of his hands wanders up to my bare shoulder or his mouth ends up on mine. The chemistry between us is intense. It feels like we're two magnets drawn toward each other, nearly impossible to separate.

Finally, I wrap it up. "I want to thank lighting tech extraordinaire Kai Chandler for being my guest today and also all my fans for the nonstop love and support. Tulsa—it's on! Nashville, are you ready? 'Cause I'm coming for you next!"

Kai leans forward to stop the camera and then wraps me up tight in both of his arms. "And I'm coming for you, Bird Barrett. Interview's over."

"Kai!" I start to protest, but his mouth is on mine immediately. He is breathing me in, and I fall into him, grabbing his head in both of my hands and matching his intensity as we kiss.

I tighten my fingers in his black hair as he pushes against me, his chest hard. He slowly presses me back, moving his hand behind my head so that he catches it as I fall against a throw pillow. I feel my phone get caught in my hair, but even as he fumbles to push it away, I don't stop kissing him. My lips move over his cheekbones, his nose, across his eyebrows. I feel his breath on my hand as he kisses my fingers. I pull his forehead to my lips and then feel his lips on my neck. He kisses me along the underside of my jaw, and I get goose bumps all over when he tucks my hair behind my ear and kisses around it softly.

"Kai," I whisper.

He brings his mouth back to mine and I melt into him, marveling at how we feel like two jigsaw pieces that snap together perfectly. One of his hands stays there in my hair, circling near my temple. The other settles on my hip.

"God, you're beautiful," he says, pulling away and staring down at me. His dark eyes search mine, his expression that of someone begging you to believe them. I take his face in both my hands and pull him toward me again, not just *wanting* to kiss him but *needing* to.

He slips the hand he has on my hip under the hem of my tank top and starts to circle the exposed skin near the top of my shorts with his thumb. It tickles. It tingles. We keep kissing, and I move my hands from his face, scratching his back with one hand, slowly, and stroking the little hairs on the back of his neck as softly as I possibly can with the other.

I grin when I feel him get goose bumps.

"Bird," he whispers.

He props himself up on one elbow right next to my head, which gives his other hand more room to . . . explore. I don't know what's coming next—or what I want to come next. I've thought about the fact that Kai is older than me, definitely more experienced. His thumb traces my belly button. My pulse pounds in my ears.

Suddenly, three loud bangs are hammered on my dressing room door, so strong they rattle the hinges.

With superhuman strength, I push Kai away and roll off the couch, landing on the floor with a painful thud.

"Ten minutes!" I hear someone call from outside the door. It's just Jordan, letting me know it's almost time for sound check.

"Bird!" Kai says, shocked. "Are you okay?"

My face is already on fire, but when I realize how badly I just overreacted to almost getting caught, humiliation washes over me. "Sorry," I say quietly. I look up at him, his expression that of someone trying desperately not to laugh. And then I do. I laugh—hard. Kai slides off the couch and joins me, laughing so much that he's holding his stomach.

"Oh man, I'm sorry," I finally say. I dab at my eyes with the base of my palms, and Kai, still chuckling, leans over and kisses my forehead. "I thought that was my dad. He would've lost his mind."

Kai nods but looks like he wants to say more. I worry the teensiest bit that he's annoyed we had to stop the moment, so I lay my head on his shoulder, just to keep a connection.

"You okay?" he asks as he brushes my hair back from my forehead.

I nod. "Uh-huh."

"Bird, if you ever—I mean—if things are ever too—"

I look up at him and smile.

"We can take it slow if you want," he finally says, though he can't keep those hands out of my hair, off my face. I feel like I can't keep my heart in my chest. "I'm really into you. I want to see where this thing goes and I'm in no rush."

"Me too," I say, nodding.

"You know that song?" Kai asks. "The one you played for me last week?"

" 'Friends Don't,' " I say. "It still needs some work."

"Yeah, 'Friends Don't.' " He nods. "Well, friends don't—"

"Make out?" I interrupt.

He chuckles. "Right. Or I was going to say: feel this way." Kai gets serious. "Bird, you are the first thing I think about in the morning, the person I always want to text, the only girl that's even been a blip on my radar in, like, two years."

My heart skips.

"So, anyway, do you—I don't know—want to be exclusive?"

I blink hard. "Do I want to be your *girlfriend*?" I ask.

He nods, looking adorably nervous.

A smile breaks across my face. "Yes, I want to be your girlfriend!" I say, too loudly, too excitedly, too not-at-all-playing-it-cool-ly. I throw my arms around him and squeeze tight. Immediately there is the electricity that always buzzes between us, but I pull far enough away that I don't leave room for more kisses. We have to go to work.

He links his fingers through mine and squeezes, looking

as happy as I am, yet considerably more chill. He stands and pulls me up with ease. When I open my dressing room door, the sounds of a busy tour greet us.

"So," he says, as we walk into the hallway, "what will your dad think about you having an older boyfriend?"

I beam at him. *Boyfriend.* "I don't think it's the age that will bother him as much as the boyfriend part," I say.

He drapes an arm across my shoulders and we head toward the stage. "Then I guess I'll just have to win him over."

I grin. "Guess so."

14

"Bird, baby, are you okay?" my mom asks softly as she peeks into my bedroom.

"Yeah," I answer groggily. I yawn wide, opening my eyes and smiling as I remember that I'm back home. Last night we played the first of our last three shows, in Nashville, and Bridgestone Arena was packed for my set. It was humbling, and a little mind-blowing, to see how dramatically five weeks on tour had increased my fan base. I really loved being back on the road, but now, as I stretch my long legs and arms, I've got to say that nothing beats sleeping in my own bed. I sit up and rub my eyes as my mom opens the blinds. "What time is it?" I ask.

"It's nearly ten," she says, sitting on the bed beside me. "We figured you'd be ready by now. Your father said you have a meeting with Dan and Anita and it's not like you to miss that stuff—"

"Oh my freaking God!" I say, throwing the covers off.

"Bird Barrett," she scolds.

"Oh, get over it, Mom. I didn't cuss," I snap as I rush past her out into the hallway. "Dad!"

"He's in the kitchen," my mom says snippily as she heads downstairs. "And I'll thank you to keep the Lord's name out of your mouth unless you can honor it."

"Ugh!" I storm past her and find my dad finishing his coffee, his car keys on the table next to him.

"Dad! We're late for our meeting. You should've woken me up."

He cocks an eyebrow. "You can work every app on your phone but the alarm clock?"

I roll my eyes. "There's no way I'm going to get ready and get down there in time. Can you call him to reschedule? See if he can meet in half an hour or something? One hour tops."

"I'll try," he says with a heavy sigh.

"I can't believe nobody woke me up," I grumble as I head back upstairs.

"*I* did," my mom calls after me. "And I'm starting to regret it."

Angry, I take the stairs two at a time. I don't have time to fight with her, and I don't know why my manager isn't on top of this. Also, it's a freaking Saturday, but Dan clearly doesn't understand the meaning of a weekend. He works 24-7, so I guess we all have to. I slam my bathroom door, grab my toothbrush, and sit down to pee at the same time, thinking that I don't have time for makeup and will probably need to wear my hair in a ponytail.

There is a knock at the door. "Bird," my dad calls from outside. "Dan's waiting. He wants to do our meeting over Skype. Let's go."

What?

I open the door, and my dad passes me my laptop. "Sounds good," he says into his cell phone. "We'll call you right back."

"I'm still in my pajamas!" I protest as he ends the call.

"Looks like sweats to me," he says. "Let's go. The man's waiting."

He leads me across the hall to his office and we sit down to call Dan. As soon as his face pops up on-screen, I notice my Albert Einstein hair in my thumbnail image and cringe, trying to smooth it as nonchalantly and yet quickly as possible.

"Good morning, Sleeping Beauty," he says, grinning.

"Dan, I am so sorry!"

"No worries," he says. "No worries."

Dan reaches for a piece of paper and snaps into business mode, his slight frown making me nervous. "I've got another meeting in a little bit so I want to get right down to it." He looks up and takes a deep breath. "We got the new song yesterday. Thank you for that, Bird."

"Sure," I say. *Please like it, please like it, please like it.*

Dan stalls, as if he's considering his words. "It's—well, it's not what we were expecting or even, quite frankly, what we associate with the Bird Barrett sound. Shannon agrees. We sort of—well, it was a head-scratcher, to tell you the truth."

I sigh heavily, feeling my shoulders droop and my heart sink.

"Have you heard it, Judd?" he asks.

Reluctantly my dad shakes his head, looking the way I feel: surprised and a little ashamed.

"Huh," Dan says, nodding. "I would figure Bird's manager would be listening to her demos before she sends them out. Maybe you'll want to be a little more hands-on in that regard in the future."

I glance over at my dad, who nods curtly.

"Bird, this track just isn't you," Dan continues, no longer worried about choosing his words carefully. "I don't even know who this is. It's—well, Shannon called it 'emo' and Anita said 'sad.' As for me," he says, "I guess I'm just confused. We talked about more of a pop sound, right?"

"Right," I say, my throat tight.

"So what happened?"

I exhale loudly. I think about my first kiss with Kai, when I played "Friends Don't" for him last week. On the way to Tulsa, he helped me finesse it, encouraging me to use a broader vocabulary and slow down the tempo. I know it's not exactly like my other stuff, and it's certainly not pop, but we wrote it together and it's special to me now.

"I was toying with the idea of when a friend becomes more than a friend," I explain.

"It's not the subject matter," Dan answers. "We love love songs."

"Right. But when I played it for a friend of mine, it sounded so mainstream and just—ordinary—that I decided to go in another direction."

"Well, if you choose a new direction in the future, make sure it's up."

Ouch.

"Remember, we were aiming for at least six new songs by the tour's end," Dan says firmly. "You aren't just a singer, Bird. You're a singer-songwriter. But I need you to let me know if I should be flagging potential songs for you, contacting publishers for material."

"No, I want to do my own stuff," I say quickly.

"Well, that's what we want, too," he says. "Listen, I have to go, but take another look at the concept and give this song some life. Or maybe just start fresh."

"Okay," I say quietly.

"Judd, everything else going smoothly?"

"Great," Dad says. He's nodding so vigorously, it's as if he's convincing himself. Embarrassed, my stomach sinks even further. It's already been a long day and I've only been awake for ten minutes.

"Okay, Barretts, we'll talk again soon. Have a good one."

"Bye, Dan," my dad and I say together. I disconnect the call and for a couple of seconds, we don't move as we let it all sink in. Then my dad's cell phone rings and he looks relieved, walking out into the hall to talk to somebody about a local morning-show appearance.

I pick up my laptop and walk back into my own room, humiliated. I shut the door, set the computer on my desk, and crawl back into bed, staring at the ceiling fan as it goes around and around. I replay the conversation with Dan in my head. *Emo* and *sad* definitely don't fit my "brand," but those words also don't describe my life at all. Since I met Kai—and especially since he asked me to be his girlfriend— I've never been happier.

"Bird," my mom says at my door, "I've made you some breakfast. Are you hungry?"

I look over at her, standing in my doorway with a tray of scrambled eggs and bacon, and feel bad about the way I treated her. "Yeah," I say, sitting up. "Sorry about earlier."

"Teenagers." She shakes her head dramatically and I

know all is forgiven as she walks into the room. She sets the tray on my lap, and I notice that she went out of her way to cut the crusts off my toast. "How was the meeting? Did they like the new song?"

And I don't know if it's this kindness that I don't deserve or the shame I feel at letting down my label, but suddenly my throat closes up and I'm on the verge of tears. "No," I say quietly.

She reaches for my hand and squeezes it. "Judd?" she calls out.

My dad paces past my door and holds up a finger. "If I'd confirmed it, I would've put it in my calendar!" he booms into the phone.

Mom shakes her head. "Always on his phone. Did you ever get to spend any time with him? On tour?"

I shrug, thankful for the change of subject. "Yeah. I mean, we shared a bus." I think about it. "We'd watch a movie sometimes, but I think with everything else that was going on, we liked to keep to ourselves on travel days so we could just rest up."

She nods and I take a bite of toast. It looks like she wants to say more, but she doesn't.

"Sorry," my dad says, storming into my room. "But, Aileen, you can't just interrupt me like that when I'm on the phone. It looks unprofessional and I'm trying to take care of our daughter here."

"I understand that, but there are a lot of ways to take care of your daughter that don't involve the people at the other end of that cell phone. I haven't gotten the details, but it seems to me that a meeting didn't go well this morning. Maybe you'd like to talk to her about it."

Cue extremely uncomfortable tension. I study my food, not daring to look at either of my parents' faces. My dad's cell phone rings again, but he doesn't answer it. Instead, he walks over to my bed and lets it ring...and ring...until it finally goes silent as he sits at the foot of my bed and sets his phone down next to him. When he gets a voice mail alert, we all glance at his screen, but to his credit, he doesn't check it.

"Are you okay, Bird?" he asks.

I nod.

I've thought a lot about what Dan and Anita said, about getting a new manager out in California, about relocating even. At the time they approached me, I wouldn't have considered replacing my dad, but their words have made me take closer notice of him the past few weeks, and I've seen how he's struggling. It's hard, but I think they may be right. And I think I was looking at it all wrong: I'm not *replacing my dad*; I'm hiring a manager and *getting my dad back*.

I take a deep breath and look up. This will be a tough conversation, but hey, that seems to be the trend this morning. "So, I've been thinking—" I start.

But then my dad's phone lights up with an alert and I see that he's changed his wallpaper to a picture of the two of us from when I was little: him strumming his banjo and me standing awkwardly next to him, my fiddle half my size. My face is screwed up in deep concentration while his is twisted in a smile that he was obviously trying to hide.

"About . . . ?" my mom prods when my words trail off.

"Um—well—um," I stammer. I decide to start with the easier sell. "I had a conversation with Dan and Anita a few weeks ago, and they mentioned that Open Highway is opening a Los Angeles office."

My parents' expressions of surprise mirror each other. Maybe this won't be an *easy* sell.

"Anyway, they think that if I move out to California, even just part-time, it would really open a lot of doors for me." My father is already shaking his head, and my mom's face is blank, like she doesn't register my words. "Think about it. TV, commercials, sponsorships, movies—it's all out there."

"You're a country music singer," my mother says slowly. "Isn't Nashville where you need to be?"

"Most of the time probably," I say. "But Anita says we should strike while the iron is hot and that a move to the West Coast could really grow my brand."

"And just how is that supposed to work?" my dad asks

skeptically. "There's no way you could get an apartment by yourself, so we're supposed to leave your brothers behind again and move whenever you get a notion to? Jump when you say 'jump'?"

"Judd."

I bristle. "Dad, it's not like that."

He shakes his head and looks out my window.

"Jacob's going to be at UCLA in the fall," I go on. "And Dylan's twenty years old. Most kids are on their own at that point anyway."

"California," my dad scoffs. "Might as well be Mars."

"It would be a big move, hon," my mom says, softer in her delivery, but I can see from her expression that she's just as against the idea. "Your father is stretched pretty thin as it is, so you go adding on a whole other house across the country and... I just don't know."

"Well," I say, "that's actually another thing they wanted me to talk to you about." I pause, trying to find the right words. "Dan and Anita know this manager who's supposed to be really great. He's based out of LA, and they think since he already knows the business and everything... it might be time to hire somebody outside of the family. Somebody who already has connections and all that."

My dad blinks as if I've just slapped him in the face. "Are you firing me, Bird?"

"No! Oh my gosh, no, Dad," I say. "I just see how

stressed out you are all the time, and this guy would have a whole office and assistants and—"

"No way," he says, standing up. "Absolutely not."

"Dad—"

"You get some big-shot manager who already has a ton of other glitzy celebrities as his clients and you think he'll take care of you better than I will?"

"Not take care—"

"Those guys are so busy you're lucky to even get 'em on the phone!" he says, picking his up. "I should know! It's ridiculous, and I'm telling you another thing, Bird. They sure as spit won't have your best interests at heart. They'll just be thinking of ways to line their own pockets while working you to the bone."

"I don't think it's like that, Dad."

He shakes his head and stands up. "Since I am still your manager, I'm going to go make some more calls. And then send some follow-up e-mails. And then maybe I'll take a good hard look at myself in the mirror and ask what in the world would make my own daughter not see how much I care about her."

"Judd!"

"And you can just forget LA," he says, really worked up now. How did this conversation get so off course? "Drugs and drinking and what is that thing they're all doing? Twerking? Hell no."

"You honestly think I'd be into any of that?" I ask, getting angry, too.

"You think Billy Ray expected any of this?"

"Dad, seriously? Get a grip."

"Oh, I've got a grip. I've got one on my baby girl and I'm holding on tight. No to LA. No to some Slick Rick manager." He stomps toward the door, shaking his head. "You have no idea what it's like out there."

"Neither do you!" I say, pushing the tray off my lap. He slams the door and I spring up, opening it behind him. He's halfway down the stairs and I lean over the balcony, calling after him, "Why can't you trust the girl you brought up?"

He stops and grips the banister and then turns back to me. He looks exhausted, worn thin, old. He exhales heavily. "I shouldn't storm off when I get frustrated," he says quietly. He clenches his jaw and looks away, then turns back to face me. "I'll think about it, okay? I'll talk to Dan and I'll think about it. But that's all I can promise right now."

I nod, feeling a huge lump form in my throat.

"I just want what's best for you, Bird."

"I know, Dad," I squeak out, and even though I'm a little mad and even though I wish he'd lighten up, I run down the steps and hug him. Because as upset as I am, honestly, he's the one who looks like he needs it.

15

"THANK YOU, NASHVILLE!" I call. I can't believe we're doing the last show of the tour already—that this is it. It's been crazy. I wave big as I walk offstage. "Jolene Taylor has a great show for y'all, so get ready!"

"Wait, wait, wait a minute," I hear Jolene say over the speakers. Astonished, I look over and see her strutting my way in her tight pants, her microphone glittering. I notice as she approaches that none of that sparkle has made it to her eyes and wonder what in the world I'm in for. "Now quiet down, y'all, quiet down," she says, laughing into the mic. She really is a beautiful woman; too bad it only seems to be on the outside. "Did y'all out there enjoy Bird's singing?" she calls.

The crowd goes bananas, thank God.

"Well, now, we want to hear our fans sing," she says, gesturing toward one of the crew in the wings, who brings out a stool. She pats it and says, "Take a seat here, birthday girl. Did y'all know that Bird Barrett turns seventeen today? She's almost a grown woman!"

Almost. Nice touch.

"Y'all know this song," Jolene says now, ever the performer. "It's a classic." As the band starts to play, the fans cheer before joining her in "Happy Birthday" (which I have to admit is really well-sung). As they go berserk on the last note, a cute roadie in a tight black T-shirt, black jeans, and a to-die-for smile brings out a big bunch of multicolored helium balloons. Kai knew about this.

I grab the balloons from him and shake my head. He winks in reply. I can't believe he didn't tell me. Grinning, I turn back to the audience and blow kisses. I couldn't dream of a better way to end my first tour. A little girl in the front row is so happy she's crying, so I walk downstage and squat, handing her a balloon. Somebody produces a Sharpie, and I sign the balloon. Then as I'm walking away, I see another little kid and do the same thing. It's not long before I've passed out the whole bunch and I'm giddy with birthday cheer.

"Thank you again, Nashville!" I call. I wave at the crowd before turning to Jolene with a sugary-sweet smile. I'm sure none of this was her idea, but like a true entertainer, she played her part, so I play mine. "And thank you, Jolene. I'm so glad I could spend this birthday with y'all, in my own Sweet Home-town."

Once I'm backstage and Jolene starts in on her first number, I glance out at the crowd again and laugh. Maybe it's childish, but I get such pleasure thinking about Jolene having to stare at those front-row balloons with my autograph during the entire set of her final show.

"Hey, guys," I say to my parents when I walk into my dressing room. My brothers, the Crossleys, and a slew of relatives got tickets for the show, and I can't wait to go join them in the crowd. "Just let me change real quick and we can head out."

"Bird, honey," my mom says, patting the couch next to her. A small box wrapped in bright yellow paper rests on her lap. "Would you mind sitting down here a minute? We'd like to give you your birthday present."

She smiles, but it's almost sad. I look at my dad, perched on the arm of the sofa above her as he finishes up a text, and something about him also seems off. I slowly sit, feeling like I'm about to be given bad news, not a gift.

She passes me the box and I unwrap it, a little confused when all that's inside is a bottle of sunscreen. The brand is California Baby and my heart flutters, although I don't want to get my hopes up. I look at my parents. "Sunscreen?"

My dad speaks gruffly. "I spoke to Dan." He clears his

throat and my mom scratches his back. "Your mother and I have come to see that he might be right. All of this may be more than I can handle." He smiles sadly. "I did my best, hon. I wanted to be a good manager. I wanted to take care of you."

"You do take care of me," I say, feeling guilty. "Dad, you're the greatest."

"You know, Bird, I wanted to be," he says. "But at the end of the day I think I can only be one thing or the other: your father or your manager. And being your father is just too important a job to let slide." He swallows hard. "So Dan set up a meeting in California, and we're going to meet this guy, Troy something or other."

"We're going back to LA?" I ask.

My mom nods. "And there's more," she says. "While we're out there, we're meeting with a real estate agent so we can look at a possible apartment to rent."

"Are you serious?" I ask, dumbfounded.

"We'd only be there part-time," my dad says. Then he smiles at me, and I see how hard these changes are—how hard it is for him to let go of the reins and let me grow up. "Happy birthday, sweetheart."

I stand up and hug him tightly, feeling so loved. Then I throw my arms around my mom, knowing she's probably been working hard to broker this arrangement.

"I'm still going to be right here," my dad says, teasing

me. "No chance you're ditching me completely. I'll be looking over contracts and overseeing your big offers. Heck, in Los Angeles, I might even turn into one of those stage moms...or dads or whatever." My mom and I laugh. "In fact, young lady, you'll probably see me a lot more now that the tour is over, so be careful what you wish for."

"I wouldn't want it any other way," I say. "You'll always be my dad, even if you aren't my manager."

He sighs dramatically. "I'm sure going to miss that fifteen percent, though."

"Judd Barrett!" my mom says, swatting him.

But we just laugh. We laugh and I think I see my dad's eyes well up, and then mine do, so we just laugh harder. That way we have something to blame for the tears.

16

"Okay, would you rather make out with Jolene Taylor..."
Stella starts. She, Kai, and I are walking down Twenty-
First Avenue playing Would You Rather. We had a blast at
the Sweet Home wrap party Sunday night and have been
like the Three Musketeers ever since. "*With tongue*," she
adds.

Kai gags dramatically. "*Or*," he prompts her.

She screws up her mouth, thinking. "*Or* perform one
of her songs at the VMAs wearing nothing but one of her
rhinestone-covered miniskirts and pink high heels?"

"Oh, ho-ho!" I hoot. I mean, Kai has an awesome body
and would look good in anything, but the image of him in
Jolene's "Pink Pumps and Purses" skirt is totally ridiculous.

"The VMAs," he says seriously. "Anything goes there,

and I'd rather stick my tongue in an electric socket than in that woman's mouth."

"Well, that's *shocking*," I say.

Kai groans, but Stella loves my corny jokes and gives me a high five. We've been playing tour guide for Kai all week, showing off Nashville the way the locals see it. Of course I took him to the Station Inn and Lower Broadway, but I also showed him around *my* Nashville: Music Row, the studio, Open Highway, our house, Stella and Shannon's apartment. He especially loved walking around East Nashville, where Stella showed him all her favorite artsy haunts.

It's been nice reclaiming Nashville from all the memories of Adam, but not necessarily easy. Kai wanted to eat at the famous Pancake Pantry, which I thought would be totally fine, but when Stella and I met him on the corner, I completely lost my appetite. Recollections of Adam and our first date came flooding back—being spotted by my fans for the first time, the car ride to the studio, our first kiss. Stella must have seen the look on my face because she suddenly campaigned for a change in venue. Thank goodness for two things: the insane line outside the Pancake Pantry and my best friend knowing how to read me. Kai was pretty hungry and was easily convinced to move the party down the block to Fido.

"Ah, so this is the place where your sordid love affair with heartthrob Jason Samuels got started, huh?"

"Ew!" I say, punching him in the arm.

He feigns pain and rubs his biceps, but Stella shoots us both a murderous look. "It's Mr. Stella Crossley, thank you very much."

Kai laughs out loud. "Oh, my bad, my bad," he says, hands up. "Tell your husband that *Twisted* was the only good movie he ever made."

She brightens. "I knew I liked you, Kai."

He looks puzzled. "But I said he only made one good movie."

She grins. "Yeah, but most guys I know say he sucks in everything. I can see that you've got a more worldly perspective on the cinematic arts."

I roll my eyes. "They're chick flicks."

"You said his last movie made you cry," she says pointedly.

I squirm, glancing up at Kai. "They're good chick flicks," I admit.

Inside, Fido is jam-packed and dark, but I leave my big sunglasses on. I think about the last time I was here and how I was conscious of all the other patrons buzzing when they realized Jason Samuels was in line. This time, I feel the stares on me. It's crazy how much things can change in a matter of months.

"I'm going to grab a table," Kai says when we join the line. "Just get me what's good. And a coffee."

He weaves through the crowd and Stella stares at the menu. "You should get him the Local Latte," she says. "I'm going to miss those when I'm gone."

I pout. "I can't believe you have to go visit your dad the minute I get back to town. You leave for school in, what, a week or something? I wanted to hang out. It's like the universe is trying to keep us apart."

"Don't be sad and don't be crazy," she says with a laugh. "You'll see me at Thanksgiving, and I promise to come visit you in LA. Plus, now you can spend some quality time with Kai without me tagging along as a third wheel."

"He's leaving me, too." I groan. "He's already booked on his next tour."

Stella throws her arm around my shoulders and squeezes. "Aw, just you and your instruments. Think how much work you'll get done."

I look at her skeptically. "Yeah, but they'll all be sad songs. Trust me. The label does not want sad."

We talk a little about her dad and his life in Seattle and a little about my upcoming move out west. The line inches along until finally it's my turn.

"May I help you?" the barista asks, smiling as if she recognizes me.

"Yes, I'll have one Warm and Fuzzy—" I start.

"Oh, that's a seasonal drink," she says, cutting me off.

"We don't carry it right now, but the current specials are on the board."

"Really?" I say, bummed. "You can't make it for *me*?" I pause. "Special case?"

"Bird," Stella says quietly, "she said it's seasonal."

The barista sighs heavily but agrees to make it.

"Thank you *so* much," I say. "You're the best." I give her the rest of my order, pay, and she tells me she'll bring it out when it's ready.

Stella places her order next, slips a pretty generous tip in the jar, and then we go to find Kai. " 'Special case?' " she asks.

"What? You don't get stuff if you don't ask for it," I say. "And it was no big deal."

Stella looks unconvinced but she shrugs.

We squeeze single file through the crowd, some people taking pictures, and I wonder if I'm being rude by not stopping. "Hey," I say. "I think word got out that I'm here. Should I just sign a few autographs to keep the madness to a minimum?"

But then a gap opens up in the wall of bodies and that's when I see her: Kayelee Ford, my supposed competition, is walking into Fido.

"Bird," Stella whispers urgently over her shoulder.

"Yeah, I know," I say, ducking my head and more than a little embarrassed that I thought the fuss was about me.

"OMG," Stella says the minute we fall into the seats at our table.

"What?" Kai asks, confused.

"Kayelee Ford is here," I explain.

He still doesn't get it.

"She's Bird's rival," Stella says as if it were obvious. "Don't you read *Us Weekly*?"

"How can she be my rival?" I ask. "I don't even know her."

Stella arches an eyebrow. "She's wearing a shirt that says 'You Want to Be Me. I Get It.'" I roll my eyes. "Exactly," Stella says.

"Okay, so she kind of seems like the worst, but that doesn't make her my rival," I say, glancing back over my shoulder. "Although she did tweet out that *TMZ* pic from the premiere with the champagne. And she totally exploited that stuff with Bex on Twitter."

"She sucks," Stella says.

Kayelee is loudly inviting people in, posing for pictures with a huge smile or biting her lower lip suggestively. Just then, one of the fans talking to her nods my way and Kayelee locks her heavily lined eyes on mine. I give her a weak smile and offer a small wave. She sneers and moves on to the next fan. "Yeah," I say turning back around. "She sucks."

Kai glances back at her briefly and shakes his head.

"What?" I ask.

He puts his arm around my chair. "Just her type, you know? Fake tan. Fake hair. Fake nails. It's so tired."

Stella nods. "I've seen YouTube clips from a couple of her shows, and she's doing full-on choreographed dance numbers, like a Dallas Cowboys cheerleader or something. News flash, Kayelee: You're a country music singer. Get a guitar."

I laugh, and when I glance back at her again, I see that she's headed my way. "Well, she's coming this way and I'm going to be the bigger person."

I take a deep breath and plaster on a smile, but she actually doesn't talk to me. Instead, she walks right past us, squeezing between our table and another, her butt right in Kai's face. "Kayelee!" I say loudly before I lose my nerve. She stops and turns around, her friends all but glaring at me.

"Oh, hi," she says, beaming. She's a very pretty girl, with deep blue-violet eyes, blond hair that cascades down her back, and the kind of "sun-kissed" skin that only comes from the tanning bed. She stands beside Stella. "Do you want an autograph?" she asks, blinking innocently.

I pause. "Um, no," I say. "I just wanted to introduce myself, you know, formally. I'm Bird Barrett."

"Oh, wow, hello," she says, sticking out her hand. I accept it, and she shakes vigorously, like a politician running for office. "I would've never recognized you. You look so...*different* in real life."

She smiles and bats her eyelashes. I drop her hand and glance at Stella, who is crinkling her nose as if she smells something rotten. I know I'm not made-up or styled, but come on. The girl knows who I am. I'm already regretting this bigger-person stuff, but as terrible as Kayelee seems, I take a deep breath and press on.

"I just wanted to say that all the stupid stuff in the magazines about us and some rivalry, it's crazy, right?" I fake a smile. "I wish you all the success in the world."

"Good," she says. "Because your wish is coming true."

I gape. *Is this girl for real?*

She turns to Kai and touches the woven band he always wears on his wrist. "That's amazing," she says in a low, sultry tone as she bends over the table for a closer look. I guess her cleavage wanted to be introduced as well. "I love tribal wear. Is it ethnic to your people?"

Kai's eyes go wide, and he looks over at me like he's holding back an enormous laugh. I shake my head and shrug my shoulders, no clue as to what she means, and frankly, ready for this interaction to be over. Her face is earnest, searching his for an answer. "Um," he says, pulling his arm away. "You mean the Los Angelenos?"

"Oh, I love them," she says airily. She puts a hand to her chest. "They're so spiritual."

Stella covers her mouth to keep a loud laugh from escaping, but I don't find any of this funny. I tried to rise above, but now I'm mad enough to spit nails. I had wanted to say something like, *Sorry Randall pitted us against each other, but I think you have a pretty voice. There's no hard feelings on my end and certainly no reason why we can't be friends.* But now, as she finally starts to back off and tosses her hair over her shoulder, exposing her abs and smiling at Kai as if she wants to devour him, I feel what can only be described as disgust blistering my tongue. How could Adam stand playing in her band last winter, even if it was for only one show?

I shake thoughts of Adam from my head and snuggle into Kai, making it very clear to Kayelee and her crew that he is taken. "Well, just wanted to say hi," I say, waving the fingers of my right hand and indicating that she can move along. I am aware of customers around us having stopped their conversations to eavesdrop, so I want to keep things civil, but if I never see Kayelee Ford again, it'll be too soon.

"I'm so glad you did," she says. "Nashville is an awfully small town, huh?"

I nod. "Sure is."

Too small.

17

AFTER AN AMAZING week in Nashville, the party's over.

I woke up with dread this morning, knowing that I had to drive Kai to the airport. He's flying to Louisiana to tour with some indie artist, Astrean, through Thanksgiving before joining one of his favorite bands, Genuine Scoundrels, until Christmas. I want to be supportive because he's obviously stoked to be on these jobs, but it's hard to be happy for him when I'm feeling so sad for myself.

"I'll miss you," I say quietly. So far I've kept my emotions in check, mainly by focusing on the road in front of me. I steer toward the lane marked DEPARTURES.

"I'll miss you, too," Kai says. He keeps one hand on my

leg. These past few days he's always had at least one hand on me when we're together, connected.

At the terminal, I pull over to the curb and pop the trunk. I kill the engine, not caring if I get a ticket, and get out of the car for one last hug. He wraps his arms around my waist and presses his forehead to mine. "We'll talk on the phone every day," he promises.

I sniff and nod, determined not to cry.

"You'll have fun in LA," he says. "And we'll be together again in a few months."

"Yeah, until your next tour," I complain.

"Or yours," he says. He pulls away and holds my head in his hands. "Bird, our lives are on the road, but that's one of the best things that we have in common. The road brought us together."

"I know," I say quietly.

"Hey, I'll miss you like crazy, but you're about to be really busy and I want to hear all about it, okay?"

I sniff and nod again.

"All of it. Everything. Okay?"

I hug him once more, laying my head on his shoulder. I kiss the side of his neck and breathe him in. And then I let him go. Kai is saying something I've heard before: My career is taking off and I'll be busy with my music. But he isn't using it as an excuse to end our relationship, like Adam did; rather, he's giving us a chance in spite of it. So I will, too. Because being busy isn't a reason to be alone.

"Call me when you land," I say as he squeezes my hand and takes a step toward the door.

"I will," he says.

"Not a text, okay? A phone call."

"Okay," he says, walking backward. He glances over his shoulder and nearly crashes into a lady and her daughter, hopping out of their way just in the nick of time. I laugh and wave. He blows me a kiss. And then he's gone.

The last thing in the world I want to do is speak to the people Kai nearly trampled, but they've recognized me and it's clear from the looks on their faces that they're fans. So I dab under my eyes with my summer scarf and plaster on a big smile as they roll their suitcases my way. Me Time is over; Bird Barrett is on.

"Hmmm," Shannon mumbles the next day as she flips through the pages of my songwriting journal. I hold my lucky pendant in my hand, twirling it back and forth between my thumb and forefinger nervously. It was only a year ago that she was blown away by the poetry I'd come up with during my time on the road with my family. It was raw and I didn't know how to shape some of the ideas into songs, but at least she had something to work with. Today I think she was expecting that same fountain from which to draw, but there has clearly been a creative drought. "Well, we could maybe piece two of these fragments together," she muses, strumming a few chords on her guitar.

"So, '*We're all born with dreams and things we're scared of*,'" she sings. My ears perk up. We've been working together for an hour and that's the first thing that's even come close to sounding like a song with potential.

She looks up at me questioningly and I nod. "Yeah, that sounds great," I say.

"So what next?" she asks.

"Huh?"

"I picked that line out of your journal," she says, her long black hair falling over her guitar as she slides my journal across the coffee table. "But the rest is a list of band names or something. Where were you going with that first thought?"

I sigh heavily and put my head in my hands. "I don't remember," I moan.

"Oh-kay," Shannon says, setting her guitar down. "Let's take ten."

It's embarrassing. I can tell that she's disappointed in me and I hate it. I'm disappointed in myself. I've had all summer to work on new material. There were a million times with Kai when a song took root in my heart, but I wasn't disciplined enough to pull away from that moment with him and write it down. And I had hours on the bus going from stop to stop where I could've been working, but instead we texted or talked on the phone or watched the same movies from different buses so we could talk about them later. It was like we were together even when we weren't together.

But right now, staring at the list of band names in my journal, the notes about Kai's favorite films from Sundance, the meals he said he wanted to make me once we were off tour...now I couldn't feel more disconnected from him—or from my music.

Instinctively I glance up at Stella's loft, but she's not here either. I sigh. Nobody is. Stella's spending time with her dad before starting school at Samford next week, Jacob's interning for Open Highway until he leaves for UCLA, and Dylan's around but already wrapped up with his new friends at Belmont. Soon, everybody will be at college making new friends and new memories. And suddenly, I feel very, very alone.

18

I DON'T KNOW when I'm going to get used to it, but ever since being discovered I am constantly reminded that a lot can change in the blink of an eye.

"Wow," I say, following Mom, Dad, and Jacob into the gorgeous condo the real estate agent found us in Santa Monica. "This is even nicer than it looked online."

"It ought to be, for as much as it costs," my dad grumbles. "The rent here is more than most people's monthly pay."

"Um, is it too late to go get my stuff from the dorms?" Jacob cracks.

We roll our suitcases into the living room and set our bags down, the four of us quiet as we take it all in. The place has gorgeous beach views through floor-to-ceiling windows, which the real estate agent promised meant we'd see some breathtaking sunsets. The two bedrooms are big enough for king-size beds and dressers, the kitchen has brand-new stainless-steel appliances and granite counter-tops, there are Jacuzzi tubs in both bathrooms, and the living room leads out to a balcony where I can totally envision myself having tea in the morning and songwriting. In fact, as I watch a couple walk hand in hand in the surf, I'm already feeling inspired.

"Let's unpack and go shopping for some furniture," I say, wanting to get settled in right away. I was jet-lagged when we pulled into the parking lot, but now that I'm officially a part-time California girl, I feel a burst of renewed energy. "We need a car and we need a couch." I clap. "Stat."

My dad looks at me dubiously. "We need groceries and we need toilet paper," he says, mocking me with a loud clap of his own. " 'Stat.' You may be making money, honey, but you still have to prioritize."

I roll my eyes. "Buzzkill."

He chuckles. "Hey now," he says, putting his arm around my shoulders, "I'm still your manager for a few more days, so I'm going to call a few more shots. Let's grab the rest of the bags from the rental car and figure out a plan for lunch. I've heard In-N-Out Burger is a Los Angeles must."

"Yeah, it's awesome," Jacob says, already the Cali pro.

"I wish they took my meal plan. I'd be, like, a gold-valued customer. Adam and I were there last night."

"Adam's in town?" I ask, whipping my head around.

"Was," Jacob says uncomfortably. "Headed back out on the road this morning. Told me to tell you hi, though."

I nod, looking back out the windows. "That's cool."

I don't know if Jacob knows exactly what happened between me and Adam last winter—what Adam may have told him or what he picked up on his own—but it seems like Jacob and Dylan tiptoe around any mention of him when I'm in earshot. It's immensely frustrating.

"So we'll grab the rest of the bags and get burgers for lunch?" Jacob asks.

"Absolutely not," my mom says breezing past us. "Might as well eat spoonfuls of lard."

"I think that's the secret ingredient," Jacob teases as he follows her out. "It's what makes them so good."

My dad winks at me and holds the door open.

"I'll be down in a minute," I say, waving him on.

The door bangs closed, and I walk to the massive windows, amazed by the view. As the waves roll onto the shore, I watch a man throw a Frisbee into the surf and wait for his dog to retrieve it. I watch seagulls circle overhead, their calls to each other like a secret language. I can't believe this is happening, that this is where I live now, that California represents so much possibility.

I wish Kai were here.

I always wish Kai were here.

I pull out my cell phone and open the patio door, taking a few pictures of the beach and the way the sun sparkles on the ocean. It's breathtaking. I laugh to myself as I text him a pic:

Can't wait until you come visit!

And then, just because Jacob mentioned he said hi, I send the same beach pic to Adam, with the message:

My view right now.

I chuckle when Adam immediately texts me a pic of an old rotary phone, a lamp that looks as old as I am, and cheesy hotel art, the frame crooked on the wall.

Trade ya.

I stretch my arms up high over my head and inhale the salty air. It was weird to go all these months without Adam popping in and out of my life, without talking or texting much, but now it's nice that we can get back to some sort of normalcy—that we can maybe just be friends.

I hear my family come back into the apartment with

the last of the suitcases and I go inside. The place is pretty sparse, no matter what my dad says. It will be air mattresses and living out of luggage for a few days.

"Did you grab my purse, Mom?" I ask.

"I didn't see it," she says. "I think we got everything."

I groan. "I left it on the console," I say. My dad holds out the keys to me. "Be right back."

At the elevator, I jab the DOWN button a few times and consider taking the stairs—the five-hour flight left my body stiff and a little sore—but then the doors open and I am totally astonished as none other than Bonnie McLain steps onto my floor. "Bonnie!"

Her face mirrors my own surprise.

"Bonnie," I say again. "Hi, I'm Bird Barrett. We met last month in Omaha. I toured with Jolene Taylor?"

"Well, Bird, I remember you, girl! You're not going downstairs for the Zumba class, are you?"

I shake my head. "Um, no."

"Good," she says, looking relieved. "I just finished spin with the girl that's teaching it and she's a drill sergeant. Had every one of us beat up from the feet up."

I laugh out loud.

"Oh, honey, it's good to see you," she says, beaming at me. She dabs her face with a small towel, and instead of getting on the elevator, I let the doors close. "Do you live here, too?" she asks, confused.

I nod. "We're moving in today, actually."

She shakes her head, her eyes wide with wonder. "Well, I'll be. Isn't it a small world?" she asks. "Y'all come on down to my apartment one of these days for some of my famous sweet tea."

"Yeah, definitely," I say.

"Six-A," she says as she starts down the hall. "Any time."

"Six-A," I repeat. "Got it." I press the elevator button again and shake my head. My mom is going to flip.

"I'll see you around, neighbor," Bonnie calls as she opens the door to her condo and heads inside.

I wave back.

When the elevator pings and the doors open, I jump on, suddenly bursting with excitement. I can't think of a better sign than bumping into a legend like Bonnie McLain only a couple of hours into my big LA move. When I get to the lobby, I stride out into the California sunshine, full of hope. It feels like things are already happening.

19

"So horses and a birdcage, huh?" my dad teases a couple
of days later as he helps Mom and me bring our flea market
finds into the apartment.

"The big stuff's getting delivered," I say, setting one of
the four wine-barrel bar stools under the counter. "And
don't worry, Dad. There were plenty of Labor Day weekend sales."

"So we're not broke?" he teases.

"Not yet," I say. "Wait until I go car shopping, though. I
saw a yellow Ferrari today with my name on it."

My dad laughs heartily and shakes his head as he goes
outside for another box.

Mom and I finally went furniture shopping, and
although it started out rough, with Anita sending us to the

designer stores on Rodeo Drive, the day ended up being pretty awesome once we texted Kai for some vintage shop recommendations. I fell in love with a triptych painting of horses inspired by the carousel at the Santa Monica Pier, and we found a modern teal-colored sofa that will look perfect against the same wall. But my favorite find was a large antique gilded birdcage that we're going to repurpose as a floor lamp.

"Well, somebody knows how to say happy housewarming," my mom calls from the front door. I turn around and see her walking toward me with an exquisite bouquet of yellow poppies.

"For me?" I ask.

She nods and hands me the small card attached. Grinning from ear to ear, I tear it open, thinking about how Kai and I texted all day and he never once let on.

But I'm floored when I pull the note from the tiny envelope:

Lady Bird,

The California state flower for a California girl. Congrats on the tour and good luck in LA.

Adam

About a billion questions race through my mind. I mean, these aren't your standard roses or lilies. Are poppies even in season right now? How did Adam get somebody to deliver wildflowers? What does it mean that he put so much thought into this? My mind is spinning, but the one question I am able to formulate aloud is, "How did Adam even know my address?"

There is mischief in my mother's eyes. "Maybe a little birdie told him."

I roll my eyes.

"Oh, not like that," she says, realizing the double meaning and waving me off. "I leave the puns to your father. I'd say Jacob told him. Aren't they just gorgeous?"

They are. And they must've cost a pretty penny, too. I play it cool until my mom goes into the kitchen; then I whip out my cell phone and take a pic of the bouquet, sending it to Stella:

What do these mean?
They're from Adam, btw.

I stare at my phone, but she doesn't write back right away. I lower my nose to smell the poppies. They don't smell like anything, but they are very pretty. And so sweet. And so thoughtful. And so confusing. And so very . . . well . . . *Adam*.

I text him:

Wow. Thanks for the flowers. They're beautiful.

Unlike Stella, Adam writes back immediately:

You're welcome. How's Cali?

My thumbs fly over the screen, texting him back easily and effortlessly, like the old days:

Great! Beaches and sunshine. You'd love it.

The minute I send that text, though, I feel guilty. I don't know why—I haven't done anything wrong—but I think about Kai on the road and feel bad as another text from Adam comes through:

Hope to visit soon. Staying with Jacob over his fall break.

My stomach flips. Again, I don't know why. I'm totally committed to Kai. I guess it's just weird that my almost-but-never-really-was boyfriend is best friends with my brother. Also weird that said brother hasn't mentioned this little visit.

I shake my head and step out onto the balcony. I'm still not used to having an ocean outside my back door. I send Kai a text:

Wish you were here. Miss you like crazy.

I click my screen off but get a text alert right away, which brings up a picture of Kai and me kissing in Nashville the day before he left. I smile as I read his short reply.

Soon!

20

"No, I DON'T want to valet," my dad barks at the young guy trying to open his door. "I'm just dropping someone off."

I cringe, not wanting to make a scene for several reasons. One, I'm outside the Ivy restaurant in Los Angeles, which Kai told me is this fancy place where celebrities and studio people always go. From the paparazzi standing around, I can see that he's right. Two, I was pretty pumped when Devyn Delaney texted me yesterday asking if I wanted to meet her for lunch, and I don't want to make a bad impression. "She's well connected to young Hollywood," Anita said. But from my perspective, she's also well suited to understanding how crazy this life in the spotlight can be.

"Do they still expect me to tip?" my dad grumbles now

as I get out of the rental car. I glance up at the cute valet again and pray he didn't hear that.

"Thanks, Dad," I say as I close the door of the Nissan Altima. I duck my head, sidestep the Mercedes-Benz next to us, and walk quickly up the brick steps to go inside.

While my dad's grouchy mood is totally embarrassing, I know he's just having a hard time after our meeting with Troy Becker this morning; we signed the papers and he's officially my new manager. Honestly, I think he'll be a perfect fit. Troy's a laid-back California guy and made us all feel at ease after only a few minutes. And even though I question a guy who wears loafers without socks, I can't question the success his artists have had. The walls of his office remind me of Dan's at Open Highway, except the stars he's posed with are all what Anita calls "cross-over artists," meaning singers slash actresses—people like Vanessa Hudgens, Hilary Duff, and Jennifer Hudson. He talked about my brand, our partnership, and being selective with my commercial opportunities while keeping my music first. Any anxiety I had about getting a new manager flew out the window: Troy Becker was our guy.

I think I maybe hear one click of a camera as I walk through the charming patio to the hostess stand. After Kai told me how "posh" the Ivy was, I stressed about what to wear, but finally decided on a gray cotton dress with a ruffled front, kind of like an old tuxedo shirt. Not too dressy, but not casual either. Looking around the patio at the white cast-iron chairs and floral throw pillows, it feels like a good choice. Until...

"Bird!" Devyn calls. I look behind me and every head on the patio turns. I see some of the paparazzi outside snap to attention and hear them start clicking. I offer a small wave, but she is already looking away, greeting a seated couple. Then right before she gets to me, she spots someone else she knows and squeezes through a couple of tables to chat them up.

Devyn looks every bit as stunning as she did on the night of her movie premiere, minus the long gown and diamonds. I guess for Devyn Delaney, a "casual lunch" means an occasion for four-inch heels and a silk lavender shift dress under a cropped leather jacket and chunky metal jewelry. Her black hair falls down her back in loose, styled waves, and her makeup is impeccable. It's only our second encounter, but I can tell that she's the kind of girl who is always glamorous, be it noon or midnight.

"Bird, it's so good to see you," she says when she finally makes her way over. She leans in to greet me and I'm momentarily anxious. Is this an air kiss or a real kiss? Air kiss. Okay. And then here she comes again, so I guess we're doing two.

"Thanks for inviting me," I say, once the whole Hollywood greeting is over.

The hostess leads us to a table inside, and I'm immediately taken with this place. I was expecting something flashy and modern, but to my surprise, the Ivy is more like a cozy country inn. The tables are decorated with fresh flowers and bowls of fruit, the walls are hung with old flags and decorative plates, and the tables are small, some of the banquettes even have throw pillows.

"I love the atmosphere," I say to Devyn as she slips her Louis Vuitton sunglasses into a case and throws them into her Fendi bag.

"Wait until you try the food," she says. "They have a grilled-vegetable salad that's to die for."

Devyn gives me a celebrity tour of the menu that could rival the Hollywood movie star tour. "Kendall Jenner loves the huevos rancheros, Lily Collins always gets the lime chicken, and Zac Efron told me the swordfish tacos are the best he's ever had," she says knowingly.

I didn't eat breakfast so I'm really hungry and everything on the menu looks good, although pretty pricey. "I heard someone compliment the fried chicken on her way out," I remark.

Devyn smirks devilishly. "The only people who eat fried chicken in LA are either behind the camera or have a lipo session scheduled in a few days."

My mouth hangs open in shock, which Devyn seems to enjoy. "Luckily, I'm naturally skinny," she says. "I mean, I can eat whatever I want because I have this superhuman metabolism, so ribs, steak, chicken, bring it on. But I'm the minority."

From most people, a comment like that would be off-putting, but Devyn's candor is kind of refreshing. I feel like she can give me the straight-up California lowdown. When she tells me that my dress reminds her of one she just saw Bella Thorne wearing, and then adds that I "totally wear it best," I actually laugh out loud. I can't put my finger on what exactly it is about Devyn, but she's magnetic, the kind of person who draws you into her orbit.

"Oh, Bird, lean in," she says, picking up her phone. "Let's tweet a pic before the food gets here and the table's a mess."

She holds out her phone and we touch heads over the flower arrangement. Once again, I don't get to see the picture before she tweets it to her fans, so I'm hoping it's a good one. I think of something my mom always says: *Some people live life asking for forgiveness instead of permission.* Devyn Delaney certainly seems to be that kind of person.

Her thumbs fly across the screen and she mumbles as she types: "Hey, my little hashtag devyls! I'm at hashtag ivy with my girl at BirdBSings, then shopping on Rodeo." She pauses and looks up at me. "You can, right? I need a dress for my *Fallon* appearance this week."

"Um, yeah," I say. "That's cool."

She nods and resumes her tweet. "Follow her! Hashtag hollywoodhotties." She looks up at me with a self-satisfied smile. "That's, like, the exact amount of characters, even with the pic of us. I'm eerily good at Twitter."

"I always have to go back and edit mine," I admit. "I type too—"

"Here, retweet it real quick, okay?"

"Oh," I say, picking up my phone. "Sure. I guess I need to text my dad about shopping, too, right? How long do you think we'll be out?"

She shrugs and gets lost again on her phone, which already feels like the third person at our table. After I text my dad, I put my own on silent and slip it into my purse. I look around the cute little restaurant until the waiter comes by and takes our order. Once he's gone, Devyn holds her phone up to me.

"Did you see *TMZ* today?" she asks, fuming.

I shake my head, leaning forward to see her screen.

"Jason supposedly went out with Emma Watson last night," she says, handing it over.

I sit back in my chair and click on the link, knowing firsthand what it's like to be caught on *TMZ* with Jason Samuels. "Maybe it was a work dinner," I suggest.

Devyn shakes her head. "I mean, that's totally what he'd say," she says. "But look—the pap caught them kissing outside the limo."

"Hmmm," I say noncommittally when a grainy pic pops up on-screen and the supposed proof is right in front of me. Emma is on tiptoes, her face right next to Jason's. "It doesn't look *too* scandalous," I say. "Maybe it was a quick peck on the cheek. You know, the whole 'Hollywood hello' thing everybody does."

Devyn frowns and holds out her hand for the phone. "I mean, we broke up so it's whatevs. I just think he can do better."

I pass her the phone and take a drink of water. *Better than Emma Watson?*

She looks at the pic again and dramatically rolls her eyes before closing the window and setting her phone on the table. "He's doing a period romance this year, so I'm sure he's just going out with her to learn her British accent, but it's pretty pathetic. I mean, Harry Potter's girlfriend? Get a life."

I nod, assuming it's a bad time to point out that Hermione was actually into Ron.

"I should be used to it. Girls are always throwing themselves at him," she says, scrunching up her nose. "Oh, but don't worry. We died laughing when all that gossip about you guys came out last year."

"I'm glad y'all were laughing because it sucked for me," I say. "There was this guy I was just starting to see, and when all of that came out, I think it made him reconsider us."

"OMG, that sucks," Devyn says, pouting dramatically.

"Yeah, I mean, it was a bunch of stuff," I admit. "I was super busy with my music. And he's a musician, too."

"Sexy," Devyn coos.

I sigh involuntarily. "He really is a great guy," I say, the thought of Adam surprisingly depressing right now. "He was trying to do his own music, and I wanted him to be on my record, but my label didn't want him, so then he played a gig with Kayelee Ford—"

"Kayelee Ford. What a fake," Devyn says, rolling her eyes again.

My ears perk up. "Huh?"

Devyn gestures for me to lean in close and she lowers her voice conspiratorially. "You know Kayelee Ford is as phony as my fingernails, right?"

"What do you mean?" I whisper.

"Her family is, like, filthy rich. She completely bought her way into the music scene."

"Bought her way in?"

"Big donations to music execs' nonprofits, paid for her own development, probably bought all of her own CDs, blah blah blah. Did you know her last name isn't even really Ford?" I gasp, and her eyes gleam. "It's actually Butts or Roach or something like that. The label made her change it so the rednecks would like it. Can you even?"

We both sit back as the food comes, and I let all this gossip sink in. "I'm not even surprised," I say once the waiter is gone. "I ran into her in Nashville and—you've heard how everybody keeps comparing us? Saying we're rivals?"

Devyn nods furiously, her eyes never leaving mine as she takes a bite.

"So I was at this coffee shop and was like, 'I'm going to be the bigger person' and, you know—"

"Squash the beef," Devyn cuts in.

"Exactly. So I stop her and, Devyn, she acts like she doesn't even know who I am."

"No."

"Yes!" I say, eyes wide. "She actually asked me if I wanted an autograph."

"Shut your face."

"And get this," I go on, happy to have someone I can talk to about all of this and who gets how messed up it is. Kai and Stella were shocked at Kayelee's rudeness, but they shrugged it off like I was above it. I am, but still. I've only known Devyn a short time, but I can already tell that she totally understands mean girls like Kayelee. "The girl actually *flirted* with my boyfriend," I say. "Right in front of me!"

"Oh, hell no," Devyn says, pursing her lips.

"I don't really want this rivalry, or whatever it is—and I'm sure country music fans don't either—but this girl is something else."

"Oh no, fans love that stuff," Devyn says, correcting

me. "You might not like what they're saying, but this thing with that trumped-up Bird-wannabe keeps people talking about you." She smiles. "And P.S., it's obvious that you're the classy one."

I sit up straighter and smile broadly. "Thank you, Devyn. I really appreciate that."

"Of course. You know I've got your back," she says. "Now show me a picture of this boyfriend. Is he the musician?"

I pull my cell phone out of my purse and look up a picture. "No, that ended," I say. "Before it even really got going, actually. But this is Kai. We met on my tour this summer and—"

"ZOMG," Devyn says, taking my phone out of my hands. "He looks like a Hollister model. Nice snag, BB."

We talk nonstop through the rest of our lunch. At first I was worried that we wouldn't have much in common. In truth, I guess, we don't. But she's only two years older than me, and she's practically a walking, talking Hollywood handbook. As I devour the absolutely delicious fish tacos, I get all kinds of insider information and she discreetly points out people in the restaurant who are big executives or agents.

When the waiter shows up with a dessert menu, Devyn doesn't even humor him. "You can go ahead and take this," she says as she slides an American Express Black Card out of her billfold.

"Wait," I say, reaching for my purse. The waiter has already walked away. "Devyn, I didn't realize. Here, let me give you some cash."

She waves me off as she digs through her bag. "Buy me a fro yo later."

She puts on lip gloss and smacks her full lips, then she gets her sunglasses out but doesn't put them on yet. Her signals couldn't be clearer—she is ready to get out of here—so I grab my phone and pull up the camera app, checking my teeth.

"Bird, that's genius," Devyn says, appraising me with an enormous smile. She picks up her own phone and checks her teeth and eye makeup, then she smooths down her already sleek hair. "I don't know how I never thought to use this as a mirror."

I shrug. "Years on the road with a very small bathroom shared with four other people. You get creative."

Devyn signs the bill with a flourish, and by the time we step out of the restaurant, the paparazzi have quadrupled in number. "Are you ready?" she asks, linking her arm through mine as she leads the way through the patio.

On the street, she beams at the cameras and waves flirtatiously as they shout, "Bird! Devyn! Over here! Bird, are you living in LA now? Devyn, what do you think about Jason and Emma?"

She manages to smile at them, giggle as if sharing a joke

with me, and power us through the crowd toward her convertible waiting at the valet stand. I give a smile or two, but mainly, I keep my head down.

Behind the wheel, she looks over at me, still smiling like a beauty queen. "You'll get used to them," she says as they keep snapping photos. "It's like this everywhere in LA."

"I get a little nervous when they're right up in my face like that," I admit. There is one guy practically lying on the car hood as he angles for a shot, and it's not until Devyn expertly pulls away from the curb that I feel the anxiety subside.

"They can be annoying, sure," she says, stopping at a red light. "But I just know to always be 'on.' Oh my God, your song!"

She blasts the radio and slams on the gas pedal as the light turns green. "Sing Anyway" blares through the speakers. My hair flies everywhere, whipping my face until I slip a ponytail holder off my wrist and pull it back. I look over at Devyn, singing along and looking every bit as put together as when she first showed up for lunch. It seems to me that always being "on" would take a lot of work, but somehow Devyn Delaney makes it look effortless.

Over the next couple of hours, Devyn gives her fancy credit card a workout. She has appointments at several shops on

North Rodeo Drive, everyone happy to see us. I didn't even know we were going shopping, but the designer boutiques have dressing rooms already stocked with clothes in my size. I'm eager to join in the fun—hey, why not?—until I see the price tags. Some of this stuff costs four times as much as we'd make for a Barrett Family Band gig…and that had to feed five people!

So I resist the urge to shop for myself and try to be a good audience for Devyn without admitting to her that my parents would go nuts if I dropped this kind of change on my wardrobe. At Gucci, she gets a white, iridescent, draped jumpsuit that looks stunning against her deep brown skin. She begs me to try on a shift dress from the same collection, but when I see that it costs $3,500, I politely decline. At Fendi, it's the same story, although it's much easier for me to try out and turn down purses than clothing. We stop at Cartier and Ferragamo before, finally, she stops me on the sidewalk outside Chanel.

"Bird, are you even having fun?" she says, with a touch of annoyance.

"Yeah," I say, surprised.

"Well, I made all these appointments and these people were expecting us. They already pulled items for us and everything, but you're, like, not even into it."

"Oh," I say, a little embarrassed. "I didn't know we were going shopping today. But no, Devyn, seriously, I'm having a great time. I just thought I was here to help you find something for *The Tonight Show*. I don't really need anything for myself."

Devyn laughs. "It's not about *needing* anything, Bird. It's about celebrating your success." She puts her hands on my shoulders, the designer bags sliding down to the crooks in her arms. She shakes her perfect waves from her face and aims the full brilliance of her wide smile at me. "Bird Barrett, my new friend, you are *crushing* the charts. Crushing them. And this week, there's a whole article about your move to LA in *People*. You are gorgeous and fun and talented and maybe you haven't realized it, but you're kind of a big deal."

I blush.

"You went on a national tour with Jolene Taylor!" she shouts, shaking my shoulders playfully. "I guarantee that diva's out shopping right now and not thinking twice about it."

"No, I'm sure," I say, biting my lip. The stuff Devyn's bought today is unquestionably gorgeous, but it was just so expensive. "My parents would kill me," I finally say, albeit halfheartedly.

"You're the one making the money," she counters. "And you're working your butt off for it, too."

"That's true."

"Come on," she says. "It's no fun having a shopping buddy who doesn't shop."

She holds open the door to the next designer store, and I feel the cool air-conditioning on my face.

"Miss Barrett. Miss Delaney," a very well-put-together woman greets us. Another girl is immediately at her side with two bottles of VOSS water. I smile at her and walk in, reasoning that I could use a couple of pairs of shoes for nights out with Kai. And after all, I am paying for my brothers' college tuition *and* I bought my folks the house in Nashville. It's about time I spend some of my money on me.

"Whoa, that's an awful big load you've got there," my dad comments when I get home later. I was hoping to hurry back to my room, but as luck would have it, he was walking out of the kitchen right as I walked in the front door.

"Yeah, I picked up a few things."

"A few?" he remarks, following me into the living room. My mom looks up from the magazine she's reading, and I can tell from the look on her face that she, too, has an opinion about all the shopping bags I'm holding. "Looks like you picked up more than a few things to me."

I roll my eyes. "Okay, so I bought a bunch of stuff. So what?"

"So what?" my dad repeats. "So I don't like your attitude is what."

I exhale mightily and walk back to my bedroom. I lay the bags on my bed, but as expected, my parents follow me.

"Jimmy Choo and Prada?" my mom asks, sitting on the bed and nosing through my purchases. She holds up a gray military-inspired coat and audibly gasps.

"Gorgeous, right?" I ask.

"I was going to say obscene," she answers. "Bird, how did you pay for all of this?"

"With the credit card," I say, shrugging.

"Do you know how many mouths you could feed with the price of this coat?" she asks.

I walk over to the bed and take the coat from her, folding it and putting it back in the bag. "I didn't buy that much," I say. "You should've seen the damage Devyn did today."

"I don't care what Devyn Delaney spent," she says, her face turning red. I haven't seen my mom get really angry in a long time, and I was actually more prepared for my dad to blow up. "That credit card is for emergencies. You shouldn't be spending that kind of money on clothes and shoes."

"Why not?" I ask. "I make the money."

"Bird Barrett, you will not take that tone—"

"Aileen," my dad says, cutting her off. He walks calmly over to the bags and empties them onto my bed: a dress, two pairs of shoes, a handbag, a metal cuff, the gray coat, and a pair of dark jeans. "Bird, look at these things. Seven things. Only seven things and you seem to have spent almost…" He checks the tags and does the math in his head. I can tell from the expression on his face that it's much worse than he'd expected. "Nine thousand dollars," he nearly whispers. "Nine thousand?" he asks much louder, looking up at me. "And you call that not buying much?"

I feel heat flaming up my neck and over my cheeks, so I sit down and focus on taking off my sandals. I had the best afternoon with an awesome new friend and they're ruining it by pinching pennies. My pennies.

"I don't see the big deal," I say. "I mean, yeah, if it were before my album was doing so well then it would totally be a lot of money."

"Nine thousand dollars is a lot of money no matter how your album does," my dad says sternly. He shakes his head. "This isn't like you, Bird."

"What is that supposed to mean?" I ask hotly. "And why can't I spend the money I'm making?"

"Because you're seventeen!" he responds, finally at the anger level I had originally been expecting.

"Well, you're not my manager anymore, so I'll call Troy and see what he thinks," I say.

My dad is in my face faster than a bullet out of its casing. "Troy Becker is in charge of deciding where you sing," he spits. "*I'm* still your father and I'll decide what's best for your future, and I hate to break it to you, but a nine-thousand-dollar shopping spree ain't it."

"Mom," I say, turning toward her for a little support.

Instead, she crosses her arms and shakes her head, her eyes full of disappointment.

"You may pick one thing to keep," my dad says through clenched teeth. He points to the pile of luxury items. "The rest is going back."

My mom stands up, giving me one last I'm-so-disappointed-in-you look before following him out of my bedroom. Furious, I throw my sandals into the closet and slam the door behind them. Then I sit on my bed and pack up the day's purchases, fighting back angry tears. My dad may not be my manager anymore, but he's certainly still running the show.

21

"It's just so hard not seeing you every day," I complain to Kai on the phone. We said we would talk every day, but it's been hard, already. Like today, I had the meeting with Troy, lunch with Devyn, and then shopping plus the parental debacle afterward. I didn't want to be in the same house with them, so I brought a blanket down to the beach for some space. And now that I finally have time to talk, Kai's squeezing me in before he has to work the show. We're both busy, and the time difference is brutal. "I mean, I'll see something and be like, 'Oh my gosh, Kai would love that,' and then I just get sad."

"Like what?" he asks.

"Um," I say, thinking. "Oh, like this heart-shaped seashell I just found on the beach."

"That's nice," he says. "Send me a pic."

"I will," I say. "But it's not the same."

He sighs. "I know."

I stare out at the ocean and watch the waves roll in and out. It's mesmerizing.

"Hey, how was your day with Devyn?" Kai asks.

"Actually, it was a lot of fun," I say. "I was worried because she's clearly so high maintenance—totally different than anybody I've ever hung out with, and surgically attached to her phone—but I was surprised. She's also really funny. And she gets it, you know? I mean she gets this *life*. She's super driven, which I totally admire, and Kai, she *knows* the Hollywood scene. I'm telling you, she knows everything about everybody."

"What do you mean?"

"You know, who's going out with whom and what projects the studios are after." I search for the right words, trying to explain it, but this is exactly what's so hard about long-distance relationships: It's never the same trying to tell him about what's going on as it would be just to experience it together. "She knows a ton of people out here. It's like getting a crash course in all things Hollywood."

"Wow."

"Yeah, and we're going to this indie film festival when she gets back from New York. See? Another thing you would love."

"That's cool," he says.

"Yeah."

And then: The Pause.

The Pause has become like a third party in our relationship. I'll tell a story and he'll chime in with "Cool," or "Great," or "Uh-huh." And he'll tell a story and I'll be like, "Why?" or "Who's that?" or "Really?" And then we segue, taking turns retelling the actual events of our lives, continuously pushing through The Pause. There were never awkward pauses when we were on the tour together. Not since the beginning, at least. The conversation just flowed, like we couldn't get enough of what the other was saying, thinking, or feeling.

"So, get this," I say now, telling him about the awful fight with my parents. "Devyn had to go shopping for her appearance on *The Tonight Show* this week. So after lunch, I went with her to Rodeo Drive."

"Uh-huh."

"And these places are pretty fancy, you know? You have to have appointments and everything. They treated us like royalty. It was so awesome."

The Pause.

"So anyway, I wasn't really buying anything at first, but then I saw this dress that was so pretty. I mean, everybody at Chanel was like, 'That is so you.'"

He laughs.

"What?"

"Oh, I don't know," he says. "These people just met you. How do they know what is 'so you'?"

I bristle. "Well, I guess they were just saying it fit me perfectly. And it's sort of mod-country chic, you know? It's black with white stitches making squares all over it, and the middle is this oval-shaped white crocheted cutout. It looks like a giant belt buckle or something at first glance. Really cool."

"I can't wait to see it."

"Well, that's what I'm telling you," I say, digging my feet into the sand. "Devyn bought, like, a trunkful of stuff—I mean that girl spent some serious money—and I only bought seven things. That dress, a couple of pairs of shoes, jeans, a coat, a bracelet, and...I don't know. Something else. Anyway, my parents *flipped* out."

The Pause.

"Kai, they flipped. My mom was all indignant, basically saying I'm taking the food out of orphans' mouths, and my dad is taking me back to all the stores tomorrow to return everything but one pair of shoes. Do you know how mortifying that will be?"

"So..." He hedges. "How much did you spend?"

"It was, like, nine."

"Nine hundred?" he asks.

"Um, thousand," I say quietly, placing the heart-shaped

shell in the sand and drawing our names around it with my finger.

"Nine thousand dollars?" Kai asks. "Bird, you spent nine K on clothes?"

"What?" I ask.

"'What?'"

"Yeah, what?" I ask, sitting up. "You're right. Nine thousand dollars is a lot of money, but we were having fun, and it just added up. And okay, maybe I overdid it a little, but I work hard for the money I make and I never, ever splurge."

"Well, there's splurging and there's nine thousand dollars," he says.

I exhale loudly. "I got the lecture from my parents, okay, Kai? I didn't call you for round two."

The Pause.

"Do you know what that kind of money could've done for me and my mom when I was growing up?" Kai asks quietly. "That's a hella lot of money, Bird."

"I get that it's a lot of money, Kai," I say. "I wasn't raised with a silver spoon in my mouth, either. But I went shopping once. *Once*. At places that weren't discount retailers. And I was treated like a princess. And it felt good, okay?"

"Well, I hate that you had to go all the way down to Rodeo Drive to be treated like a princess."

"That's not what I meant."

The Pause.

"I know," he finally says. He sighs. "Look, I'm not trying to be all judgy or treat you like your dad or anything. And it's not like you did anything inherently wrong. It just doesn't sound like you. You spent a lot of money on materialistic stuff." I bite my lip, staring out at the surf. "And you *are* only seventeen," he says delicately, "so your parents do still have a say in what you buy."

I shake my head, annoyed all over again, and think it best to change the subject. "Whatever. What'd you do last night?"

"Oh, it was pretty cool, actually," he says. "Astrean played this intimate space in Raleigh, crazy small and cozy. And she convinced the owner to kill the overhead fluorescents and hang these vintage chandeliers. It was so beautiful. You would've loved it."

"Sounds amazing," I say halfheartedly.

"Nothing but her voice, the piano, and the violin," he continues. "It was like she cast a spell, Bird. It was like the rest of the world stood still and the only people breathing were in that room, listening. And when the show was over, everyone just lingered, you know? Because they were so moved by the music."

"Wow."

"Yeah. It was mind-blowing. Have you ever felt like that?" he asks, really worked up now. "So inspired that you literally could not keep living unless you wrote the song in your head?"

I immediately think back to "Sing Anyway," the last song on the *Wildflower* album, the one I wrote right after Adam called things off. I had terrible writer's block, but once the idea sparked, it wrote itself in ten minutes. I tweaked it and worked it over, but the essence of the song was so gripping when inspiration struck that it nearly took my breath away.

That's not exactly a story I want to share with Kai, though.

"Bird?"

"I'm here," I say. "That sounds amazing. I'm so glad you're enjoying the tour."

"Yeah, this is really where I belong," he says. "The big tours pay the bills and set me up, which is good and all, but this...this is an experience...this is, well, it's just *life*."

I know he doesn't mean to, but that hurts my feelings, like he's diminishing my music in some way. This is life, too. My life. My shows may not be in cozy little lounges, but people all over America—all over the world, even—are inspired by my music.

"Bird, I have to go," he says. "My call is in half an hour, and I need to eat first. Talk after the show?"

"Yeah, I'll be up."

"Sweet. Miss you."

"I miss you, too. Bye." I press END on my phone quickly. Maybe I'm reading into it because I was already in a bad mood, but I can't help feeling like Kai just called me immature and superficial, writing music that's too commercial to be good.

And maybe it cuts a little deeper because I've got another album due and lately I've felt anything but inspired.

22

"BIRD, IT'S ALMOST time," my mom yells from the living room.

"Be right there!" I holler back as I finish brushing my teeth.

Last night I was pretty quiet at dinner, not just because of the clothes fight with my parents but also because of how crappy I felt after my phone call with Kai. Before going to bed, I nursed my ego by reading fan posts on Twitter and Facebook about how I was a shoo-in for the Country Music Awards nominations this morning. Then I handed over my laptop, iPad, and cell phone to my dad. We all agreed we wanted to experience the announcements on *Good Morning America* for ourselves instead of hearing the good or bad news over the phone or online.

The minute I woke up to the smell of my mom's buckwheat pancakes this morning, I felt butterflies. Open Highway is counting on me. My fans are counting on me. It would be so freaking spectacular to be nominated for a CMA.

"Bird, it's on!" my mom calls again. "It's on!"

I nearly trip over a pile of dirty clothes in my bathroom as I race to the TV. My dad sits on the couch next to my mom, both of them clutching mugs of coffee, with their eyes glued to the flat-screen, and it hits me that they're as nervous as I am. I grab a throw pillow and plop down beside them, then stand up again, then pace a little. I can hear my heart pounding in my ears.

"And the songs nominated for Single of the Year are," Kacey Musgraves finally says, " 'Hold You Tighter,' Mom and Pop's Shop; 'Notice Me,' Bird Barrett—"

The second we hear "Notice Me" is nominated for Single of the Year, we scream. We all scream. My mom spills her coffee all over her blanket, and my dad pumps his free hand in the air as if he just saw the Titans win the Super Bowl. We stand up and hug, acting like lunatics, jumping around in a circle.

My dad kisses my forehead. "I'm so proud of you, sweetheart."

"Oh, Bird, I'm so happy, baby," my mom says, hugging me tightly. "You deserve this. You work so hard." Tears are streaming down her face, and we all laugh.

"Mom, stop crying," I say. "You're going to make *me* cry."

"Hush, y'all," my dad says. "They're still going."

"Oh right," I say breathlessly. "I didn't even hear who else was nominated."

We settle back onto the couch and this time I squeeze between my parents. We listen to Blake Shelton, Miranda Lambert, and Keith Urban rack up nominations, and I see on a news ticker that Kayelee Ford was also nominated for Single of the Year. It doesn't matter, though. Doesn't even faze me.

When they get around to announcing the New Artist of the Year category, I am once again on pins and needles. I want this one. I really want this one. They announce Kayelee right off the bat, but my own name is called just after, and the circus in my living room begins again. This time we're all unabashedly crying. I was nominated for two CMAs. *Two* CMAs!

When the announcements are over, we immediately power up our phones. I laugh at the sounds they make, the pings and beeps of about a hundred message alerts confirming that many of our Nashville friends and family tuned in earlier. My dad's calling my brothers and then my granddad. Mom calls my gramma and then probably half of Jackson. I go to my room and call Kai, the one other person I most wish were right here at this very moment. I wish

I could see the look on his face. I wish I could have a hug, the huge kind where he swings me around in a circle. I wish I could have a big, romantic, dip-me-down-low congratulatory kiss.

"Hey, Bird."

"Good morning!" I sing into the phone. "Guess whose girlfriend is nominated for two CMAs!"

"Wow! Bird, congratulations," he says.

"Can you believe it?" I yell. I jump up onto my bed.

"Yeah," he says, not even close to my level of enthusiasm.

"Kai, I'm jumping up and down over here. My pillows are falling off the bed. Answer me like you mean it. Can you freaking believe it?" I shout.

He laughs hoarsely. "Yeah, I can, Bird. You're amazing."

I know he worked a really late show last night and then had to load up and get back on the road right after, and I imagine him in his tour bunk, shirtless probably, the covers thrown everywhere and his hair a mess. A pang of longing grips me. "I wish you were here," I say, flopping down. "I so wish you were here right now."

"Me too," he says. "I'm really happy for you."

"Thank you."

"We'll definitely celebrate when I'm back in town."

I flop onto my belly and trace the pattern on my comforter, already imagining it. "I can't wait."

He chuckles. "Me neither."

"I wish I could just come meet you out on tour," I say. "I could get to know your tour mates and Astrean, put names with faces, and they could get to know me as your girlfriend and not just the girl on the radio or whatever."

"Oh, yeah," he says uncertainly. "That'd be cool."

The Pause.

"Wait," I say, a weird feeling taking over. "You've told them about me, right?"

"Bird, yes," he says. "Of course they know I have a girlfriend."

"And you've told them that it's me?"

"What do you mean?"

"Kai."

"No, it's just, you know, a lot of the people on this tour don't really do country music. I don't want to be that guy that's like, 'Oh, I'm dating Bird Barrett.'"

"Why not?" I ask quietly, feeling like a popped balloon.

"Well, I don't know. I mean, I thought you wanted to keep us quiet and not let the tabloids in on it."

"I thought *you* wanted that."

"Right, well, we both did. So..."

I wait. "So what?"

He exhales loudly.

I shake my head. I can't believe Kai hasn't told his friends about me. I can't believe my boyfriend is embarrassed by me. I know new country's not really his preferred style of music, but—

"Hey," I say, hoping he can't hear the tightness in my throat, "Dan's beeping in on the other line, so I should probably go." It's a lie, but my feelings are hurt, I might cry, and I don't feel like talking anymore.

"Bird, I really am happy for you," Kai says. "A CMA is a huge deal—"

"Yeah, it's a pretty big honor," I squeak out. My eyes get blurry because I can't help but expect my *boyfriend* to be over the moon for me instead of making me feel like my music isn't legit—or even worse, that *I'm* not.

"Bird, I'm so proud of you. I really am."

"Uh-huh," I manage. "I'll call you later, okay? I really do have to go."

"Okay, call me anytime today. I'll have my phone right here, okay?"

"Yep. Bye."

I press END before he can say another word.

Before this phone call, I was on the high of my life. Adrenaline was racing through my body and I felt like I could rocket myself to the moon. But now I feel silly. I was ecstatic when they announced my name. I was happy for myself and for my label and for my family. I was already imagining Kai on the red carpet with me.

Tears fall down the sides of my face and into my ears. *Maybe if a few hundred thousand fewer people liked my songs, then the one person on earth I really want to like them actually would,* I think bitterly.

My phone beeps and I check a new text from Kai:

Not sure how the convo got weird, but I really am happy for you, okay?

I start a text back, typing:

You're not sure how the convo got weird? Maybe because you're embarrassed that

but I don't get a chance to send it because a phone call comes through and I accidentally answer it with my thumbs.

"Hello?" I hear Adam say. "Bird? Are you there?"

Unbelievable. I close my eyes and wipe my face with one hand before bringing the phone to my ear and faking the appropriate perkiness.

"Adam, yeah, hi!"

"I just heard the news," he says excitedly. "Two CMA nominations? That's amazing. Congratulations!"

"God!" I say, exhaling loudly. "Thank you."

"Yeah! Of course."

"Seriously," I say, snatching a tissue from the box on my dresser. "Freaking thank you."

"Um," he says, thrown off. "You're welcome?"

I MUTE my phone real quick and blow my nose.

"Bird?" Adam says. "Are you okay?"

I press UNMUTE. "Totally," I say, as my eyes fill up with tears again. Leave it to Adam to call and see through me right away. "Yeah, of course I'm okay. I'm just...so happy."

My phone beeps and when I see that it actually is Dan this time, I pull myself together.

"Adam, I hate to do this and it really is awesome of you to call," I say, "but Dan's beeping in on the other line."

"Oh, yeah, sure. I'll let you go," he says as if he doesn't really want to. The concern in his voice makes it nearly impossible to keep my tears in check. "I'll be in LA in a few days, but I just wanted to call now—say how proud I am. And how much you deserve it."

I sniff. "Thank you," I say. The call waiting beeps again.

"Call me back if you want to," he suggests. "I'm around pretty much all day."

"Oh yeah, okay. Cool."

"Okay."

"Bye, Adam."

"Bye, Lady Bird."

I can picture him, his slow smile, his shaggy hair...

I shake my head, end the call, and take a deep breath. "Dan! Hi!" I say, my voice full of false pep.

"This is Dan Silver, president of Open Highway records, the label built by incredibly talented and CMA-nominated artists like Bird Barrett," he says as his way of greeting. "How may I help you?"

I laugh despite myself, wiping my face with my sleeve. "Dan, *you* called me."

"Oh, Bird! Is that you?" he says, laughing. "I must have pocket dialed you."

"Ha-ha."

He chuckles and I can imagine him in Nashville, kicking back with his boots on his desk. "What a morning, huh, kiddo?"

Tell me about it, I think.

"I can't believe it," I say instead, focusing on the nominations. "I really can't believe it."

"Oh believe it, baby," he says. "We are so proud of you. I can't say that I was surprised, but it's still nice to hear it out loud."

"Yes," I say firmly. "It *is* nice to hear it. It's really nice to hear it."

This was just the phone call I needed. He sounds as excited as a little kid. "My in-box is already flooded. Open Highway really showed up this year—thanks very much to you. I'm ecstatic. Couldn't be prouder."

"I haven't checked all my messages, but I guess Anita's happy," I say.

"Happy? She already sent out a press release!" He laughs. "I'm sure she'll connect with you later."

"Did you see that Kayelee Ford was nominated in the same categories as me?"

"I did see that," he muses. "And you know what, speak of the devil, an e-mail came in from your old buddy Randall Strong right this very minute."

"Really?"

Dan laughs again. "Oh, I love it."

"What's it say?"

"The subject is 'Awards,'" he says. "And the e-mail is one line: 'Looks like we've got ourselves a horse race.'"

"Oh, great."

He laughs again, a big booming laugh so that I have to hold the phone away from my ear. "Oh, Bird. I'm not a betting man, but I've never felt better about my odds."

23

"So, you think I should let it go," I say to Stella over Face-Time. We've hashed out the CMA day a billion times this week. I've called her immediately after every attempt at a make-up conversation with Kai. It's been tense. Every time I try to explain to him why I'm hurt, I come off sounding needy, which makes me even more frustrated. But if I can't even tell him how I feel, how is he supposed to get it?

"Yeah, I do," she says. "You're crazy about Kai and he's crazy about you, and this was understandably really hurtful, but I think he realizes he messed up. He was prob-ably just trying not to be 'that guy,' you know? The type who brags about a famous girlfriend. Also, a lot of guys are intimidated by strong, successful women."

"Maybe," I say, not totally convinced. I look at the

vase of two dozen long-stemmed red roses from Kai on my dresser and can't help but compare them to the poppies that Adam sent last week. The roses were a nice apologetic gesture, sure, but not original at all—and not really me. "I just feel like my music is *me*. It's my heart that I put out there, my real experiences, and if Kai is ashamed of that, then he's ashamed of me."

Stella nods sympathetically on the screen. "You're right," she says. "And you should tell him that."

"I mean, I kind of have, you know? Like, he knows I write my own songs—"

"No, no, no," she interrupts. "Boys are dumb and they need everything spelled out. Explicitly. Like you're talking to a child."

I laugh.

"I wish I were joking."

"Knock, knock," Devyn sings from my bedroom door, looking as rocker chic as ever. I glance down at my yoga pants and oversize jersey-knit shirt and frown. "Are you ready for a day of pampering?" she asks.

"Definitely," I say. Devyn invited me to a day at the spa, and the timing couldn't be better. Even the Money Boss—as I now not-so-affectionately call my dad—okayed it. "Hey, this is my best friend, Stella," I say, eager to introduce my two closest friends. I aim the iPad toward Devyn. "Stella, Devyn. Devyn, Stella."

"Hi-yee!" Devyn says, wiggling her fingers. "I've heard so much about you."

"Same here," Stella says. "Nice to meet you." I glance at the screen and frown. The average viewer would see a perfectly polite person, but I know Stella Crossley and that is her faking-it face. I hope she gives Devyn a chance. "Bird, call me later?"

"Totally," I say. "And thanks for listening...again."

"That's what I'm here for," she says. "Dr. Stella Crossley: psychiatrist to the stars."

"And no doubt a hell of a lot cheaper than my shrink," Devyn quips.

Stella rolls her eyes and fake gags. Quickly, I turn the screen away, but Devyn is preoccupied with her phone anyway. "Bye, Stel." I close my iPad cover and grab my purse. "Let's do this," I say to Devyn, and head for the living room. "If anyone's earned a massage, it's me. You aren't going to believe the drama with Kai."

"OMG, I thought something was up," she says. "Your eyes look terrible."

I hesitate, glancing at myself in the big mirror in the hall, but I don't have much time to respond because I hear deep voices laughing in the kitchen, one in particular that makes the tiny hairs on my arm stand up.

"And then he got on the skateboard anyway, just to impress the girl," I hear Adam hoot.

I round the corner, completely flummoxed that Adam is in my condo and nobody thought to tell me he was coming over. "Hi," I say in the doorway.

My mom is wiping tears out of her eyes, and my dad's face is red from laughing so hard. Jacob's is red, too, but not from laughing.

"Hey, Lady Bird," Adam says, his demeanor softening. His eyes are fixed on me as if I am the only person in the room. "It's good to see you."

His focus is a little unsettling, and I feel the blush rise up in my cheeks right away. This is the first time I've seen Adam in person since our pseudo–movie date last winter, and I am definitely not prepared. He looks good. He's leaning against the kitchen counter with that same ease he always has about him, as if he's been here a thousand times before. He's wearing a simple gray V-neck and he needs a shave and a haircut, as usual, but it all works for him. When he straightens up and takes a step toward me, his arms open for a hug, I awkwardly step forward.

"Yeah, you too, Adam," I say, putting my arms around him. He always smells like fresh laundry, and my heart skips a beat at the familiarity. I pull away quickly. "I didn't know you were coming over," I say, looking pointedly at my brother.

"We just got here," Jacob says, averting his gaze. He's clearly uncomfortable, and I realize that Adam *has* told him at least something about what happened between us.

"Hi, I'm Devyn Delaney," Devyn says, pushing past me with her hand outstretched. She flashes Adam her million-dollar smile and then works the rest of the room, my brother drooling all over himself while Adam keeps his attention on me.

"Sorry I didn't get to call you back after the CMA announcements," I say. "It was so crazy and—"

"Oh, yeah, I'm sure—"

"The label was calling and Anita had...stuff," I say lamely. I should've called him back. He gives me a lopsided grin and I involuntarily sigh, remembering how easy he is to be around. I snap out of it and busy myself with grabbing a bottle of water from the fridge. "So how was Austin?" I ask.

"Good," he says, leaning back against the counter again. He's standing unnervingly close to me. "Really good. I got a lot of writing done, actually. The songs were pouring out of me. I've never been so inspired. And I met a guy who's helping me make a demo, so things are really going well."

"That's great," I say, thinking about how unproductive my own summer was, writing-wise.

"Not CMA great," Adam says with a nudge.

I look him in the eyes, remember how pretty his are, and blush. "Thank you."

"You and Kayelee both," he says, shaking his head. "I may not have made a name for myself yet, but I'm starting to think I'm a good-luck charm for the girls I hang around."

"You still hang out with Kayelee?" I ask bluntly.

He shrugs. "Eh, not really. You know how it is on the road. We text every now and then, but that's about it," he says. I frown. He and I text every now and then, too. "She asked me to tour with her—and the experience would've been great—but I really need to focus on my own stuff right now, you know?"

"Yeah," I say frankly. "I think you made the right choice."

"Me too," he says, nodding. "It sure was hard to turn her down though."

"Hmph." I snort. "I bet."

Devyn smirks at me.

"What do you mean?" Adam asks.

"Well, I think she's pretty used to getting what she wants."

Adam crosses his arms. They are lean and strong, not like Kai's, whose arms bulge with muscle, but like those of someone who grew up hauling hay and now hauls his guitar everywhere. He looks down as if considering his words. "She's a little spoiled I guess. I'll give you that. But it was really nice of her to offer me the spot."

"Sure," I say.

"She's talented," he goes on. "She has a great voice." He looks up at me. "You don't like her stuff?"

I shrug. "It's all right, if you like that mainstream pop sound."

"*Oh*-kay," Adam says, glancing over at my brother like I'm crazy.

I sigh. "Look, she and I don't really get along," I explain. "Of course she's nice to you. You're a guy and you're—cute or whatever. And maybe she does have a good voice."

"Maybe," Devyn pipes up. "But you wouldn't know with all the auto-tuning."

I laugh out loud, but Adam looks a little annoyed.

"Her label is pressing her for a commercial sound, but I've heard her live and, believe me, she can sing," he says.

It completely astonishes me that Adam is defending Kayelee, so I put my hands up and step back. "Okay, okay, sorry," I say. "Agree to disagree."

He doesn't respond, and in the silence that follows, I become incredibly self-conscious. The people in this kitchen are supposed to be in my corner, but the laughter that filled the place moments ago has been sucked out of the room and now everybody just seems uncomfortable. I look over at my parents.

"She practically threw herself at Kai," I finally say, feeling like I have to explain. And as good as it is to see Adam, I also get a twinge of satisfaction at letting him know that I've moved on. "She's the worst."

"She really is, like, always talking smack about Bird," Devyn chimes in.

"Thank you," I say. At least one person has my back. "Trust me, Adam. You dodged a bullet."

"Yeah," he says, as he scratches his scruffy jawline and nods slowly. "Maybe I did, Bird."

The weight behind his words stings.

"Okay, so we're going," I announce, frustrated with everybody in my house. *My* house. "Good to see you again, Adam."

He takes a seat at the table with Jacob, his back to me as they help themselves to the snacks my mom has laid out. "You too, Bird," he says, raising a hand in the air, but not looking back.

I don't even understand what just happened.

"So that's your ex?" Devyn asks once we're in the hallway. I nod. "He's super cute."

"Yeah, but I can't believe he was sticking up for Kayelee."

"He just doesn't know her," Devyn says. "Girls like Kayelee Ford are always sweet to hot guys and mean to girls they're threatened by. Don't take it personally. He'll see."

"Well, if anything, I feel like that just reaffirmed his decision to call things off," I say at the elevator. "Not that it matters now that I'm with Kai."

I grab my phone from my purse and text Kai:

Hey. I miss you.

And I feel instantly lighter when he replies right away:

So much it hurts.

I smile and lower my sunglasses as we walk through the lobby and step out into the sunshine.

24

"You look great, Bird," my dad says as he double-parks beside the line of town cars queued up for Hollywood Howls, an annual Halloween charity event supporting the Gentle Barn. "I'll be back around eight, and if you want to stay longer, I'll come inside and chaperone you girls."

I cringe. "Um, thanks, Dad. See you later."

I step out and walk to the curb, scanning the crowd for Devyn before my dad changes his mind and decides to come in now. Devyn told me that the whole event will segue into a rager later tonight once the money's been made for the Gentle Barn, but I'll be long gone by then. Still, as photographers and entertainment reporters line the barricades, I gear up for another red carpet, excited to be attending a fancy LA event on my own, even if only for a few hours.

I text Devyn that I'm here, and when I spot her getting out of a long black limousine up ahead, followed by Bria and Bridget, the statuesque twins I so often see photographed with her, I head her way. Devyn wanted us all to get ready together and was clearly annoyed on the phone when I told her I couldn't get out of brunch at Bonnie McLain's with my parents. She insisted we at least walk the step-and-repeat together, posing as a group for the paparazzi so our costumes make sense. We're the four seasons: I'm fall, Devyn's winter, and Bria and Bridget are spring and summer.

"Devyn!" I call, hustling over to my group.

She waves halfheartedly and adjusts her bikini top, which is covered in silver sequins. White organza flows from behind her neck, down over one cup, and over her toned stomach to blend with the shredded-organza skirt, gorgeous against her dark skin. She looks stunning, except for the obvious distaste on her face. I wonder what's the matter.

"You look so pretty," I say as we exchange air kisses.

"I can't believe you have wings," Devyn replies, her full lips turned down in a frosted-white pout. "I'm wearing wings. These are custom-made. And now I don't stand out." She sighs tremendously and looks away.

Speechless, I turn to my summer and spring counterparts, introducing myself as if everything is okay, but to tell the truth, I'm a little taken aback by Devyn's attitude. I am in love with my costume. I found a long, copper-toned, off-the-shoulder dress with a shimmery sheer overlay that looks really pretty with my skin and hair. My mom added leaf details and tiny pearls, and she made me a pair of almost transparent wings to give my autumn look an ethereal feel, but I never imagined they'd be an issue.

"Okay, ladies, let's turn it on," Devyn says. She takes a deep breath and lets it out slowly. "I just want to walk this carpet, get a ginger ale, and find a dark booth to crash in."

And without another word, she struts off as if she were about to walk the Victoria's Secret runway show. I look inquisitively at Bria, who is exquisite in a floral two-piece dress, her big blue eyes shadowed with pinks and greens. "Hangover," she explains.

"Devyn! Over here! You look amazing!" the photographers call.

I follow the girls to the red carpet and watch Devyn dazzle. She is radiant, and as she flashes her perfect smile at the cameras, her hip cocked out at the most flattering angle, I wouldn't have known in a million years that she'd partied too hard last night.

"Bird! You look amazing! Bird, over here!"

The photographers snap me from my trance, and I stop a few feet away from her, promptly posing in my beginner's go-to, the ankle crossover. I smile demurely as the camera shutters audibly open and close. I'm still not a pro at this red carpet stuff, but one of the things Troy's done in the last two months is set me up with an acting slash modeling coach, and after all the publicity Anita's had me doing since the CMA nominations, I'm getting used to it. I always thought modeling looked easy, but in actuality, it's anything but.

"Bria! Bridget! Gorgeous!" the photographers call out as the twins pose in sync on my other side. Effortlessly, they loop limbs around each other, angle their shoulders, and point their toes in a way that makes their legs seem to lengthen right before my eyes. They are both rail thin and taller even than me in their Louboutins.

I continue down the red carpet, taking big strides between poses, ready to get inside. I'm almost there.

"Bird, we need to pose together," Devyn suddenly squeals, sliding up to me and putting her arm around my waist. She beams at the cameras and with near ventriloquist perfection, she says through her teeth, "I'm sorry about the wings comment before. What do wings have to do with winter? Or fall? It was stupid. I just have a headache and you look gorg. Forgive me?"

Instantly, I relax. "Forgiven," I say, relieved.

"I'm so glad you're here," she breathes, flashing me an indebted smile. She glances over at Bria and Bridget and then links her arm through mine. She lowers her voice even more, and I have to stoop a bit to hear her. "I was, like, best friends with the twins in high school, but we've really grown apart since then."

"But I thought you graduated in May," I say.

"Exactly." She sighs dramatically. "Like, forever ago." She turns and leans against me, giving the photographers a side view of her wintry gown. I mimic her pose, back to back, and smile at the mass of cameras. "Bria and Bridget are great," she says over our shoulders, "but they're reality stars and I am a *professional* actress. I've worked with Tom Hanks."

"You have?"

"It was a voice-over, but yes. And the point is, the girls and I just don't have as much in common as we used to."

Uneasy talking about them when we're all here together, I glance their way. Maybe they haven't worked with Tom Hanks, but from where I stand, it's clear to me that Bria and Bridget certainly aren't hurting for exposure. Their family got a reality show because their half brother, Lil' Thunder, is a preteen rap sensation, but now both of the girls have legit modeling contracts and have been in all the major fashion magazines. Watching their lithe figures work the red carpet, it's easy to see why.

"So why do you still hang out with them?" I ask Devyn. There's a lot of noise on the red carpet, but I still whisper.

"Oh, Bird, there's so much history there," she says

leading me down the carpet. We pose again, completely avoiding interviews as reporters call to us. "Plus, their dad is this big music exec who I totally need to stay on good terms with because I want to record another EP. *And* they have ten million followers on Twitter, collectively."

Shutters click double-time, and I grin at her. That sounds like the Devyn I know.

"Let's get the four seasons together!" a photographer shouts.

The twins join us and urge me to mimic some of their poses, although I'll never feel comfortable making a pouty face. We start to have fun, getting a little silly with it all, and Devyn, who seemed cold as ice when she arrived, melts under the spotlight.

"So Dacari Waddell was there last night with some of the cast from *Teen Wilderness*," Devyn says once we're sitting down inside. She has pulled a tiny flask from her clutch and is spiking her ginger ale. "Want some?"

I shake my head, having learned that lesson fast. "Who's Dacari Waddell?"

She gives me a look of disbelief and then shares a condescending laugh with the twins. For a moment, I'm worried that she's about to make me feel bad for not drinking, but then she says, "Bird, do you live under a rock? Dacari Waddell is on MTV's *The Challenge* spin-off."

"He's, like, a god," Bridget chimes in.

"So hot," Bria confirms.

I glance at my iPhone. We've been here for an hour and haven't moved from this booth. There are superstars everywhere—Portia de Rossi just walked by my table—and I want to mingle. I want to talk to the people who run the Gentle Barn, the charity we're supposed to be here for, but Devyn just wants to chill at our table taking pics and posting them online. Her Twitter feed looks like we're having a blast, when in reality, we're the most boring people here.

"So yeah, Dacari is smokin'," Devyn says, her ice-queen eye makeup sparkling. "I'll totally admit that. But it's not like I'm going to go out with Jason Samuels, who was *People*'s Sexiest Man Alive, don't forget, and then rebound with a reality star." She looks at Bria and Bridget without a shred of remorse. "No offense."

"Whatever," Bria says, shooting Devyn a cold look. "Dacari is a billion times hotter than Jason."

Bridget cocks her head and mimics, "No offense."

Devyn gives them both a demeaning smile. "Dream on, girls." Then she turns to me, scooting closer in the booth and grabbing my forearm as she essentially freezes them out. "So Bird, this guy is coming at me hard and basically ruining any potential game I might have from major players, so I go to the bathroom, and that's when I see Austin Clark. I wasn't sure if he'd be into me since he and Jason shot *Over Getting Over You* together last year, but we started talking and..."

She cocks an eyebrow and purses her lips suggestively.

"And...?" I ask.

"And we hooked up," she says, her eyes gleaming. "Jason would die, especially since Austin just signed on for the next *Batman* remake, but I can't worry about his feelings and I don't even think they really hang out anymore."

"So...you just...hooked up?"

She beams at me. "Yes, and he is ah-to-the-mazing."

Bridget rolls her eyes and stands up. "We're going to the bathroom," she says, grabbing her sister's hand.

The girls leave, gliding through the crowd gracefully, and Devyn sits back, self-satisfied as she takes another sip of her spiked soda. "They're mad about the reality show comment, but they'll get over it," she tells me. "And they're probably jealous about Austin, too. He's gorg."

"So what exactly is your definition of 'hooking up'?" I ask. I've wanted to ask her this question several times, actually.

"Nothing major," she says, shrugging. "I think he's dating Rachel something-or-other, and he's, like, pseudo-serious with her, so we just made out in the VIP room."

My chin hits the table. "Devyn!"

"What?" she asks, raising a frosty eyebrow. "It's not like I slept with him."

"Um, I hope not!" I exclaim. Like that had even crossed my mind. I can't imagine going at it with a guy at a club, not to mention one who's taken and ten years older than me.

"Bird," Devyn says, frowning. "Don't judge. It's gross."

"I'm not judging," I say, snapping out of my, well, judgment.

Then Devyn squints at me and leans in closer. "Bird, tell me you've done it with Kai?"

I look down but feel the blush creeping up my neck. I shake my head slightly.

"Are you serious?" she asks, slapping the table. "He's older, right?"

"He's not *thirty*," I say. Devyn shoots me a cautionary look, so I back off. "But yeah, he's twenty. And we're taking things slow."

"But you've had sex before, right?" she asks. I just stare at her, not even sure how the conversation about her illicit VIP make-out somehow became about me. "OMG, Bird Barrett! You're still a virgin, aren't you?" she asks loudly.

"Now who's the one judging?" I fire back. I cross my arms and sit back hard in the booth. I hear my wings crunch and look up at the ceiling. This event is so not what I'd imagined.

"Oh, Bird, I'm not judging," Devyn says, cozying up to me. She lays her head on my shoulder and squeezes me around my waist. "I think it's sweet how innocent you are. It, like, goes with you. The whole good-girl country-singer thing." She sits up and looks at me with a genuine smile. "I thought it was part of your image, but it's, like, real." This oddly amazes her.

"I'm just waiting for the person I'm going to be with forever," I say quietly.

"But you love Kai, right?" she asks.

"Well, yeah."

"And he loves you?"

"I think so," I say. I stretch my neck, suddenly very antsy.

"Okay, so you waited for love, which is totally admirable, but now you love each other, so what's the problem?"

"There's no problem, Devyn," I snap. Her eyes widen and she holds her hands up in defense. "Sorry. It's just—" I exhale loudly and look down at my hands. "We love each other, yeah, but I mean, we haven't said it. And also, it has to be *right*, you know?" I glance up at her. "I mean, he's never here. I haven't seen him in over two months."

"Wow."

"Yeah," I say. "So we're just taking it slow, okay?"

"I get it," she says. She squeezes my hand, but it feels like she's patronizing me.

I've had enough. I didn't get dressed up to sit at a table the whole time and be antisocial, so I grab my purse and stand. "I'm going to check out the silent auction."

"Bird, wait!" Devyn says, scrambling to get out of the booth. She grabs my arm, partly to stop me and partly to steady herself on her four-inch heels. "I wasn't being mean. You know how I am, vomit mouth, no filter. I'm sorry."

"It's fine."

"No, really," she says, batting her long, frosted eyelashes at me and pouting. "I really am sorry, okay?"

"Okay," I say, somewhat exasperated.

"Come on," she says as she links her arm through mine. "Let's have some fun."

Finally, I think as we weave through the crowd. We stop at a tall cocktail table to snag a mini-quiche and suddenly "Notice Me" comes on over the speakers.

"OMG, your song!" Devyn squeals. She holds up a fake microphone and sings:

"Maybe you like me, or do you like me not?
May be wishful thinking, but wishin's all I've got."

As she sings, people near us start to point and turn their heads. It's crazy, but it still feels so good to hear one of my songs in public, to see people singing along and dancing, especially famous people. As annoyed as I am with Devyn, there's a reason she got a song on that movie sound track. She belts out my country song with gospel soul, doing it justice while giving it a new twist. I feel myself soften toward her as she serenades me.

Soon Bria and Bridget have found us, and they start singing along, too, although it's painfully clear that their little brother is the one with the musical talent. *"If I'm a wildflower, then you're the blowin' breeze!"* they yell. *"I could get swept away, don't know where you'd take me."*

"Come on, Bird," Devyn says, leaning into me and holding up her phone for a quick video of us. *"Is it real? Do you see? Say—you notice me,"* we sing together.

She immediately posts the Vine and sighs. "You know, Bird, you're like the Katy to my Rihanna."

I laugh out loud and shake my head. Only Devyn.

25

"How's it coming?" my dad asks from the patio door. I had a conference call with Troy and Dan this morning, and they both agreed that I need to be recording again. Problem is, record what?

I sigh heavily. "Not great." I gesture to my journal lying in front of me with a million black scratches across both open pages. "The lyrics are so generic and the sound..." I set my guitar down and flop backward on the chaise. I've been out here on the balcony all afternoon thinking the backdrop of the beach would be the perfect place to work, but that's just it: Songwriting never really felt like work before. "Please! Put me out of my misery."

"Oh, Bird," he says, picking up my guitar. "It can't be that bad."

He starts strumming a few chords, just playing around.

"You working on a love song?" he asks, not looking me in the eye. "Maybe something about Kai?" It's been a lot easier for my dad to accept that I have a boyfriend now that that boyfriend is hundreds of miles away.

I turn my head on the cushion and smirk. "Dad. No. You're safe."

He grins. "So nothing too mushy."

"I'd take mushy," I say. "I'd take anything."

Then the chords he's playing morph into something I recognize. "Maybe you need to get back to the basics," he says. He scoots my legs over and sits down with me on my chair. He is playing "Before Music," the song Dylan and I wrote about life before our little brother, Caleb, drowned. It's the simplest song I ever wrote, the purest, just raw emotion. To hear my dad strum it now seems to quiet even the crashing waves. "You know, hon," he says, "the best songs ever written are the ones that come from the heart. I think you know that. I think you're feeling too much pressure, looking at it all like a business, showing up to write songs with your journal and your guitar and your mind, but you keep leaving your heart at home."

He plays softly and I pull my legs up to my chest, rest my chin on my knees, really stop and listen. I hear my song, remember the heartbreak, listen to the waves crash and the seagulls call out to one another as the chords float away on the wind. As my dad plays, I think about what the phrase *before music* means to me now, what my life was like before I was discovered, before I was compared to anyone else. What was my music like before I knew anyone would ever hear it? My dad, a very talented picker, works out an intricate melody where the bridge usually is, and I close my eyes, hearing something sweet and special there in his riff. This idea of life before fame has me gripped, makes me consider who I was before, who I am now, who I want to be, who I want to be with—which makes me think of Kai. Who was I before I was in love?

When the song comes to a close, we sit together in silence as the sun dips low on the horizon. For the next five minutes, we just watch, my heart and mind spinning around with the idea of "Me Before Love."

Finally my mom breaks the spell.

"Supper?" she asks from the patio door.

"Yeah," my dad says, standing up.

"Bird?" she asks.

"I think I'm going to keep working," I say, finally inspired. My dad passes me my guitar and gives me a knowing grin. "Turn the light on for me?"

He nods, and they go inside. I start to pick out a melody, basing it on his riff, the phrase having taken hold in my fingertips. I play something fun but not overly uptempo—something I think Kai would like but Dan would, too. I let my fingertips dance over the strings and then slap them quiet, adding percussion between the halting phrases. Already, I like this song better than anything I've written all summer. I don't have lyrics yet, but my heart is full, so something will definitely come.

Once I've got a good idea of the music, I grab my iPhone to record it. That's when I see the text from Devyn:

Hey BB, hitting up Greystone Manor tonight.
Mary Jane & Molly will be there ☺ Meet at 11?

I don't know who Mary Jane and Molly are, but after the lame Halloween event last night, I have no desire to go clubbing with Devyn and her friends. My answer is immediate:

Have to write. Label needs songs, like, yesterday.
Have fun!

Knowing Devyn, she'll text me a million times, tweet at me, and beg me to come, so I turn my phone on AIRPLANE MODE and pull up my recording app. After the champagne incident, I had to plead with my dad to let me go to Hollywood Howls by myself, and the only reason he agreed was because it was for charity. There's no way he'd let me go to a nightclub where there is definitely drinking and probably drugs. And honestly, that's just not my scene. I'm happy to stay home and write, especially when the air is buzzing with creative energy.

I pick out the melody, working a little with tempo, waiting for the words to come. Right before I read Devyn's text, I was thinking about sunsets and sunrises, about beginnings and endings, about how much you can love somebody but how hard it can be, too. But now my anxieties are taking over again. What if Devyn was right about Kai? I mean, I wasn't surprised when he said we could take things slow—it made me like him even more and it was the biggest relief—but maybe he was just saying that? Or maybe it's too slow? I mean he *is* twenty. And he was raised in a major city, not like me in an RV where I was overprotected by my parents and older brothers. And I know I'm not his first girlfriend, although I hate to think about that.

I finish the instrumental recording and decide to shoot for lyrics after supper. I smell something good through the screen door, and I know there's no way I'll conquer this writer's block over the noise from both my mind and my stomach.

26

"WHAT'S YOUR FAVORITE thing about being on the beach?" Kai asks me over the phone.

I stand on the hard, wet sand, letting my feet sink with each pass of the waves. "Just this feeling of serenity. I've never felt anything like it."

"Yeah?"

"And watching the ocean," I say, putting my hand over my sunglasses to block out the bright afternoon sun. "It's massive. Think how much water. Think how someone thousands of miles away might be looking right back at me from another shore. Think how many feet have been right where mine are."

"But don't your toes get cold?"

"Huh?"

"Right where your feet are," he says. "Just stuck in the sand like that."

"How do you know my—?" It's crazy, but I look around. And then I see him. I see Kai and I scream. He is running toward me, full speed.

"Kai!"

I jump into his arms, and the force knocks us both down. His face is in my hands, his lips on mine. It feels like a dream.

"What are you doing here?" I ask when we come up for air.

"Astrean has the flu, so she canceled this week's shows," he says, smiling.

I beam at him. "Poor Astrean."

He laughs. "Your empathy is touching."

He brushes my hair from my forehead and just stares at me as if taking me in, the sun backlighting his head. Is it possible that he got more handsome while he was on tour? He kisses me again, and I let my head fall into his hands. Kai is here. I laugh out loud, laugh right into his mouth and he pulls away, laughing, too. Kai is home.

"Okay, so the ingredients you e-mailed me are in the crisper drawer of the fridge, Kai," my mom says, her eyes twinkling.

"You knew about this?" I ask my parents. I am still in shock that Kai is here.

"Oh yes," she says, kissing me on the forehead. "And we're going down to Bonnie's for dinner, so we'll see you two later."

My dad waves at me as he walks past and then takes Kai's hand in what looks like a pretty firm handshake. When the door closes, Kai turns to me and shakes his hand out dramatically. "I think that was a warning," he says with a smile.

"Whatever would he be warning you about?" I ask coyly.

"This," he says, rushing over. His arms are around me and his mouth is on mine in an instant. My pulse races. I run my fingers through his hair, taking pleasure in messing it up when I know he likes it styled just so. We back up until I am against the wall by the front door, his hands moving down to my hips. "God, I've missed you," he whispers.

His kisses start to migrate, leaving my lips and making a trail across my cheek and under my jaw. Soon, he is kissing my neck, and every single part of my body is humming. But when his fingers start moving up my side, I get self-conscious. It's like as soon as our lips aren't touching, connected, then my mind starts to circle like a Ferris wheel, the thoughts spinning slowly: *Is he going up my shirt? Do I want him to? My parents could come back. Will he get weird if I stop him? Do I want to stop him?*

His hands are still on top of my shirt, moving upward, inching their way toward my chest, and I pull his face to mine again, keeping my elbows tucked in tightly so that he has to stop just at the base of my bra. I kiss him hard, trying to shake the questions from my brain and just be in the moment, just enjoy the kissing. I could kiss Kai for hours. He matches the intensity of my kiss and leans against me, the weight of him so powerful that it's as if he could fall into my own body, that we could become one.

He certainly seems happy to see me, and the thought makes me laugh. "What?" he asks.

"Nothing," I say, shaking my head and kissing him again. My hands stay in the cheeks, head, neck area, but his are on tour again, this time traveling south as he starts to rock against me. At the top of my shorts, his hands hesitate. Involuntarily, I stop kissing him, stop breathing as his thumb dips beneath my waistline.

"Kai," I whisper urgently.

It means *yes* and it means *wait* and it means *I want to* and it means *I'm not sure*. I say his name and it means everything and it means nothing. It means *I love you, but I'm scared and I don't want to be, but I am*.

"Kai," I whisper again, calmer.

And then, all at once, his hands flatten on the wall at either side of my head and he pushes his body back from my own. I breathe again. He leans his forehead against mine and searches my eyes. "You okay?"

I nod. "Uh-huh."

He watches me for a couple of seconds, and I can see his mind working, the wheels turning as if he's having an argument with himself. His cheeks are flushed, his hair is a mess, and his lips are wet and red. I realize that I don't want to stop.

"I'm okay," I insist, breathless as I gather the material of his T-shirt in my hands and tug gently.

But he must see something in my eyes that tells a different story because he kisses my nose and takes my hand in his, pulling me from the wall and leading me into the kitchen. "You know you drive me crazy, right?" he says with a crooked grin.

He exhales, loudly, almost like shaking something off. "Oh-kay," he says when we get to the fridge. He stands in front of the open door for a moment, not really focusing on anything as the cool air flows out. I turn to the cabinet next to the stove to grab us a couple of glasses for water.

Then, we get to the work of cooking dinner. We waltz around each other in the kitchen, stealing kisses here and there, but mainly talking, the conversation spilling out, natural and effortless like before. I'm so relieved. The easiness is reassuring after two months of forced telephone conversations and texts that have been getting shorter every day.

242

Long-distance is tough, but when we're together, the energy between us is palpable, the chemistry intense.

As Kai puts the food on our plates just so, paying careful attention to the placement and even wiping the edges with a paper towel like they do at a restaurant, I go to the dining room and set up the perfect ambience. I bring out a candle from my room and plug my iPhone into the sound system, pulling up the very first playlist that Kai ever made me.

"Dinner is served," he says, bringing over our plates.

"It smells delicious."

He holds my chair out, which is so cute I could die.

"So?" he asks when I take my first bite.

"Mmmm...delicious."

He grins and allows himself to dig in, his relief adorably evident. "I'm no chef, but I pay attention at the restaurant. I've actually cooked some for Astrean and the band. She's been to Makana and was saying how much she loves it, so I offered to cook for everybody. I called Matt, and he gave me some of his recipes. It was fun."

I stiffen at the thought of Kai cooking dinner for Astrean, hanging out on her tour bus. I've Googled her and she's beautiful, has traveled all over the world, and plays a slew of instruments. I try not to be jealous, but it wasn't so long ago that Kai was on *my* tour bus.

"That's cool," I manage.

"Yeah, I think you'd really like her. I told her all about you. I told *everyone* all about you," he clarifies, grinning.

I blush a little. "Good."

"She loves your music."

"Aw, that's nice," I say, feeling better.

"And she's a classically trained violinist."

"Yeah, you mentioned that," I say. "A couple of times."

"Oh," he says, frowning. "Well, I just think you have a lot in common. I mean, she's older, but she writes her own songs, moved to Nashville, then LA. Maybe we can all meet up the next time she's out here."

"Do you always get close with the artists on tours?" I ask, trying to sound nonchalant. I take a drink of water as he studies me and try to keep my features smooth and my face expressionless.

"*No*," he says, drawing the word out.

The Pause.

Ugh, no! The Pause.

"You know, speaking of meeting up, I'd love for you to meet Devyn," I say, changing the subject.

"Oh." He takes a bite and looks out the window. "Yeah, sure."

"I'm heading back to Nashville tomorrow for a while, but I'm sure I'll be back and forth a couple of times before Christmas," I say. "Don't you get a break around Thanksgiving?"

"Yeah, but then I'm going out with the Genuine Scoundrels."

"Right, I know, but we can see each other if we time it right. And maybe we could all go to Makana or something," I say, perking up. "Devyn could bring some of her friends, maybe Bria and Bridget, or no, even better, she knows Zac Efron and Jennifer Lawrence. I don't know who, but she would definitely tweet about it to all her fans." The more I think about the idea, the more excited I get. "The paparazzi might even show up. Wouldn't that be the best press for the restaurant?"

I look at Kai expectantly, but he doesn't seem nearly as excited as I am about the idea. "Um, I don't know that they're desperate for business or anything."

"No, of course not," I say, a little stunned. "That's not what I meant. I just think it'd be cool to meet up there. And I could meet your folks again, I mean, officially."

"I'm definitely going to introduce you to my parents, Bird," Kai says. He reaches across the table and squeezes my hand. I smile, not wanting to make things weird, but I don't understand why he's not more eager to meet my friends.

When he turns his focus back to his plate, I do the same, my mind going a mile a minute. I think about my conversation with Devyn, about Kai being older and not wanting to wait forever to have sex. I think about all this time he's spent with Astrean, this sexy woman with a sultry voice who also happens to be a violinist but is "classically trained"—*blah*. As I chew, I sneak glances at Kai and want those moments on the beach again, that pure joy of seeing each other after so long, of being so happy. Devyn is right; I need to be sexier.

I take a deep breath. "When we're finished, you want to go to my room and watch a movie?" I keep my chin down the way I've seen Devyn do a thousand times, her hair falling over one eye and her head just slightly tilted.

"Yeah, maybe," he says. "Honestly, I was hoping you'd let me hear some of the new stuff you're working on."

"Oh," I say, pleasantly surprised. "Definitely."

He picks up my hand from the table and kisses it. "Are you finished?"

I nod and follow him into the kitchen with my plate, but he shoos me away. "I'll clean up. You go get your guitar."

"Okay," I say, but I stand behind him, wrapping my arms around him as he starts rinsing the plates. I thought it would be hot—I always see Devyn wearing guys like shawls in photos, their arms wrapped around her tightly—but I just feel awkward. Kai's back stiffens, like he's bent too far over the sink. I pull away. "I'll meet you on the balcony," I say.

On the way to my bedroom, I unplug my phone, not at all surprised to see messages from Stella and Devyn. I texted them both a pic of Kai and me on the beach, back when I expected tonight to be perfect and not, I don't know, a little awkward.

Stella wrote back first:

OMG that's so sweet.

I write back:

He made me dinner.

And then check the text from Devyn:

OMG tap that! lol #sohot #iwillifyouwont

I roll my eyes. Leave it to Devyn to use hashtags in a text. And she's not exactly helping. A reply from Stella comes through:

Dying. Turn off your phone and have fun!

Followed by another text:

Then call me in the morning with all the deets!

I start to text her about how weird things got toward the end of dinner, but Kai knocks on my door frame. "Bird?"

"Oh, hey, sorry," I say, sliding my phone into my pocket.

"I like your room," he says, walking in and looking around, and I realize for the first time that he's never seen it before. When he stops in front of my old Hatch Show Print posters and photos of Johnny Cash, June Carter, and Loretta Lynn, the appreciation is evident on his face. "These are so cool, Bird."

I walk over and grab his hand with both of mine, leaning my head on his shoulder. "Yeah, I brought those from home."

"A little country with the city," he says, nodding. "Really cool. Johnny Cash was sort of a country revolutionary, you know? Nonconformist. Dark."

"Your kind of guy?" I ask, amused.

"Exactly." He kisses me on the lips—a quick peck—but I wrap my arms around his neck and pull him back in. He is slow to respond, but as I run my hands down his spine, he shivers and wraps his arms around my waist, holding me tight. Before I know it, he is leading me back toward my bed, and I marvel at how suddenly we feel like "us" again, at how quickly the disconnect vanishes. We *need* each other. Maybe Devyn was right: I need to *show* him how I feel.

"I missed you so much, Kai," I say as we sit on my bed.

"I missed you, too," he mumbles through the kisses. His lips barely leave mine. His hands are everywhere.

"Kai, I…" I start to say it—the *L*-word—but then I chicken out. "I *really* missed you."

"Bird," he says, looking into my eyes. "I really missed you, too."

Okay, so this is it, I think as he kisses my neck and squeezes my thigh. I grip my hands around his shoulder blades, holding on tightly, my breathing shallow. As he lays me back, a loud thump from upstairs shakes the chandelier above me.

"Agh!" I scream.

"Bird!"

"Sorry," I say, extremely embarrassed. I cover my face with my hands. "Sorry. Sorry. I just—that totally scared me." I peek up at him. "I'm sorry."

Kai hangs his head. Then he leans back on his palms and clears his throat. "We probably shouldn't be in your room, huh?" he says, getting up from the bed. "I mean, since your folks are right down the hall and everything."

Desperate to save the moment, I look up at him and say in what I hope is a sultry voice, "Afraid they're going to catch us?" Immediately, I know I just made things worse.

He looks at me strangely. "Are you okay?"

"Yeah," I say with a nervous laugh.

He stands a few feet away from me and I stay put on the bed, not really knowing what to say or do next. I have never felt more awkward. Finally Kai's eyes land on my guitar and he walks toward it. "You were going to play me something, right?" he asks as he picks it up.

"Yeah," I say. "Sure."

I grab my journal and follow him out to the living room. We settle on the couch and I start tuning, avoiding eye contact. Not only did I just embarrass myself—again—but tonight is not going at all the way I'd imagined. Plus, I'm incredibly nervous about some of my new stuff, especially the pop undertones that I know Kai won't like. I decide to play the song I wrote the other night, hoping like crazy that he'll approve. Out of the very little new material I've come up with, it's the only one I'd categorize as mellow.

"You excited about the CMAs?" he asks, breaking the silence as if everything were perfectly normal.

If he's willing to pretend the bedroom fiasco didn't happen, I'm on board. "I can't wait," I answer truthfully.

"I'm so proud of you, Bird. Really. It's incredible."

I don't know why it's so important to me that Kai see my music as "legit," why I feel so desperately that I have to prove myself to him, but this compliment means the world. I feel my shoulders relax. "I hate that I can't bring you as my date," I say, looking up at him with a frown, "but Anita thinks it'd be better for me to take my dad. You know, with the whole firing-him-as-my-manager thing. Shows there's no ill will."

"Hey, I totally get it," Kai says. "It's really not my scene anyway."

I pause a sec, gritting my teeth as I move the capo on the fretboard of my guitar while his words sink in. *I get it already*, I want to say, *my world's too "mainstream."* But isn't loving someone showing up when you don't want to and having an open mind to the tastes of the other person? Doesn't it mean being so proud of the person you love that you shout it from the mountaintops, not caring what your too-cool friends think? Aren't you supposed to love the other person the way they are instead of trying to change or diminish them?

"Bird, are you okay?" he asks.

I snap out of the argument I'm having with him in my head and meet his cocoa eyes. He is completely oblivious to my anxiety. He didn't mean anything by his comment, and in all honesty, he's probably right. As much as I want him to be on my arm at the CMAs, I take in his skinny black jeans and bright graphic tee, his faux-suede Clarks and bold wristwatch, and realize it's probably the last place he'd want to be. He's not a country guy and not a musician, which makes me think of a guy who would be the perfect date for an event like the CMAs: Adam.

Of course he'd probably rather go with Kayelee Ford.

I shake my head and take a deep breath, exhaling

slowly. I want to be present. As I start to strum, I focus all my energy on the song. "This is rough," I warn Kai. "It's something I just wrote this week and it needs work, but I hope you like it."

The Pause.

"'Cause I wrote it for you," I admit, feeling my cheeks redden. Before he can say anything, I start singing:

> *"You—*
> *Got me wrapped, you*
> *Got me rolled, you*
> *Got me restless.*
> *And you—*
> *Got me waiting every day."*

I glance up at Kai, who is actively listening, his forehead creased in concentration, but he's not nodding or smiling, which kind of freaks me out. I keep singing:

> *"You—*
> *Got me hooked, you*
> *Got me hung up, you*
> *Got me helpless.*
> *Then you—*
> *Had the nerve to go away."*

252

I really liked the song, but now that I'm singing it live—
to the very person it was written for—I am way more nervous than I ever was in any of the sold-out arenas.

I glance up as I start the chorus and Kai smiles at me.
Ah. I am flooded with relief and I feel my body unwind.
Just that smile of his, it gives me everything I need. I sing
with strength, with confidence, enjoying myself as I belt the
hook:

> "*And I—*
> *Knew better than to fall in love.*"

I beam at him:

> "*But you—*
> *Make it worth being in love.*"

I bend over my guitar and all self-doubt vanishes as I
lose myself in this moment. I basically just told Kai how I
really feel and my heart feels like it could grow wings and
fly around the room. I can't control it. *I just told him how
I feel.* For me, music was always something that brought
people together, and right now, I am bursting with joy. Kai
is finally here. A song is finally working. All is right with
the world.

Then, before I start the next verse, his cell phone rings.

"Oh man, Bird, I'm so sorry," he says, scrambling to get it out of his front pocket. I keep strumming for a minute, but the look on his face when he sees the caller ID shows that he's clearly conflicted. "Bird, I should...um..."

"No, no, answer it," I say, the euphoria instantly gone as I slap my strings quiet. "Really. This one is so new and that's all I've really got anyway."

He looks at me skeptically, glancing down at my journal, but I close it and look away as his phone rings for the third time. The silence between the rings is resounding. Finally, he lets the call go and we sit in stillness until a voice mail alert sounds. I try to swallow back the lump in my throat and focus on the rounded edges of my pick in an attempt to cover up the stinging sensation in my eyes.

Kai takes a deep breath. He gently pulls the guitar from my hands and lays it against the wall. "I'm sorry, Bird," he says. "I didn't want you to stop. I just—that was about a job—" He shakes his head. "Whatever. I'm sorry. That was rude and I'm sorry."

"It's okay," I say quietly.

He sighs.

He wraps an arm around my shoulders, and I resist a little as he brings me in next to him. When he leans back against the cushions, I tuck my head and lie on his chest, feeling exposed, and honestly, a little hurt.

"Nobody's ever written a song for me before," he says softly. I listen to the sound of his heart beating as he runs his fingers through my hair. "Thank you, Bird."

I gulp hard. He puts a finger under my chin, forcing me to look at him. He searches my eyes with his own and then brings my lips to his, kissing me slowly like I'm something to be savored. I have so many emotions at war in my heart—Kai is back and so everything should be better, everything should be right, and it's not, it's just not—but as his lips gently dance over mine, I give in and let go of the negativity. What we have when we hold each other is worth holding on to.

27

"AND THE CMA for Single of the Year goes to…"

Hunter Hayes takes his sweet time opening the envelope, and I'm squeezing my dad's hand so tightly that it very well may fall off. There is a cameraman kneeling in the aisle next to me, ready to catch my reaction, win or lose. Anita scheduled a special PR meeting about the CMAs with me, my dad, Troy, and my styling team yesterday, and although it seemed silly at the time, she had me role-play this very situation. Now that I'm here in the Bridgestone Arena, surrounded by country music legends and stars whose music I really admire, with a camera in my face that basically represents all of America, I thank the Lord once again for Anita Handler and her control-freak tendencies.

"'Be Like Me.' Kayelee Ford," Hunter says.

My heart drops, but my smile doesn't. Just as I was taught by both my parents and my publicist, I play the part of a good loser, applauding along with the rest of the audience. I beam across the aisle at Kayelee, who is bending over in her short, red, skintight sequined dress, kissing everybody around her and dramatically shaking with her hand over her big mouth. *Give me a break.*

When she finally quits with the theatrics, she takes a step toward the stage and glances over at me. She shoots me a patronizing look, her fire-engine-red lips in a quick pout, and then sashays up to the stage sunny as a Miss America contestant. She thanks her label, "especially Randall Strong, the best in the biz," and I try not to read too much into it; but when I make the mistake of glancing across the aisle again, Randall winks at me, making my skin crawl.

Kayelee talks for so long that the music starts to play, and I imagine Hunter Hayes grabbing a long cane and pulling her offstage. The thought makes me giggle. Then I feel my phone vibrate through my clutch, so I fish it out and see a text from Devyn:

WTF? You totes deserved to win. And what is she wearing? 👎

I laugh, then drop my phone and applaud as Kayelee finally finishes.

"You've still got New Artist," my dad says next to me.

I smile at him, thinking he was the perfect date for the awards show after all. He was the first person on his feet after I performed at the beginning of the show, his enthusiastic cheering both sweet and a little embarrassing. And unlike the last time we walked a red carpet together, he wasn't multitasking, instead letting Troy and Anita do their jobs. Plus, my dad loves country music, so we've sung along to all the performances... well, all but one. We coincidentally both went to the bathroom during the newly named Single of the Year.

The awards show progresses, and I try to enjoy myself as best I can, especially since Carrie Underwood and Brad Paisley are funny hosts, but I'm fidgety and nervous. Open Highway artists were also in the running for Musician of the Year and Song of the Year, losing both. As the program gets closer to the New Artist category, I start to feel hopeful glances from Dan and Anita, and the pressure of helping to grow a small label mounts. I am freezing cold, but my palms are sweating as last year's New Artist takes the stage. If I win, I'll be handing out the award next year. I am covered in goose bumps.

"This award changed my life," Olivia Brooke says into the mic, as cherub-faced and wide-eyed as ever. I'd say winning *The Voice* did a number on her average day as well. "To be named New Artist of the Year is a great big welcome into the world of country music, but no matter who wins tonight, all five nominees deserve a hand."

Olivia steps back from the mic, allowing the audience to applaud, but it only makes me feel more restless. Finally, she steps forward again and smiles into the camera as she reads from the teleprompter. I grip my dad's hand. "The nominees for New Artist of the Year are: Brayden Paul, Bobbie Jo Weston, Kayelee Ford, Quinn Moore, and Bird Barrett."

When I hear my name, my heart stops, my palms sweat. I feel like everybody in my row is holding their breath.

"And the CMA award for New Artist of the Year goes to..." Olivia fumbles with the envelope, dragging out what is already the most excruciating moment of my entire life. "Shouldn't have gone with these fake nails," she jokes into the mic.

Yeah, yeah, ha-ha. *What's it say?*

"Bird Barrett!"

I scream. I know that wasn't what we rehearsed, but I scream. I stand up and turn to my dad, hugging him tightly and not even trying to fight the tears. Dan gives me a hug next, woo-hooing like he's the one whose name was called, and Anita gives me a thumbs-up...and a pink hankie that just happens to match my dress. I beam at her, fist-bump Troy, and then hug my dad again. I couldn't be happier.

"Go get it!" Dad says, snapping me out of my enraptured haze.

I turn around and step into the aisle, nearly running into the cameraman. "Sorry," I say, giggling like a kid. I dab under my eyes with the hankie, delicately, the way Sam showed me so as not to ruin his dramatic eye masterpiece. At the stairs to the stage, Tim McGraw actually reaches out to give me a hand up, and it all feels even more dreamlike.

"Thank you," I say as Olivia Brooke hands me the award. Then I turn to the crowd and shout into the mic, "Thank you! Thank you! Thank you!"

And then I scream again.

Words start tumbling out of my mouth, none of it coherent, I'm sure. "Oh my gosh, this thing is so heavy! I love it. Oh man, I just—yeah, wow—you know? I'm—ah! I'm so happy!" I shake my head and take a deep breath. I need to thank people. "I just have to thank Dan Silver and all the people at Open Highway Records for believing in me and giving me this chance to be New Artist of the Year. Thank you, Anita Handler, Troy Becker, and Judd Barrett for taking good care of me. Oh my goodness, I'm going to forget everybody. I couldn't have written this record without the support of the superbly talented Shannon Crossley." I think about my inspiration for *Wildflower* and add, "Also,

Adam Dean." I pause and see Jolene Taylor in the front row, texting and looking magnificently bored. I beam down at her. "Oh! And thank you to my new friend Jolene Taylor for taking me on tour and teaching me so much." A cameraman immediately swings around for her reaction, and the kiss she throws me makes me laugh heartily into the microphone. "Oh, what a night!" The music starts to play softly, an indication that my time is up, so I rush to finish. "Thank you to the fans who filled up stadiums all over the country this summer! Thank you, Kai and Stella and Jacob and Dylan and sweet Caleb." I throw a quick kiss up to the ceiling. "I love you all! Thank you to my mom and dad, the best parents in the world. I love you so much!" The music swells as I take the award in both hands and hold it out to the crowd. "Thank you, everybody! You've made my year! Woo-hoo!"

I step back and wave, feeling like my lungs are full of helium and that I would float away if the award weren't weighing me down. *I'm country music's New Artist of the Year!*

The press waits for me backstage, and I don't even have a chance to catch my breath. Immediately, a microphone is in my face.

"Bird, how does it feel to win this award?"

"Oh, um, it feels—I'm still in shock, you know?" I say. "It feels amazing."

"Were you surprised?"

"Yeah, actually. I didn't realize it was so heavy."

"No, were you surprised to win it?"

"Oh," I say, laughing. I can hardly focus as the adrenaline courses through my veins. "Yes, of course. The other artists who were nominated are exceptionally talented. I mean, to even be invited to perform on this stage tonight was a dream come true. But this? Taking this home?" I hug the award tight to my chest. "I can't even comprehend."

"So it looks like you and Kayelee are all even this go-round," the reporter says. "She won Single of the Year and you won New Artist. Anything you want to say about your much-talked-about rivalry?"

"O-M-Please," I say, rolling my eyes and borrowing a phrase from Devyn. "I don't even see her as a competitor." Karrie Kinney is walking by, and she interrupts us for a quick hug. Karrie-freaking-Kinney! Hugging me! When I turn back to the reporter, I am ready to get this interview over with. "Look, Kayelee and I have totally different styles. If fans want authenticity, that's what they'll get from me—*real* music. I happen to think it's a waste of time to compare us, or to try to *be* like anyone else," I say, referring to the silly rivalry as well as her awful song. The reporter starts to ask a follow-up question, but someone is moving me toward the pressroom and I go with it.

During a break in the show, I am escorted back to my

seat. I can't help but feel the win is even sweeter knowing how badly Randall Strong was hoping to snuff me out, so I flash him and his posse a brilliant smile as I pass their seats. I am surprised to see Karrie Kinney talking to Kayelee Ford like they're besties and then not so surprised when my supposed rival shoots me a death stare.

I feel my smile falter.

"Bird, let me get a look at that thing," my dad says excitedly. He hugs me again and reaches for my CMA. "Wow, it's heavier than I thought."

I glance over at Kayelee. Thank God looks can't kill. When I turn back toward my team, Dan, Troy, and Anita are all standing in the aisle, huddled close and visibly unhappy.

"Was that really necessary?" my new manager asks.

I squirm, feeling like this may not be the best way to start our working relationship. "What do you mean?"

Anita holds up her phone and reads quietly, "Karrie Kinney just tweeted this: 'Hashtag birdkayeleerivalry is real, y'all. Saw it firsthand. CMAs getting ugly. Glad I'm drama free. Hashtag phew.'" Anita rolls her eyes and mumbles to herself, "Drama free, my ass. And she clearly has no idea how to use a hashtag."

Dan glances over at the other label and pulls me close. "Bird, what did you say backstage?" he asks. The look on his face makes me want to crawl under a rock.

"Nothing, really!" I say. "I did a quick interview. Karrie maybe overheard part of it."

"What did you say *exactly*?" Anita demands. "How much damage control is necessary?"

"No, just—" I gulp. This is spinning out of control. "Just that I write my own songs and my music is authentic. And something about how fans shouldn't try to 'be like' anybody else, but are great just how they are."

Dan purses his lips. "Bird, not only do you look like a bad winner now, but you've also fanned the flames." The warning music starts to play, cueing everyone, stars and seat fillers, to move back into their rows.

"I'm sorry," I say, clutching my award like it could save me. As my team files into our row, I wait in the aisle, anxious. "I'm so embarrassed," I tell my dad as I finally sit.

"Don't be," Anita commands from his other side. "The cameras are about to start rolling again, and we've still got a lot of awards show to watch. The way 'BirdKayeleeRivalry' is trending online right now, you need to sit up straight and be a model of grace." She is clearly disappointed in me, which somehow stings as badly as if she were my mother. "It was catty, Bird, and not what we talked about, but be embarrassed later. Right now, remember your aura. 'Friendly,' right?" she asks, using air quotes.

Then she sits back primly and starts to clap with the crowd as Lady Antebellum takes the stage. I feel light-headed. My phone buzzes in my purse and I open it, checking my messages as discreetly as possible so as not to draw more ire from Anita or Troy.

I scroll through the texts, feeling better as I read all of the congratulatory messages from my friends and family. Stella loves me, Kai is happy for me, my brothers are stoked, my mom couldn't be prouder, Adam says congrats (although he probably sent the same text to Kayelee), and Devyn says I look prettier than KF, which makes me feel really good, actually. Then I am surprised to get a text from Anita:

Enjoy your night. You deserve this win. Sorry I was
harsh. You made us proud.

And then, in true Anita fashion, she sends a follow-up text:

#rivalriessellrecords

I lean forward and catch her eye. She cocks an eyebrow and smiles, making me feel a million times better. I'll deal with the aftermath tomorrow. For tonight, I'll just steer clear of Kayelee and hold tight to my shiny new trophy.

28

"First the CMAs, and now the Grammys," Dan says jovially when I walk into the Music Row offices of Open Highway. Christmas music plays over the speakers and I think how cool it'd be to do a holiday album one day. "How does it feel?"

"Surreal," I say truthfully. It's been a month since the CMAs, the excitement of which hadn't worn off before I got a Grammy nomination for Best New Artist. "Sometimes I feel like my life is one big hallucination," I say with a grin.

Dan chuckles. "I knew you were something special." He walks around his desk and gives me a hug, then holds me away from him, grinning like a proud papa. "California looks good on you, Bird," he says.

"Do these bags under my eyes look good, too?" I ask.

He laughs as he makes his way back to his chair. "The red-eye is rough."

"Brutal. It feels like all I do is fly back and forth these days."

"I know Anita and Troy have had you doing a lot of press, but that's awards season. We're building momentum and have to keep you front and center."

"Hey, I get it," I say, taking a seat across from him. "I still can't believe I got nominated."

The truth is that when I heard about the nomination, my first reaction was wanting to text Kai, *See? My music is legit.* But that felt dumb, especially since Kayelee Ford was nominated in the same category and her music is anything but. Now the press is all about how odd it is for two country artists to be nominated in the same category for a Grammy, especially females, but I'd say most people lump Kayelee in with pop.

"Well, congrats again," Dan says. "We're very proud of you."

"Seriously, I still can't believe this is my life," I say.

"You better believe it, Miss Barrett," he says, grinning. "And you better be ready to win a lot more of those trophies. I have big hopes for your next album."

I tense up. I've been on pins and needles all night, listening to the demo tracks on the flight and trying to hear them the way he would. "Have you heard the new stuff?"

"Yes. I have," Dan says, breaking eye contact as he looks down at a memo on his desk. "And we need to talk about it."

Uh-oh.

"The A and R guys you've been working with out at Open Highway LA really have their finger on the pulse of current music trends, and we feel this follow-up album needs to go in a bit of a different direction."

He pauses for my reaction, but I can only blink, waiting for more.

"*Wildflower* was a beautiful introduction," he explains. "It was, 'Hello, world. I'm Bird Barrett.' And for that matter, it was 'Hello, world. We're Open Highway Records.' But for this next one, we want a slightly more inclusive sound. We talked about a pop influence. Now, I don't mean anything like Kayelee Ford, although her new single is at the top of the charts—" he adds grudgingly.

"Right, but I'd argue 'Hashtag on My Heart' isn't even really country," I interject hotly. It makes me so furious that a stupid song like that is number one on the Billboard. "I mean, my singles have been out for a while, so they were clearly going to fall eventually, but for a song like that to skyrocket?" I sit back in my chair and cross my arms. "It makes me worried about the future of music in general."

Dan chuckles. I know I sound like Kai, but seriously.

"You make a good point, Bird," Dan says, nodding.

"And listen, I'm not saying you should try to adopt her sound—" he says.

Thank God.

"But I am saying that I only hear *potential* in these demos. I don't hear singles, Bird. Not yet. They're not there and they're not in line with where we want this one to go."

I clench my jaw and look over at the fireplace. I'm so frustrated, not at Dan really, but at the whole process. At myself for knowing in my heart that these songs weren't going to cut it, and at the label for comparing me to other artists, especially one like Kayelee, who has about as much depth as a kiddie pool.

"We'd love it if you could infuse some of that West Coast experience into your songs," he continues. "Like this one, 'Worth Being in Love.' It feels like it's right on the brink. The idea is there and I even like the phrasing, but it's so slow, almost...indulgent." He is trying to be gentle, but he might as well take a big red stamp and put *this sucks* on that stupid memo he's holding. "And then I like the concept of 'Shine Our Light,' but it feels overworked to me. I think it could be a hit as more of a power anthem. Give it some life. I guess I'm just looking for the fun in these demos, Bird."

I feel a lump form in my throat. I do not want to cry.

"Can you up the tempo? Play around with the lyrics?"

I nod curtly. I know Dan has my back and I know he

only wants me to do well, but this criticism is hard to hear. The first album felt so easy compared to this one; there was nothing to liken it to, and I wrote a lot of the songs never dreaming that anyone else would hear them. But the second album has been like banging my head against a wall. I don't want to let down my family, my label, my fans, but that's exactly what's happening.

"I called Shannon Crossley, and she's got a fairly open schedule these next few weeks before Christmas," Dan says gently. "Should we schedule some sessions?"

I blink hard before I buck up and admit that I desperately need help. In fact, a couple of weeks on her couch, staying put and buckling down, might be just the push I need.

29

"Happy Christmas Eve!" Stella calls when I answer our door.

"My two favorite elves," I say, hugging both her and her mom as they come inside. We're hosting the First Annual Barrett Family Christmas Bash tonight, and obviously the Crossleys were invited.

"We brought eggnog and pie," Shannon says.

"And presents," Stella adds, her eyes twinkling. "Listen, don't pick mine during the White Elephant exchange. Seriously."

"What did you bring?" I ask, narrowing my eyes.

"I've already said too much."

We laugh and walk through the living room, where all

the guys are watching *Christmas Vacation*. Stella intentionally blocks the TV as she sets her gift under the tree, and everybody—including my uncles and cousins—shouts for her to move.

"Stella, you are so obviously the Cousin Eddie," Dylan remarks, shaking his head.

She blows him a kiss. "I've missed you, too, Clark," she cracks.

In the kitchen, my mom and aunts are cooking up a storm. Alabama's Christmas album plays in the background, and a folding table is set up for us kids. I can't think of anywhere else I'd rather be.

"So, did you get your grades back?" I ask Stella as we sit.

She glances up at her mom, who is already washing her hands to help make mashed potatoes. "Not great," she says quietly. "I don't think I'm cut out for college."

"What do you mean?" I ask, floored.

"I hate English, I hate Com, and I still have to take Math, Art History, and all these other stupid Gen Ed courses," she says.

"Well, what about the design class you were so excited about?"

"I don't even love that, truthfully," she says. "I just want to go with my gut, you know? But it's like all my instincts go against what they're teaching. Plus, design was fun for me before. Now it's...I don't know...stifling or something."

272

I nod knowingly. "I'm going through the exact same thing."

Luckily for me, though, over the past two weeks Shannon and I have finally fallen into a groove that works. My demo was really ballad heavy, so we upped the tempo on a few songs and scrapped two altogether. She reminded me that some songs are only meant to be written, not recorded. She had me change keys, rewrite verses, add hooks—you name it, we tried it. And as hard as it was to pick them apart, we both think A and R will like the revised tracks a lot. I'm still a few short of an album, but Shannon thinks I'll get the green light to book a studio, which will be a relief. Once I'm recording again, I'll at least feel like I'm working toward a tangible goal.

Stella and I commiserate about her course work and my album until my mom says it's time to eat. All sixteen of us cram into the kitchen and circle up to say grace.

"Let's bow our heads," my granddad says. He mutters his standard prayer, thanking God for His Son, our country, freedom, family, loved ones far away, and the troops. I could tick them off on my fingers I've heard the list so often. "Amen," we all say when he wraps it up.

My mouth is watering by the time I fill my plate. The adults eat in the dining room, and I squeeze between my brothers at the kids' table in the kitchen. Dylan is so focused on stealing a roll from my cousin that he completely misses Stella swiping one of his stuffed peppers.

When he looks over, she takes a bite of the stolen pepper and closes her eyes as if it's the best thing she's ever tasted. "Yum. Dylan, you've *got* to try these. They're amazing."

Jacob and I laugh, and Dylan glances down at his plate, realizing at once he's been robbed. "Who even invited you?"

"I'm a VIP," she says.

Dylan shakes his head and smiles. "I'll get you back, Crossley."

He jabs his fork toward her plate, and she puts both hands up, blocking it.

Just then my phone rings, and I quickly pull it out of my pocket. "Oh!" I say, backing my chair from the table.

"Let me guess," Stella says. "Kai?"

I nod. "Hello?"

"Oh, Kai!" Dylan calls in a high-pitched voice.

"Kai, I love you," Jacob teases, making loud smooching noises.

"So obnoxious," I say as I walk into the living room. "Hey, Merry almost Christmas, babe."

"You too," Kai says. "Are you having fun with your family?"

"Yeah. Sorry my brothers are so annoying."

He laughs. "I think that's how they're supposed to be to their little sister's boyfriend."

"I guess," I say. I flop down onto the couch. "How's Makana?"

"Oh, it's great," he says. "We're slammed actually, so I don't have long. They need me in the kitchen. But I wanted to call because I have some bad news."

"Oh no. What?"

"Well, it's good news and bad news," he says. "I just found out that I get to work the Times Square New Year's Eve concert and ball drop."

"Oh, wow," I say. "That's big time."

"Yeah, it's going to be pretty incredible," he says. "The city on New Year's has this amazing vitality."

"That's cool, I guess," I say, not nearly as excited for him as he is. "But I thought we were going to spend New Year's together."

I really had my heart set on being with Kai next week. I couldn't get away from Nashville over Thanksgiving, and he joined the Genuine Scoundrels' tour right after. We haven't seen each other since he surprised me in California and that feels like forever ago. This New Year's was going to be the first time I've had someone to kiss when the ball drops, and ever since we've been dating long-distance, the kisses have been too few and too far between.

"I know, me too," he says. "I mean, you could come up, I guess, but we really wouldn't get to see each other. I'll be working the whole time. It's a pretty intense day, and the NYPD is strict about who they let into the stage area in Times Square. And it'll be cold."

"Wow," I say sarcastically. "Sounds like you really want me to come."

"No, Bird, I do if you want. I'm just being honest. We probably wouldn't see each other much."

"Ugh, this sucks," I say.

"I know. I knew you'd be bummed, but I just found out, and I really can't afford to pass it up," he says. "I have to pay the bills, you know?"

"Well, what if I could help you out?" I suggest.

"What do you mean?"

"Like, what if I just gave you the money for your bills or whatever?"

"Hell no," he says. "Are you kidding me?"

"No, I'm serious," I say. "I really want us to be together."

"Listen, Bird, I don't need money from my sugar momma," Kai says. "I can take care of myself. I get opportunities like this because other people have noticed how hard I work."

Shocked at his tone, I slowly reply, "I realize you work hard, Kai."

"Yeah, well, maybe you don't realize that not everybody gets paid thousands of dollars just to get out of bed every morning."

My jaw hits the floor. I'm speechless. I want to remind him that I'm not some trust fund kid—*I used to live in a freaking RV*—and that I work hard for my money and that my music is my heart, but I really don't want to fight on Christmas Eve.

The Pause.

I am fuming as I stare at the white lights on our Christmas tree, listening to my family laugh and enjoy themselves in the next room. I just wish Kai were here. I wish we were together. Everything always seems easier when we're face-to-face, when we can hold hands and talk things out without a million distractions. That's when we're really *us*.

"I'm coming," I hear Kai yell to somebody in the background. I hear dishes clattering and somebody calling out orders in the restaurant kitchen. "Listen, Bird, I have to go. I'm really sorry, okay? But I need to work this show. It's good money and good connections. I know you're disappointed, but surely you know the business well enough to know that it's all about networking. If I turn down this gig, they'll skip over me for the next one."

I sigh heavily. "I know."

"Okay. So I'll call you later. Okay?"

"Yeah," I say, my throat tight. The doorbell rings.

"I miss you," Kai says.

I uncurl myself from the couch and get up. "Miss you, too. Bye."

"Bye," he says, but I barely hear him because I'm trying to hang up first.

I walk to the front door, deeply disappointed. And then, when I swing it open, I gasp.

"Merry Christmas, Lady Bird," Adam says with a grin. His black fleece is zipped all the way up, and his cheeks are pink. His brown hair is shaggy, his jaw is covered in stubble, and his hazel eyes twinkle brighter than the lights my dad strung up in the yard.

"Adam."

It's all I can bring myself to say.

"Hi. May I come in?" he asks.

"Oh, um, yes. Of course," I say, stepping back. We haven't been face-to-face since that day in my kitchen when he defended Kayelee, and I worry that things will be weird.

"Jacob invited me," he says by way of explanation as we share an awkward side hug. "And, hey, congrats again on the Grammy nomination," Adam says as he sets down his gift bag and guitar case. He unzips his jacket. "How awesome is that?"

"Yeah, thanks, it's—it's incredible," I say as I take his coat and hang it in the closet. "Sorry I haven't been that great about keeping in touch. I've been doing all this press and then trying to get songs ready for the next album and—"

"You're busy," he cuts in.

"Yeah."

We stand there in the entryway, looking at each other

the way you do when you haven't seen someone in a while and you're cataloging what's different...the way you do when you have more to say than you ought to say...the way you do when there is chemistry between you that you know there shouldn't be.

"Something smells good," he finally comments.

"Oh, yeah, everybody's eating," I say, turning around and leading him through the living room. "You can put your gift there. And your guitar anywhere."

He adds his gift to the pile and follows me into the kitchen. Jacob and Dylan get up and exchange bro hugs with Adam, and when he ducks his head into the dining room, my dad gives him a hearty slap on the back and a healthy handshake, while my mom is near to tears when she comes over to hug him. Stella's eyes nearly pop out of her skull when we make eye contact, and although I wasn't expecting him and although things were a tad tense last time we saw each other, I have to agree with my mom when she says he sure is a sight for sore eyes.

"Sit, sit, eat," she says now.

Chatter fills the kitchen again as Adam fills a plate. I sit down and try to resume eating, but my thoughts are all over the place, my head reeling from the horrible call with Kai followed by the surprise visit from Adam.

"How's Kai?" Dylan asks annoyingly.

"Good," I say quickly. I glance up at Adam, whose back

is to me, and then over at Stella. Jacob gets up for more food, and I start to slide over next to her, but Adam takes his place, squeezing right between us.

"Move your feet, lose your seat," he says and immediately starts to eat while Dylan launches into his take on the Titans' play-off chances.

It takes me a few minutes to get comfortable next to Adam. I sit with my back ramrod straight and try to think of anything normal to say. It doesn't help that our legs keep touching accidentally under the table. *Why am I buzzing like this? I have a boyfriend.* I shake my head and try to relax. Fortunately, Adam makes it easy. It's not long before he's telling stories and making everybody laugh, and I resolve not to let my phone call with Kai ruin my night.

After dinner, my dad suggests a good old-fashioned jam session, just like the old days. We play a few bluegrass standards and several Christmas carols. I close my eyes and lose myself in the songs, completely content as I make Maybelle sing, wishing the music would come this easily when I'm writing for the new album. As we wrap up "Go Tell It on the Mountain," I feel a surge of inspiration and turn toward my brothers, playing the first notes of "I'll Fly Away," the sweet bluegrass hymn that was played at my little brother's funeral. It's Christmas Eve and Caleb should be remembered.

After that song, we move on to the gift exchange. My

favorite part is when Dylan gets stuck with Stella's gag gift: The Gentleman's Fart Button. Every time he pushes it, the button makes a loud, obnoxious sound and then a very polite British voice says something like, "Who cut the Brie?" I laugh so hard that tears stream down my face. "I wish we'd had that during your teenage years in the RV," my mom tells Dylan, making me laugh even harder.

By the end of the night, my cheeks hurt from smiling so much. Eventually, everybody makes their way back into their coats and out the door, or upstairs to the guest rooms. After I walk Stella and Shannon out, I head up to my own room and get ready for bed. The house is still. I am exhausted. I brush my teeth and wash my face, pulling my hair back with a thick headband. I put on a pair of PINK sweatpants and a long-sleeve T-shirt, then climb into bed and snuggle under the heavy comforter with my cell phone. But before I can call Kai, my mom knocks on my door.

"Bird, did you rinse out your skirt?" she asks.

"Ugh, I forgot," I say, throwing my head back against my pillows.

"Well, you don't want the stain to set," she says. I dropped a Rudolph the Red-Nosed Cupcake on my skirt at dinner, and as exhausted as I am, the article of clothing in question was the recent catalyst for yet another argument about my shopping habits. Not only did my dad think it was too short, but my mom claimed it was too expensive. *When will they realize that I can afford this stuff now?* "There's a bottle of Mean Green under the sink in the laundry room," she adds.

"Thanks, Mom," I say through a forced smile.

I throw the covers back and climb out of bed, picking the skirt up off the floor and breezing past her. I walk downstairs and hear the faintest music coming from the living room. When I turn the corner, I am stunned to see Adam strumming his guitar on the couch. I didn't realize he was still here.

I try to tiptoe behind him, but he turns around.

"Hey, Lady Bird," he says.

"Hey."

"Jacob's on the phone with his girlfriend," Adam explains.

"Jacob has a girlfriend?"

"Uh, never mind," he covers. "Anyway, I'm leaving soon. Just messing around with this new song I'm working on."

"Cool. I'm just grabbing the stain remover from the laundry room," I say, holding up the skirt. "It's Prada, so, you know..."

Adam looks amused. "Oh, well, if it's Prada."

My cheeks flame. I scurry down the hall, feeling ridiculous. I grab the bottle and berate myself as I treat the stain, wondering why I can't be normal around Adam. I remind myself: I've moved on. I'm with Kai. I'm in—

"Hey, Bird?" Adam says.

I jump a mile.

"This song, I don't know, it feels like it's missing something," he says. He runs his hand through his hair. "You care to listen? Maybe let me know what you think?"

"Oh, um, sure," I say, hanging the skirt on a drying rack. I follow him down the hall and glance at my cell phone. It's only nine thirty in LA. Kai might not even be off work yet. And anyway, I think as I pocket my phone, he ought to be the one calling me after the New Year's blow off.

In the living room, Adam sits and picks up his guitar. I sit on the other end of the couch, bringing my knees to my chest.

"Being here tonight kind of got me inspired," he says. "I was waiting for Jacob and this song was just brewing, you know?" I nod. "But the lyrics—I don't know. I'm hung up a little."

"Okay."

"And so it's really new," he continues. "Like minutes old."

"Okay, okay, Adam," I say, grinning. "I'll be gentle. Just play it."

"Okay." He takes a big breath, and I tuck my chin to hide my smile. I can totally relate. Sharing something before it's ready is the most vulnerable feeling in the world, but there's also this *need* for someone to listen to it and tell you if it's working or even worth pursuing.

He starts to strum. Immediately, I am rocking to the beat and can easily imagine a guy like Jason Aldean singing it.

Adam belts:

"I know a girl who's from every town,
Kinda girl who shakes you up without letting you
down.
From Georgia to Kentucky, New York to Caroline,
I'm right there in her shadow, but always a step
behind."

He glances up at me nervously, so I smile and motion for him to keep going. It's already so catchy. He changes chords and sings louder:

"Gotta prove myself, gotta make her see,
Gonna sing across the miles."

Then, abruptly he stops. "See, I hate that line."
I swat his arm. "Keep going!"
He shakes his head, grinning as he finishes the chorus:

"That I'm the man for her, she belongs with me,
I'm the one who needs her smile."

He strums and starts in on the second verse. The song is actually really awesome; I can't believe he just wrote it a few minutes ago. I see what he means about the chorus being a little corny, but the song is so good that it'll be easy to fix. Excitedly, I get up and grab my guitar from where Shannon left it propped by the bookshelf during our impromptu jam. He starts in on the chorus again and I play with him, singing quiet harmonies here and there. By the time he strums the final note, we are both invested.

"It's good, Adam," I say. "It's really good."

He nods. "I think it's got legs," he says. "I just—there's something…"

"The chorus?" I ask delicately.

He laughs. "Yeah. Okay. So you hear it, too."

I reach out and squeeze his arm. "It's not bad!" I assure him. "It's just—the rest of the song has this kind of tough, almost cowboy roughneck feel to it and that 'sing across the miles' and 'one that needs her smile' stuff is a little… soft."

"I know!" he says, laughing. He scribbles on the envelope in front of him, and I wonder briefly if that's a piece of our mail. It reminds me of how I would sometimes scramble to write lyrics on beverage napkins in the honky-tonks where we used to play. "So what if I was like, 'if I have to walk a mile' instead?"

I chew my lip, strumming the chorus again as an idea forms. I sing to myself softly, *"Gotta prove myself, gotta make her see, gotta stay the winding way..."*

"Oh, that might—"

"That I'm the man for her, she belongs with me, and I'll make her see one day," I finish, looking up at him for his thoughts.

"Or better," he says determinedly: *"And I'll make her mine one day."*

"Yes, I like that," I say enthusiastically.

"Oh, I'll make her mine one day," he repeats. He stares at me, unblinking, his smile gone. I don't know if he's waiting for more feedback, but I think it works. I smile at him encouragingly. He finally grins and looks away, leaning back against the couch cushions as he plays.

And then I am struck with a crazy thought: *Is this song about me?*

I turn my attention to my guitar and feel my cheeks flame. If it's about me, then I could've been his, like, *already.* Does he regret calling things off? Maybe he hasn't moved on?

We sit still for about a minute, my mind spinning. I never did finish that song I was working on before I went on tour, the one about Adam, back when they were all about Adam. I met Kai. I fell for Kai. So why do I feel a little sad now that Adam's finally writing songs about me?

I shake my head and focus on the chords I'm playing. More than likely, the song is about another girl, somebody he's met in Texas, another touring artist maybe, so I settle back into the couch and do what I always do when I can't figure guys out: turn to my music. The Christmas tree lights twinkle against the glossy finish of my guitar, like little fairies in the room, sprinkling us with creative energy as Adam strums softly and I pick a little riff that complements what he's playing.

Then he turns to me and asks, "Bird? Are you okay?"

"Yeah," I say, looking at him with a contented smile. "It's just so nice to have the music come easy again."

"No, I mean—" He stops playing. "I don't want to overstep or whatever, but you seem a little down lately. And this whole thing with Kayelee. It just—I guess it just doesn't feel like you. Are you doing it for publicity?"

I frown. "No. Not at all," I say, eager to defend myself. *She's the one that keeps provoking me*, I want to say, but then I stop and think about it from Adam's perspective. He's known me a long time, and honestly, the old me never criticized anyone else's music. Why am I so caught up with her beating me on the charts? That's energy that could be better spent writing songs like the one Adam just cranked out. Songs sprung from inspiration rather than imitation. Embarrassed, I look down. "It's so stupid."

Adam nods. "It's hard being under constant scrutiny,

I'm sure," he says graciously. "I just don't want you to get lost in it."

I sigh.

"And I don't want to make you mad or anything," he continues, "and I feel like maybe I did when I saw you in LA, but Kayelee really isn't the villain she acts like."

"Aha!" I say. "So you *do* think she's a mean girl."

"No," he says. "I don't. I think she tries to be, but I don't think that's who she is inside. Honestly, I think she's jealous of you, and I think her label has pitted you two against each other and you're both buying in. And Bird, her mother is hands down the worst stage mom I have ever encountered, and her dad is this huge jerk who keeps reminding her how much he's 'invested' for her to 'make it big.' To tell you the truth, I think she's terrified that she's going to let everybody down."

I blink. "Oh."

"And I just don't see how the bad blood helps either of you," he says, shrugging. "Seems like a waste of energy and a huge distraction to me."

I chew my bottom lip and look down at my guitar. I shake my head and sigh, feeling tension I didn't even realize I was holding loosen its grip from my shoulders. He's right.

"You know, my label wanted me to write six new songs while I was on tour, and I thought it would be so easy," I say. "But I've had the worst writer's block of my life."

"Really?"

"Yeah. Luckily Shannon cleared her schedule for me the past couple of weeks and managed to help me get back on track, but this album has been brutal."

"What's going on?" he asks.

I shrug. "Maybe I've been distracted, like you said. But also, I think there's just so much pressure this time." I glance up at him and confess, "Adam, it got so bad that I actually wrote a song called 'Friends Don't Snuggle.'"

Adam guffaws, a loud hearty laugh that makes me jump. We both crack up laughing and I'm not even embarrassed. "Bird, I shouldn't laugh," he says as he collects himself. "I once wrote a song called 'You Make My Heart... Burn.'"

"No!" I say. He hangs his head in shame, and I kick back against the couch with glee. "Oh, Adam. Tell me that was while you were in Texas. The chili too hot?"

"Ha-ha," he says dryly, rolling his head on the couch to face me. We are only a foot apart and when he blinks, I am reminded how long his eyelashes are. He really is a good-looking guy, but he's also just a good guy. I am not stirred, not nervous or giddy or overcome by an old crush. Instead, next to Adam, I feel at home.

"You know, if you want to return the favor, there's a song that I really want to work, but it needs some help," I say.

"Yeah," he says as if coming out of a daze. "Let's hear it."

"It's in G," I say.

He nods, and I start to pick the melody of "Worth Being in Love," the song I tried to write about Kai. "So Dan wants it to have a pop sound," I explain as I strum, "but Shannon thinks it's too schizo, like the verse and chorus are really two different songs. And my boyfriend—" I say, pausing to glance up at him. If he's jealous or if it bothers him that I've moved on, his face betrays nothing. I look back down at my fingers and start to pick out the melody, thinking how I never could tell what Adam was thinking. "Anyway, Kai thinks it's too teenybopper or not deep enough or whatever."

"You know what I think?" Adam asks.

"What?"

"I think you ought to stop stalling and sing."

"Okay, okay," I say, grinning. I sing:

"You—
Got me wrapped, you
Got me rolled, you
Got me restless."

As soon as Adam gets a feel for the song, he joins in, slapping the strings and adding an almost doo-wop sound that makes me laugh out loud. But then, when I realize that he's being serious, I see that it actually works. I loosen up and we have fun, joking about other awful symptoms of being in love and weaving them into the lyrics.

Adam suggests a pre-chorus to transition between the distinctive styles of the verses and chorus, and as he plays, a lightbulb goes off. From there, the song totally comes together. I grab his pen and flip over the envelope he was scribbling all over, correct in my assumption that it is our electric bill, and start to scrawl out lyrics. We work together, hammering out a pre-chorus in five minutes. Then we tweak the third and fourth verses and add some percussion in the hook. It's not a long song, but the final product is more heartfelt than anything I've written yet for my new album.

When we finally play it all the way through, the deep tone of his voice the perfect complement to the softness of my own, it's inspired. I'm so glad I didn't give up on it.

With Adam here, it all falls into place.

30

"Whoa, this place is no joke," Stella says to me under her breath as we pull up to Bria and Bridget's New Year's Eve party. I've been to their house a few times before, as well as to Devyn's ginormous house, and the girls have invited me to brunches and get-togethers at a few other Hollywood homes since we started hanging out. I guess the grandeur of it all has kind of worn off for me already, but now, as I look at the mansion through Stella's eyes, I realize why she's awestruck. Her entire apartment would fit in the twins' dining room. She's seen a few episodes of their reality show, but this is the first time Stella has visited me in Cali, and I don't think she was prepared for how different life is out here.

"Wait until you see the inside," I whisper as I climb out of the limo behind a very drunk Devyn. Apparently the best way to ring in the New Year is to black out on the old one, which really stinks because this is not the way I wanted my two closest friends to meet face-to-face. The girl taking shots in the limo and screaming out the sunroof is not the same always "on" Devyn that I've come to know. Then again, I've never partied with her before.

I've spent most of my time in Nashville since the CMAs, only coming back to LA for a couple of pre-Grammy press events. When I am in town, I'll shop or get my nails done with the girls, but I also see Devyn tweeting a lot from clubs and parties where I'm not allowed to go. Her dramatic eye rolls let me know exactly how lame she thinks my parents are, but I try to brush it off. Honestly, I wasn't sure they'd let me come tonight, but it helped that Stella's in town and that the twins' parents are going to be here.

I follow the entourage up the path to the gorgeous, white, three-story super-modern Hollywood Hills mansion and try to get as excited as everybody else is. A Pitbull song is blaring from inside the house and colored paper lanterns hang around the pool. It looks and sounds like the place is packed, but the one person I would give anything to see is in New York.

"Do you think Mr. Crossley is here?" Stella whispers excitedly as we step into the mansion.

"Devyn said he's shooting in Vancouver," I say.

She shakes her head dramatically. "I'm finally in LA and now he's off to Canada. We are such star-crossed lovers."

"I completely understand," I say, showing her my phone: 8:55 PM. Almost a brand-new year on the East Coast.

Stella fake pouts and puts an arm around me. I lean into her as we follow our crew toward the pool out back. Devyn may be short, but she stands out in her backless, red, shimmery mini, and she certainly knows how to steamroll her way through a crowd.

"Happy New Year!" she shouts when we finally find our hostesses among the throng. The twins are stunning in matching illusion dresses, Bria in silver and Bridget in gold, with sequins covering just their bustlines and short skirts. My dad wouldn't let me out of the house dressed like that, but with their light blond hair smoothed over one shoulder and their makeup light and shimmery, I think the effect is breathtaking.

"Happy New Year," they say as we all exchange air kisses. I glance at my phone. It really is a new year for Kai. It's midnight in New York.

"Thanks for inviting us," I say with a big smile. No sense ruining anybody else's night with my bad mood. I turn toward Stella—my rock—genuinely happy to finally introduce her to the people she's always hearing about. "This is my best friend, Stella Crossley."

"Well, *Nashville* best friend," Devyn corrects as the twins move in for air kisses with Stella. "We're like divorced parents. You get Bird half the year, and I get her the other half." Devyn laughs at her own joke, but Stella looks at me with an expression that conveys her colossal irritation. I cringe. This night is already anything but what I expected.

"Oh, you guys, there's Josh Hutcherson," Devyn says, narrowing her eyes as if closing in on a target. She grabs a glass of champagne off a cocktail tray as a waiter walks by, flips her wavy black hair over one shoulder, and completely ditches us all as she power walks toward the *Hunger Games* star.

"She's the best," Stella says wryly.

Bria and Bridget exchange a look.

Uncomfortable, I try to defend my friend. "Devyn was pregaming," I explain to the twins. "I think she saw that 'Who Wore It Best' shot in *Us Weekly* and clearly—"

"Gisele," the girls say in unison.

"Right, so that," I say, turning to Stella, "plus I think being single on New Year's Eve has really gotten to her."

"Sure," Stella says, nodding. "It's probably that. Or maybe she's just awful. One or the other."

Bridget's eyes are twinkling as she looks at Stella with both admiration and disbelief. Devyn isn't necessarily nice to the sisters, but she's still their queen bee. "We need to go check with the DJ about something," Bridget says, clearly wanting to distance herself from any Devyn bashing...as well as pass it along.

"Right," Bria says. "Have *so* much fun, guys."

I force a smile and drop it once they're gone.

"So now what?" Stella asks. "Want to walk around?"

"Sure," I say, already dialing. "And I want to call Kai."

We walk toward an enormous ice sculpture, grab a couple of mocktails, and follow the crowd of people gathering around a small stage by the pool. Kai answers, but he's right in the thick of things in Times Square, not to mention that Lil' Thunder himself takes the stage here at the party, complete with voluptuous backup dancers at least twice his age. Kai shouts, "Hello?" right as the reggaetón blasts on a speaker near me. I hold one ear and yell into the phone, "Happy New Year!" I wait for his response, see that our call is still connected, but can't hear a thing. "Kai!" I shout. "Kai?" After a minute, I hang up and just text him, but the whole thing is stupid and anticlimactic.

I feel my throat tighten, but Stella grabs my phone and puts it in my clutch. Then she kisses me on the cheek and holds up an air mic, scrunching her face as she raps along with Lil' Thunder. The lyrics are super fast and a little crude, and it cracks me up that she knows them all.

"Dance with me," she commands as the song segues into his newest single. "This was an amazing year! Let's celebrate!"

I nod. "You're so right," I say. And she absolutely is.

I grab Stella's hand and let loose as we shake our hips shamelessly to his hit, "Make the Room Boom." This was the best year of my entire life. I'm at a Hollywood mansion right now, I'm dancing with my best friend, and I have an amazing boyfriend, even if he is far away. Not so long ago, I would've killed for any of those things, and now, I've got all of them.

"Happy New Year!" I shout to no one...to everyone.

For the next few hours, Stella and I mingle and start having a really great time. We try not to make it obvious, but we are more than a little starstruck when we run into Rihanna in the bathroom and overhear her talking to her friend about Drake and Chris Brown. That sparks the idea to tweet snippets of conversation we overhear as we wander through the house with the hashtag overheardnye, like: Can you tell this is a spray tan? and: So that's when I knew I needed rehab. My fans keep tweeting back, asking who's saying what, which just spurs Stella and me on.

"*TMZ* should hire us," she says.

"Oh crap," I say, reading a new post. I feel a quick stab

of worry. "Someone just tweeted me, 'Is it Devyn Delaney? I heard she's always wasted.'"

Stella shrugs. "I heard that, too. And now I've seen it."

I glance around the room for her. "Devyn's addicted to Twitter, and this would kill her. And then she'd kill me." My thumbs fly across my phone screen, and I mumble as I type: "Not Devyn, you guys. She's just high on life!"

Seemingly out of nowhere, a couple of cameramen appear. "Paparazzi?" Stella asks over the music. "They need to fire the gate guard."

Lil' Thunder walks by with a girl on each arm, and I fit the pieces together. "Ah, it's probably for their reality show. Thunder is a preteen play-ah."

Stella and I are cracking up at that when I hear Devyn squeal, "OMG, you made it!" When I turn, she runs toward me with her arms stretched wide, her face ecstatic.

"Um, we came together," I say, but then she whisks past me and embraces none other than Kayelee Ford, who looks like she just walked off the cover of *Maxim* magazine in a slinky, provocatively draped pink dress. I wasn't expecting to see her here, and I *definitely* wasn't expecting to see Devyn hugging her like they're besties. Suddenly Bria and Bridget also magically appear with their air kisses, and I feel so betrayed—and lost. Since when are they friends with Kayelee? They're supposed to be *my* friends.

"Let's go check out the upstairs," Stella says, linking her arm through mine. "I'm always interested to see how rich people decorate."

We start to walk behind the cameramen, but I make the mistake of glancing over at Kayelee one more time. Her lips curl into a mean smile. "Oh, don't fly off, little Song Bird," she says loudly. A couple of heads turn, and Devyn covers her mouth, trying not to laugh.

"Hi, Kayelee," I say, determined to be the bigger person. "It's nice to see you."

She rolls her eyes. "Oh, I'm sure. I saw what you said about me in *Star*. You think I'm too skinny? You're worried about me being anorexic?"

"What?" I ask, shaking my head. I know exactly what she's talking about: another of the endless side-by-side comparisons that basically said I was a thicker girl than Kayelee. "If anything can be taken from that article, it's that you called me fat. But it's a rag. I'm sure they made stuff up to stir the pot."

"No," she says with a gleam in her eye. "I did say that. I'd step away from the hors d'oeuvres if I were you."

"Oh!" someone calls from the crowd. I realize that all eyes are on us and a microphone boom is hanging over our group. Her comment stings and I suddenly feel very self-conscious, but I take a deep breath and force a smile.

"I hate that you wasted any of your pre-Grammy press

time talking about me," I say, batting my lashes. "I've done lots of interviews, but somehow, your name just never comes up."

Stella squeezes my arm. "Let's get out of here," she says quietly.

"You guys, you have to make up," Devyn whines with a dramatic pout. She grabs Kayelee's hand and drags her over until she can reach one of mine, too. "You're my very closest friends and this feud is killing me."

I do a double take at Devyn. "You and Kayelee are friends?" I ask. "Since when?"

She shrugs. I can't tell if she's avoiding my gaze or just too drunk to focus. "I don't know. We did an appearance on *Kimmel* the same night a couple of weeks ago. I think you guys would really like each other if you buried the hatchet."

"There shouldn't even be a hatchet!" I say, pulling my hand away from Devyn. "This whole rivalry thing is so stupid."

"Then stop talking trash about me," Kayelee says.

"Me?" I ask incredulously. "*I'm* the one who talks trash? You called my performance at the CMAs 'amateur hour.'"

"Well, you basically said I'm not a good role model."

"First of all, I didn't say that, and secondly, you told the world I'm a high school dropout."

"What school do you go to, then?" she asks.

"I was homeschooled."

"Even worse."

"Argh!" I exclaim, grabbing my head in my hands. "You are so ignorant."

"Oh yes, call me stupid again."

"I've never called you stupid, Kayelee!" I cry, completely rattled. "Why do you believe everything you read in the tabloids?"

Devyn makes a face. "Well, you did say that when you hear 'Hashtag on My Heart' you feel your brain cells deteriorate."

My eyes bulge. "Devyn, what the hell?" I'd told her that in confidence.

Kayelee cocks a hip smugly as she ticks off two more insults. "You told *InTouch* that my music hurts your ears and you told *Seventeen* that my CMA dress was slutty."

"No, I said it was 'revealing,'" I correct her, so mad now I'm seeing stars. "And I stand by that assessment due to your nip slip on the red carpet."

"Bird," Stella says softly.

Kayelee smirks. "So you think I'm a ho."

"I wouldn't use that word, no..." I say through gritted teeth, "but the first time we met you *did* flirt with my boyfriend right in front of me."

Kayelee sneers. "It's not my fault if your man likes what he sees."

I clench my fists at my side and step toward her.

"She's baiting you, Bird," Stella says, grabbing my arm. "Walk away. You don't need them. Let's go."

My pulse is pounding in my ears, but I know Stella is right. I *know* she's right. I start to turn away, feeling sick to my stomach, but the crowd is thick around us.

"Oh look, D, there's Jason," Kayelee says. "I thought he was shooting in Vancouver."

Devyn shrugs. "I thought so, too," she says, her deliberate nonchalance proving that she undoubtedly knew otherwise.

"Come on," Kayelee says, "let's go say hi."

"No way. He can come to me," Devyn says, slurring her words a little. "Oh, smile!" She holds up her phone and takes a pic of the two of them, then drops the smile and shoos Kayelee away as she tweets it. "But go over and say hi and, you know, tell him I'm here or whatever if it comes up."

" 'Kay. Bye, Song Bird," Kayelee says as she breezes past me. Then she stops suddenly. "Oh! You hear that?" she asks. "I love this song. It should be your anthem."

As "Be Like Me" blares over the speakers, she blows me a kiss and walks off, bulldozing her way through the crowd. I feel my shoulders start to shake. I am seeing red, madder than I've ever been in my entire life. "How can you be friends with her?" I demand of Devyn.

"She's actually pretty cool," she replies as she puts her phone back into her purse. "And I know you don't like her, but her music is crazy fun to dance to. This song gets in my head and I can't get it out. You should give her another chance, Bird." Her glassy eyes go wide. "Ooh! Wouldn't it be cool if the three of us recorded a song together one day? Maybe for my next movie or something. OMG, my fans would love that."

My mouth hangs open. Is she serious?

"Bird Barrett," Jason declares when he makes his way over. "You look as pretty as ever."

I take a very deep breath and plaster on a forced smile. "Thank you, Jason." My mind is in a fog as we hug, barely able to comprehend the last five minutes. As though on autopilot, I say, "This is my best friend, Stella Crossley." I've been looking forward to the moment when I can finally introduce my best friend to her celebrity crush, but this is not at all how I imagined it going down.

"Stelllllaaaaaa!" Jason wails. Heads turn, and I flinch, looking at him like he's lost his mind. "It's Marlon Brando," he tells us like it should be obvious. "From *A Streetcar Named Desire.*"

"Yeah," Stella says. "I get that a lot actually."

He leans in and flashes her a cocky grin. "But probably not so spot-on, huh?"

"*Right.*"

Stella looks at me, and it's abundantly clear that the crush is over. That's Jason Samuels: a very good-looking, really nice guy, but cluelessly self-involved.

"What's up, Devyn?" he asks his ex. He rubs his jaw and tries to be nonchalant.

"Hey," she says, twirling a lock of hair and trying to look bored.

He starts bobbing his head to "Be Like Me." "Man, I love this song."

"Oh my God, I can't," Stella says. She grabs my hand and pulls me along behind her, roughly pushing through the crowd and past the cameras, bumping guests on her way back into the house without a care. When we get inside, there are more famous and semifamous people working the room, more fake smiles and fake body parts, and just a general sense of NYE suckery. "Can we go home?" she asks. "Pop popcorn and watch the ball drop on the TV with your folks?"

"You read my mind," I say, following her out the front door.

We get into Devyn's limo and ask the driver to take us home, not even bothering to check with her first. I'm over her after tonight, wondering how I was so blind to what a crappy friend she is. I lean my head back on the seat and look over at Stella, thinking for the millionth time how lucky I am to have her.

"Sorry tonight was miserable," I say.

"There were fun moments," she replies. "And it was definitely an experience. I don't think we're going to make it back for the ball drop, though." She pulls her phone out of her purse and shows me the time: 11:58 PM.

I sigh heavily and look out the window. "This night was doomed from the start."

"Can I tweet this?" Stella asks a few seconds later. She holds up her phone:

Doesn't auto-tune, writes own songs, plays
2 instruments. #belikebird #teamBB

I laugh. "Go for it. The rivalry is ridiculous, but it's obviously not going away, so go for it."

When my phone flashes 12:00 AM, I send a quick text to Kai:

Happy New Year!!! Missed you so bad tonight.☺

Then Stella grabs my arm. "Ussie!" she calls, holding out her phone, clearly mocking Devyn. She shows me the pic and we both look so pretty and happy. It's instantly one of my favorites ever.

" 'Hashtag hollywoodhotties,' " I joke.

We laugh and once we start, we can't stop. It was a terrible party, but as the New Year begins, I know that it'll be a good one as long as I've got Stella in my corner.

31

"SO ARE YOU going to talk to him about it?" Stella asks as we look at Kai's Instagram the next morning. It's covered with pics he took at some indie concert last night after he got off work.

"Oh, he's going to hear about it," I say as I scroll through the images. I am seething. "The whole reason I didn't fly out there was because he told me he wouldn't have any time to spend with me, but he obviously found time to go out."

Kai never texted me back last night when it turned midnight on the West Coast. I figured it was because he was already asleep—it was three AM his time, and he'd been working all night. But when I woke up this morning, I had four texts sent at six AM his time:

Happy New Year, Bird!

And:

Hope your night was as great as mine! Got to meet
Sween Machine!!!!!

And:

Finally in bed but too hyped to sleep. What a way to
start the year!

And finally:

I miss you. See you soon!

"It's crazy, but the last text makes me angrier than any
of the others," I tell Stella. "Oh, you miss me? Then how
about you act like it. How 'bout you don't lie to me? How
'bout you freaking text me back at *my* midnight? He was
obviously out at three AM. Why didn't he text me 'Happy
New Year'?"

Stella shakes her head. "I don't know, Bird. I like Kai
and everything, and I know I told you to go for it at the
start, but..."

"But?"

"I don't know," she says, selecting her words carefully. "It just seems like you guys are bickering a lot lately. Like, a lot."

I bite my lip. I'm hurt that Kai didn't want to be together on New Year's Eve. I offered to come meet him. I offered to help with his bills. I was willing to do whatever it took to be together. Why wouldn't he want the same? "I don't want to fight," I tell her. My voice quivers. "I'm crazy about Kai, you know? I really think I love that boy."

"I know you do."

"And it's like, on tour, he was this fascinating and intriguing guy who gave me nonstop attention. We were always together or texting or on the phone. All summer."

She nods and rubs my back. I feel tears in my eyes as I open the folder of pics Kai gave me of us sightseeing in Chicago. "We were so happy a few months ago," I say as I click through. "How do relationships fall apart so fast?"

"Long-distance is hard," Stella says. "And people change."

I sniff and shake my head. "It's like, all he cares about are these bands that no one's ever heard of. And he acts like the music I make isn't valid. And—" I stop and look out the window. Stella doesn't say anything; she just keeps rubbing my back and we stare at the waves as they crash against the shore and wash back out to sea. In and out. Constantly starting over.

"Hey, beautiful!" Kai shouts.

I look up from the bench I snagged on the always-busy Venice Beach and smile. Kai took the red-eye home last night, but he still looks amazing. I feel my resolve weaken. I knew this was going to be hard, but as I take Kai in now, walking toward me with his hands in the pockets of his gray jeans, the teal V-neck he's wearing snug against his chest, I'm not sure I can go through with it.

"Hey back atcha," I say. I stand up to hug him and the strength in his embrace makes me a little woozy. I smell the Moroccan oil he uses and think sadly that I will miss that soothing scent. "Thanks for meeting me down here," I say as I pull away.

"Definitely." His fingers still grip mine. "I couldn't wait to see you."

"Right," I reply with a wry grin. "You couldn't wait, but you had time to go to the gym this morning and stop by Makana for lunch."

He looks taken aback. "Um, I wanted to see my mom, Bird."

"No, I know," I say, nodding. "But if you 'couldn't wait' to see me, you could've invited me to go to lunch with you."

He looks away. "Oh-kay."

We stand there in The Pause. Awkward is our new usual.

I pull my hands away and sit down on them. He stands for a minute and then sits next to me. Skateboarders and bikers pass. People run and walk. I know what I need to do, but when I look at Kai's face—at his gorgeous face that I have kissed all over—I am overcome with sadness.

"I don't feel like this is working anymore," I say quietly.

Kai clenches his jaw by way of response. I keep my hands under my legs, knowing that I'll lose my resolve if I touch him. Our relationship never suffered from lack of chemistry, but after talking to Stella, I've come to realize that maybe it's survived on that alone. Once the miles separated us, the differences that I loved in the beginning began to wedge their way between us. I was so intrigued by Kai's emotional openness, by his cool, obscure tastes, by his upbringing that was so different from my own; but now every conversation feels forced, and it's like we have no common ground.

"Are you going to say anything?" I finally ask.

Kai turns to me, searches my eyes, and smiles sadly. "If I say what I'm thinking, then I may not ever see you again."

"What are you thinking?"

He inhales, holds it, then hangs his head and sighs. "Aw, Bird." He looks up at me and then he says something that breaks my heart in two. "I'm thinking that you're right."

32

"BIRD?" MY MOM asks as she taps on my bedroom door.

I set my guitar down and lean back against the huge pillows on my bed, grateful for the interruption. "Come in."

"How's it going in here?"

"Not great," I say. I gesture to the heap of balled-up paper all around me: abandoned songs and forced lyrics. The label is really pressing me for the second album now, especially since I've finally laid down a few tracks in the studio. "They want snappy and fun and upbeat stuff, and Mom, I'm trying, but I just broke up with Kai." I close my eyes and throw my arm over my face. "And I'm just . . . sad."

"Breakups are hard," she says, walking over to my bed and sitting next to me. "Even if you're the one doing the breaking."

I feel a lump in my throat and try to swallow it down. Every day I check Kai's Instagram, Twitter, Facebook, all of it. And I've almost texted him a million times, but I never know what to say. I've had two relationships bite the dust now. Is this how it will always be: having to choose between my career and my love life?

I hear my mom unwrinkle a discarded page of lyrics, and I open my eyes. There is obvious amusement on her face. "Don't, Mom," I say, sitting up.

"'Getting off the Ferris Wheel of Love'?" she reads aloud, trying not to laugh.

"Mom!" I say, embarrassed. "Throw it away. I was trying to get inspired at the beach and saw the rides going on the Santa Monica Pier. It's terrible." I snatch it from her and wad it up again.

She looks away, but her shoulders start to go up and down, as she tries with all her might to keep it together. "Mom, seriously," I say, throwing it at her the same moment she turns back to face me.

"Ow," she says, flinching.

"Oh!" I cover my mouth. "Sorry!"

"No, I'm sorry," she says. "I should be more sensitive." She purses her lips, but her eyes are still shining. "But honey, how much is a ticket for the Ferris Wheel of Love?"

I try to be mad, but I can't. I finally crack a small smile, and that gives her the green light to bust out laughing. She pulls me in for a hug, and soon I, too, am laughing so hard that tears run down my face.

"Oh, Bird," she says once she catches her breath. "You're just in a rough patch. You know what you ought to do? Call Bonnie."

I grab a tissue and wipe my face, considering the idea.

"We just did yoga downstairs this morning, and I think her husband's out fishing. You ought to call her. If nothing else, you can get a little advice from somebody who's been there."

"Where?" I ask as I climb out of bed. "On the Ferris Wheel of Love?"

She snorts. "Oh honey, we've all been there. And one of these days, you'll sit in the bucket with the right guy and you won't ever want to get off."

I pick up my phone to text Bonnie and smile at my mom. "I hope you're right."

"So what's going on, girl?" Bonnie asks as we settle into her super-comfy sofa a little later.

"Just writer's block," I admit. "Still."

She nods knowingly but doesn't say anything, so I go on.

"It's like, A and R wants this fun pop stuff, but—I don't know if my mom told you—I just broke up with my boyfriend. Everything I write about him is so sad, and everything I write for the label is so fake." I drop my head into my hands. "I feel like I'm losing my mind."

"My second album was by far the hardest," she says. "I felt so much pressure, and I was writing songs that didn't even make sense, like square pegs in round holes."

"Exactly!"

"Well, it's simple, honey. You've got to write what you feel. That's what they want to hear; sometimes they just don't recognize it right away."

I shake my head. "They really want pop."

She doesn't even flinch. "Good for them. I want to be a size two again, but we don't always get what we want."

I laugh out loud. She does, too. It feels good.

"You know, Bird, that pressure? Well, it can get to you. It got to me," she admits. "I got all caught up in the fame, the perks, and especially the scene out here with the partying and stuff. It was not good."

"My mom, um, told me you went through some hard times," I say delicately.

Bonnie runs her hand through her feathery bangs and nods. "I sure did. Bird, honey, I saw some dark days. If it wasn't for Jolene, I might not be sitting here today."

"Really?" I say, completely shocked.

"She drove me to rehab," Bonnie says with a sad smile, "and helped me through a very depressing time. Jolene and

I wasted a lot of time hating each other, only to find out that our differences made us a pretty good fit. You know, Bird, sometimes people are only flashy because they're insecure."

I nod, not knowing what to say. The Jolene Taylor I know is certainly flashy, but also self-centered and in love with herself. I don't think she has an insecure bone in her body. I definitely can't imagine her going out of her way to help someone she didn't like, but that's not for me to comment on, so Bonnie and I sit in silence for a few minutes, enjoying the sweet tea and watching the stormy ocean.

"I saw you and that Ford girl got into it again," she finally says. "Some New Year's Eve spat?"

I feel my cheeks flame. Bria and Bridget's reality show crew caught it all, and the promos for that episode have been airing nonstop this week.

"I should've walked away," I say regrettably. "I let her goad me, and I shouldn't have."

Bonnie nods. "Hindsight's twenty-twenty."

"Devyn and Bria and Bridget were supposed to be my friends, you know?" I say, still smarting. "But looking back on it, it's like the whole thing was this big setup for ratings or something. I'm dreading the episode. I should have risen above it. Troy, my manager, is trying to see what he can do to have it cut."

"What'd you say to her?"

"I don't know," I answer truthfully. "I was so mad that it's like I blocked a lot of it out. I was just trying to defend myself and say how everything's gotten blown out of proportion, but then I got really angry and—" I sigh mightily. "That girl hates me. She's hated me long before she ever had a reason to."

"What do you wish you'd said?"

I pause and look at her. "Huh?"

"If you could do it all over, what would you say?"

I chew my lip and think about it. "I guess I'd tell her I'm not against her the way she thinks I am. And I'd want to know what makes her so hard. Like, why does she hate me? Why isn't there room for both of us to succeed? Bonnie, the girl is beautiful and, honestly, her songs *are* catchy even if they aren't anything I'd sing. I mean, we're nominated for the same Grammy, so it's not like she doesn't have talent."

"So why don't you say that?" Bonnie suggests.

I shake my head and look down at my pink toenails. "Because every time we see each other, it's like everybody around us starts fanning the flames," I say. "And I think Kayelee actually enjoys the rivalry."

"There's nobody here now," Bonnie says. She leans over and grabs her guitar from the corner. She starts to strum, and I find myself bobbing my head. Once she has something she likes, she looks up at me. "Okay, Bird. Tell her. Say it in a song."

I feel my heart swell, my brain connect in a way that it hasn't since writing *Wildflower*. I think about the way Adam described Kayelee, about the pressure she feels from her label *and* her family. I try to put myself in her shoes, close my eyes, and sing:

> *"You look at me like it's a natural rivalry,*
> *Like there's just room for one to succeed,*
> *But who's the one that spun the lie we both*
>   *believed,*
> *That if you rise, I would have to sink?"*

I hum as Bonnie strums, and let the raw emotion spill out as she plays. "Just rise and fly," I sing. "You've just got to shine your light, shine, shine, shine."

When I look up at Bonnie, she is grinning from ear to ear. She picks out a fun instrumental solo and then stops. "I think you've got more to tell her," she says, her crow's-feet deep as she smiles. "Go grab your guitar. There's room for both you girls to fly."

33

"BIRD, YOU LOOK fabulous," a fashion correspondent on the red carpet says. "Who are you wearing?"

Without missing a beat, I smile at her and say, "Catherine Malandrino. I wanted something glamorous, of course, but still me. When I saw this dress, I knew it was the one."

My brothers snicker beside me, more like little boys than grown men, but I totally get it. This life really is lightyears away from the one we were living a little over a year ago, and as much as this has become old hat to me, they are totally out of their element. "And these goofballs are in Burberry," I tell her.

"It was so hard to choose," Dylan says with a straight face. "Sequins, lace, something with a high slit? In the end, I played it safe with a standard tux."

The correspondent actually giggles. I glance over at Dylan and can see why. He may be my brother, but even I see that he's a really handsome guy.

"And I went with James Bond," Jacob says leaning into the mic with his best attempt at debonair. We all laugh.

"Well, Bird, our readers will love the ruffles," the woman gushes. "And guys, the classic tuxedo is never a miss when worn with confidence, so we give you both A-pluses as well."

The guys fist-bump each other, and we continue down the press line, stopping here and there to pose. I'm so glad that Anita let me bring both of my brothers tonight. I'm the only girl here with two dates.

Getting ready was fun, too. At my fitting last week, Amanda showed up with a rack full of the most beautiful designer gowns and shoes I've ever seen, iconic labels like Armani, Christian Dior, and Gaultier, but the Malandrino took my breath away and we all agreed it was the perfect red carpet choice. To top off my fairy-tale evening, Vera Wang designed a second gown especially for my performance later, the delicate lace and light pink color absolute perfection. Tammy pulled my hair back in a loose bun while Sam kept the makeup classic. I don't know how my styling team manages it, but I feel more glamorous every time we do an event.

"Oh, there's Caitlyn's Cradle," Jacob says as we near the trio on the red carpet. His tastes have always gone beyond the boundaries of bluegrass and country, but this band was one of Kai's favorites, too. I feel a sudden stab of longing when Jacob points them out. "I can't believe you're nominated in the same category as those guys."

"Come on," I say, walking toward the group. "Let's say hi."

Jacob is clearly starstruck as we make our introductions, but the best part for me is when Caitlyn herself says that she loves "Sing Anyway" and listens to it on days when she doesn't feel like working. And although it doesn't matter what Kai or anybody else thinks, it feels good to have an accomplished artist appreciate my music. "I love your album," I say truthfully. "Good luck tonight."

Her publicist pulls her toward Mario Lopez, and we say good-bye as Anita and Troy direct us back toward the press line.

"That was so insane!" Jacob says, turning around. "How are we even at the Grammys right now? Tonight is, like, inconceivable. Bird, thank you." He gives me a big hug and when he pulls away, his eyes pop. "Oh sweet Yeezus, there's Kanye West."

"When you win tonight, don't let that man take your microphone," Dylan says protectively.

I throw my head back and laugh, loud and happy. The night is young, but I'm already having the time of my life.

Once inside, an usher escorts us toward the stage, where I know we have prime seats in the fourth row. Troy, Dan, and Anita have already taken their seats, but I stop cold when I see they are directly behind the on-again couple Devyn Delaney and Jason Samuels. And down the row from them, laughing obnoxiously at something Bruno Mars is saying, is none other than Devyn's new BFF, Kayelee Ford. *Of course.*

"Bird, you are a vision," Anita calls as she stands from her seat in our row. She walks quickly over and embraces me as if we didn't just spend the last half hour on the red carpet together. I freeze. The woman doesn't hug— it's not in her DNA—but she can read me like a book and must see that I am unnerved because she whispers in my ear, "The cameras will be on you all night. Smile, wave, *shine.*"

I pull away a little. "You heard the new song?"

She nods, smiling wide. "Dan played me the demo. It's my favorite so far."

"Barretts!" Dan booms when he turns away from a conversation with a GAM exec in front of him. "Bird, you look beautiful as always, and boys, you clean up well."

"You don't do so bad yourself, Dan," Dylan says as they shake hands.

We take our seats, and briefly, Kayelee looks over her shoulder at me. I smile. She rolls her eyes. When she faces forward again, I catch Dylan's eye. He gives me a wink, which makes me feel better. A moment later Devyn holds up her iPhone to take a pic of Jason and herself, and Jacob leans over for a magnificent photobomb. I cover my mouth to suppress a laugh. My brothers should be nominated for Best Grammys Dates Ever.

The show is spectacular. Jay Z and Justin totally destroy it, Imagine Dragons bring the house down with their new hit, and Adele's performance gives me goose bumps from head to toe. Jolene Taylor is clearly reading from the teleprompter when she introduces "an exciting new artist who deserves to win a slew of Grammys," and then she looks pained when Kayelee takes the stage. I think about what Bonnie said and wonder if maybe Jolene *is* insecure under all those rhinestones. Kayelee performs "Be Like Me" on a revolving stage with mirrors everywhere, and although the effect is cool, I personally feel that one Kayelee Ford is more than enough for this world.

Soon, it's my turn to perform, and as I go backstage to change, my stomach is in knots. Right before the cue for my three-song mash-up, I send out a tweet:

Birdies! Wish me luck. This one's for you!
#singanyway #noticeme #yellowlines #grammys

I throw my phone down on a pile of my stuff as Sam touches up my lips, but then I bend down to double-check once more that it's on silent. That's when I see the text from Bonnie:

Live this moment, girl. Fly!

I smile and take a deep breath, ready to get out there. With Bonnie's help, I made a demo of "Shine Our Light," and we even wrote a couple more together. It was totally different than writing with Shannon. Bonnie was full of funny stories and had me cracking up the whole time. She's adamant about not receiving songwriting credit, but I don't know what I would've done without her. I'll get back in the studio Tuesday morning, and I'm finally pumped about my album. We're calling it *The Road to You*, which I love. It's the real me: the country girl, the California girl, the girl who messes up, the girl under the microscope, the girl who falls in love, the girl with a broken heart. It's the pretty and the ugly. It's everything.

Anita and Dan suggested I play my fiddle tonight to differentiate myself from Kayelee, who doesn't play an instrument, although she sometimes holds a guitar for promo pics. With Maybelle in my hands, I feel like the old Bird again—the one who got discovered at the Station Inn a year and a half ago—the one who deserves this nomination. I grip my fiddle in one hand and my lucky rock pendant in the other. I bow my head, whisper a super-quick prayer, and when Martina McBride begins my introduction, it's go time.

With the stage lights low, I follow the glow-in-the-dark marks on the floor. For more good luck, I'm wearing the custom Justin boots that my stylist gave me at my very first promo shoot last year. I take my place on a bench at center stage and prop my legs up. As I listen to Martina talk about my incredible year, I get chills. "So it's easy to see why this New Artist was nominated. Please put your hands together for Miss Bird Barrett!"

The room swells with applause, and a small spotlight finds me. I tilt my head as though I am daydreaming about the guy of my dreams, when in reality, I am keenly aware of cameras on long booms zooming near me around the stage. I have sung these songs a thousand times this year, but I am suddenly as nervous as if it were the first time.

The music starts and I look up at the crowd forlornly, just like in rehearsal. I've found that being "in character" really helps calm my nerves.

"*I shake the sleep from my head, I drag myself out of bed, you're still gone,*" I sing sadly. "*My heart can't handle this pain, how do I sing in the rain? The mic's on.*"

I kick my legs off the bench and slowly walk up the T of

the stage, marveling when I see Nicki Minaj singing along to "Sing Anyway" in the front row. I clutch Maybelle to my stomach as I sing the chorus, focusing on the fans at home when the cameras pass by, and giving every part of my heart with this performance. As I sing, I think about mega fans like Bex; my parents who moved to California to support my dream; and my granddad, who started an Old Farts Love Bird Barrett Facebook group. I marvel at the hit makers in the room and the fact that they are rapt over my performance, singing along.

I still can't believe this is my life.

When I finish the chorus to "Sing Anyway," I smile broadly and walk backward toward the band. As the slower song picks up pace, it morphs into something more upbeat, and the energy in the room kicks up a notch when the instrumentals for "Notice Me" fill the theater. A fan blows my hair back from my face, and all kinds of wildflower images flash onto the floor and the massive screens behind me. I sing:

"If I'm a wildflower,
Then you're the blowin' breeze.
I could get swept away,
Don't know where you'd take me.
And maybe we could shine
So bright in the sunlight.

Is it real? Do you see?
Say—you notice me."

Flower petals float from the ceiling like confetti. I tilt my head back and raise my arms, Maybelle out to one side, my bow to the other. *"Notice me,"* I sing again. *"Oh notice me."*

Then I look at the audience with a playful smile. I tuck my chin and pull my bow across Maybelle's strings, finally giving her a moment to shine. She is a thing of glory in the spotlight, her tone pure, her liveliness catching. At first I play sweetly, but as the instrumental break goes on and the petals fall all around me, I give more, take more, push the solo. The music morphs into the melody of "Yellow Lines," and I play like a woman under a spell, like my fiddle and I are the only two things in the room, in the entire world. I play with passion, almost in tears when I finally fling the bow back and look up at the ceiling. My chest heaves. The band stops, too, barely long enough for a few people to start clapping, but then I look back at the crowd and sing a cappella, just one slow phrase that sums up my entire journey to this very moment:

"Adventures wait and life unfolds along these
yellow lines."

The lights dim and the room erupts in applause. I breathe it all in, feeling their love and filling my lungs with it, before I take a humble bow.

"I love this category," Fergie says, holding the envelope for Best New Artist. I am still riding my performance high, just barely having had time to grab my acceptance speech notes and tuck Maybelle into her case before Fergie started the introduction. "It's a glimpse into the future of music. So, to all the nominees, congratulations. And if you don't win, don't worry. I was never even nominated for this award, so you already beat me!"

I watch the audience laugh from where I stand in the wings, a cameraman right in front of me to capture my reaction, win or lose. I try to keep my expression calm, just like Anita coached me, but none of this postperformance adrenaline was coursing through my veins when we practiced.

"The nominees for Best New Artist are..." Fergie looks into the teleprompter and announces, pausing slightly between each name so that we can smile at the fans at home. "Kayelee Ford. Bitter Boyz. Caitlyn's Cradle. Bird Barrett. Calusa."

Here we go. Here we go. Here we go.

"And the Grammy for Best New Artist goes to..." She opens the envelope and quickly puts me out of my misery. "Bitter Boyz!"

Immediately, I clap and smile even broader into the camera. I am momentously disappointed—I really wanted that Grammy—but I have to look unruffled on TV. As the rappers take the stage, the cameraman finally moves away, and I find myself grateful for one thing as I head back to a dressing room: I didn't lose the Grammy to Kayelee Ford.

Unlike the other nominees, I get the opportunity to hide from the world for a few moments. As Amanda zips me out of my costume, my styling team gushes backstage about how much they love me and how much I deserved to win. Still, I am disappointed. I go from the extreme high of giving the performance of my life to the ultimate low of losing a greatly coveted award. I suddenly have a headache.

Once I'm in my gown again, we return to the auditorium. I make sure to keep a big smile on my face, determined to show the world how happy I am just to be at the Grammys. When I take my seat, Jacob squeezes my knee and Dylan puts his arm around my shoulders. I know they are proud of me, and I abruptly remember that they would give anything to be in my place.

So I cowgirl up and clap as Jimmy Fallon and the Roots take the stage and do a hilarious bit mocking the Bitter Boyz's music video. I look at the bright side: My next album will be from a Grammy-nominated artist, which isn't half bad.

34

"I KNOW YOU'RE exhausted," Anita says as she paces the greenroom of *Good Day LA*. They just switched to a live-audience format so I need to bring my A-game, but I keep yawning, and I think it's setting Anita on edge. "And Bird, I know you wanted to win that Grammy last night, but this talk show is a perfect way for you to show your fans how grateful you are for their support and the nomination."

"I know," I grumble, "but getting up at the butt crack of dawn for this appearance sounded a lot better when I had a chance of winning."

"Don't mope," Anita scolds. "I want to see sweet and sunny."

I bat my lashes theatrically.

"You know they're going to ask you about Kayelee," she

goes on. "So no mouthing off. Do you know what you're going to say?"

I look at myself in the mirror and think about the song I wrote with Bonnie, about people's backstories and what makes them act the way they do. "I'm just going to tell the truth," I say with a shrug. "I think Kayelee Ford is a good singer, and I think this rivalry is silly. I wish her the best and I look forward to her new album. That's it."

Anita cocks an eyebrow skeptically. "Surprised but impressed."

I grin. "I keep telling you about my aura."

She actually cracks a smile. And then, uncharacteristically, she displays a little maternal nature by squeezing my shoulder before click-clacking out to the hallway.

Alone in the greenroom, I take Maybelle out of her case. After my Grammys performance last night, the hosts want me to fiddle on air, so I practice while I wait for Anita to come and get me, letting the energy exchange with Maybelle calm my jitters. As I play an old Bill Monroe tune, I let the bluegrass fill the small room and study myself in the mirror. In a silk jumpsuit and three-inch heels, I don't look like the typical fiddler, but then nothing about my life has ever been typical. I got my start in music from tragedy, and I got my shot at celebrity from circumstance.

As my bow moves back and forth across the strings, I start to loosen up, the melody so familiar that it practically plays itself. I close my eyes and think about everything I've achieved this year. I toured America with a country music legend, I loved a boy and I think I was loved in return, I helped my family put down roots, and I won a CMA. So I lost the Grammy. *I was nominated for a Grammy!*

I feel a smile work its way across my lips and the song transforms into something different, something new, something energized and fun, something for my new album maybe. One day, I will win that Grammy. I just have to keep making *my* music.

"Bird," Anita says at the door. "It's time."

I nod and follow her down the hallway, letting my mind wander as I hear her mumbling about a headline tour this summer. I'm actually looking forward to getting back on the road again, and she's right: It is time—it's *my* time.

"Our next guest is a CMA winner who gave a phenomenal, foot-stomping performance at the Grammys last night," the morning show host says into the camera. "Please welcome Grammy-nominated artist Bird Barrett!"

The crowd applauds, and I turn the corner, confident that it is, indeed, my time to shine.

ACKNOWLEDGMENTS

I thought writing a series sounded great. Over the course of three books, I would really get to sit with the characters and *know* them. While that proved to be true—Bird and her family feel so real to me now—what I didn't realize was that writing follow-up novels is no easy task. When I sat down with the outline to *The Road to You*, it felt like trying to start a push mower that was out of gas: No matter how hard I tried, I couldn't get going.

Luckily, I had my early readers, Bobbie Jo Whitaker and Becky Bennett, to urge me on. After reading *Wildflower*, they bombarded me with messages: "What's happening with Bird? Has Adam called back? And how is her album doing? Platinum? Gold?" Wait, did I say these ladies urged me on? What I meant was they blew up my phone, texting and leaving voice mails asking where "their" pages were, to the point that I thought I may have to avoid running into them socially. So thank you, crazy gals, for loving Bird's story enough to beg for pages and letting me send you each chapter, raw and unedited, the minute it was written. And thank you for not turning this into a *Misery* situation.

To my *real* editing team, Pam Gruber of Poppy and Kathryn Williams and Dan Tucker of Aerial, thank you for the guidance as we crafted this novel. Each time we pass the pages back and forth, it sort of feels like we are on our own little journey. And to

Alissa Moreno, thanks once again for helping me with the particulars of the songwriting business and for bringing another one of Bird's singles to life in the back of the book.

To Alyssa Reuben of Paradigm, thank you. I feel so blessed to have you as my agent, my advocate, my friend. We did it again. Now let's go eat.

Enormous gratitude to the people who helped watch my children while I worked: Glen and Vicki Whitaker, Joe and Loretta Fryman, Kim Pace, Paul Maguet, Jeff Maguet, Rhonda Moore, Tom and Becky Lundy, Denise Kirtley, Liss Marie and Mariah Mendez, Alisa Siwacharan, Michelle Goodman, Savannah Robertson, Ashley Buenaflor, David Cross, Kendra Wilkins, Melissa Mott, Chitra Bisraj, Kendra Wilkins, and Cindy Johnson. It takes a village.

It was hard work plotting out Bird's touring schedule, and I have my Little, Brown copy editors, Wendy Dopkin and Chandra Wohleber, to thank for keeping the story on track. As for my personal copy editors—Momma, thanks for the encouragement, and Mamaw, I cut out a few instances of the adjective *freaking* especially for you. ☺

Thank you to Kristi Hall for the title to Kayelee's song "Hashtag on My Heart." Ridiculously perfect. Lisa Mantineo and Mike Brown, thanks for the Twitter character count help and day-making selfies. It's the little things that got me through.

To Gwendolyn Heasley, Rebecca Serle, and Jen Calonita, thank you for the sweet *Wildflower* blurbs. Lending your name to this series means the world.

To Tracey Sinclair at Chase Bank on Park Avenue and Dennis Green of Westwood One radio, thanks a million for a desk when I was desperate. And to all the folks at NashFM, thanks for bringing country music back to NYC!

To my fans, thank you for loving my books, for the words of encouragement on social media, and for the sweet e-mails you send. To the schools who have hosted me in Kentucky and New York, thank you so very much. Your students left lasting impressions on me, and I hope that I've done the same.

Finally, I must shout from the rooftops about the men in my life: my husband, Jerrod Pace, and my two young sons, Knox and Rhett. I could've never predicted where life's road would lead me, but I am so happy that it was to you.

John 13:34

TURN THE PAGE FOR
THE COMPLETE LYRICS
AND SHEET MUSIC
FOR BIRD'S SONG
"SHINE OUR LIGHT."

SHINE OUR LIGHT

You look at me like it's a natural rivalry,
Like there's just room for one to succeed,
But who's the one that spun the lie we both believed,
That if you rise, I would have to sink?

We're all born with dreams and things we're scared of,
And we're all made to live these stories out.
Nothing's wrong with being who you really are.
Take a chance, don't let drama get you down.

Just rise and fly.
Live your life out loud, yeah, live it outright.
Just ride and smile.
On this crazy roller coaster in a whirlwind storm,
We just gotta hold our own, be bold,
And shine our light.

This world is wide. They tell us it's a one-trick town,
Not big enough for the both of us,
But I don't buy it no matter how they sell it.
You don't have to fall when I stand up.

Just rise and fly.
Live your life out loud, yeah, live it outright.

Just ride and smile.
On this crazy roller coaster in a whirlwind storm,
We just gotta hold our own, be bold,
And shine our light.

BRIDGE
[FIDDLE SOLO]
Could be so beautiful if you . . .

CHORUS
Just rise and fly.
Live your life out loud, yeah, live it outright.
Just ride and smile.
On this crazy roller coaster in a whirlwind storm,
We just gotta hold our own, be bold,
Yeah, we just gotta hold our own, be so bold,
And shine our light.
Shine your light.
Yeah, shine your light.

Shine Our Light